Black Friday

By Nick Russell

Copyright 2015 © By Nick Russell
All rights reserved. No part of this book may be reproduced in any form or by any means, electronic or mechanical, including photocopying, recording, or by any information storage or retrieval system, without permission in writing by the publisher.

Nick Russell
1400 Colorado Street C-16
Boulder City, NV 89005
E-mail Editor@gypsyjournal.net

Also By Nick Russell

Fiction
Big Lake
Big Lake Lynching
Crazy Days In Big Lake
Big Lake Blizzard
Big Lake Scandal
Big Lake Burning
Big Lake Honeymoon
Big Lake Reckoning
Big Lake Brewpub
Dog's Run
Black Friday

Nonfiction
Highway History and Back Road Mystery
Highway History and Back Road Mystery II
Meandering Down The Highway;
A Year On The Road With Fulltime RVers
The Frugal RVer
Work Your Way Across The USA;
You Can Travel And Earn A Living Too!
The Gun Shop Manual
Overlooked Florida
Overlooked Arizona

Keep up with Nick Russell's latest books at
www.NickRussellBooks.com

Author's Note

While some locations in this book are real, all persons portrayed here live only in the author's imagination. Any resemblance in this story to actual persons, living or dead, is purely coincidental.

*To Terry, without whose constant love,
support, and encouragement, I am nothing.*

Chapter 1

The rain wasn't just pouring, it was coming down in sheets. And with the wind it was blowing sideways, beating against the side of the Pathfinder as he drove down Cheney Highway. Raymond hated rain, he hated wind, and he hated the Nissan. But most of all he hated Black Friday.

"Who the hell wakes up at 4 a.m. to drive through the rain and stand in line to get inside a store so they can fight the mobs to buy junk at sale prices for people who don't appreciate it and that will be even cheaper in just a few days when all of the Christmas nonsense was over?" he asked himself. Then he answered his own question; *"Me, apparently."*

Of course, just like last year when Sheila announced that they would be up early the morning after Thanksgiving, she said they were both going to go shopping early to get the best of the Black Friday deals. And, just like last year, Sheila woke up with a migraine and said she needed to stay in bed until it passed. So Raymond was on his own. Again. Just like last year.

Sheila had a lot of migraines. They always seemed to hit when she didn't want to do something. Like going to visit Raymond's mother at the nursing home, or when the house needed cleaning, or when there was grocery shopping to be done, or when Raymond wanted sex.

"Can't we just get the stuff later in the week, after all the crazies are done shopping and have it out of their system?" he had suggested, not wanting to leave the comfort of his bed.

"No, Raymond. You know all of the deals will be gone by then. Don't you even care about your kids? God, you are so selfish!"

"What deals? You stand in line for two hours to save ten bucks. It's not worth it."

"So what you're saying is that your children are not worth a little bit of effort on your part, Raymond? I can't believe you!"

"Come on, Sheila. Don't start that again. We'll still get them everything on the list. Just not this morning."

"Go," she shouted. "Just once in your life Raymond, think about somebody besides yourself. Can you do that? Just once?"

He started to protest, but knew it would be a waste of time. She pressed the heels of her palms over her eyes and said, "You're not helping my headache, Raymond."

So he had given in, like always, and gotten out of bed and trudged across the room to the bathroom to brush his teeth.

"Do you have to turn the light on?" his wife had complained. "You know it hurts my eyes."

"The door's shut."

"The light still comes under the bottom of the door. But I guess that doesn't matter to you, does it?"

Raymond had muttered, but dutifully turned the bathroom light off and finished his morning ablutions in the dark. When he came out of the bathroom and was getting dressed, Shelia said, "Don't forget to make your bed!"

He did and then left the bedroom, cursing when he stepped in a wet spot in the hallway carpet where Buttons had peed again. He hated the dog, a mixed breed rag mop of a thing that weighed six pounds and barked incessantly, when it wasn't busy chewing up everything in sight. Books, magazines, shoes, the TV remote control. If Buttons could reach it, it was gone. He hadn't wanted a dog. That was Sheila's idea, and she adored the ill-mannered mongrel. And when he had tried to teach it obedience she had screamed that he was abusing her baby. He should have known better. They had two teenagers who were just as undisciplined, for the very same reason.

Raymond went into the kitchen, where he poured the last of yesterday morning's coffee from the glass carafe into the cluttered sink, then opened the cabinet door to find the can of Maxwell House empty. "*Son-of-a bitch!*" Was it too much to ask to at least have a cup of coffee in the morning, even if he had to wash the cup and brew it himself? Apparently so.

He had walked back through the living room, where one of the kids had left the TV on overnight, stepping over discarded clothing and shoes along the way, and gone out into the rain.

***

The traffic signal was out of order and Raymond had to stop while

Black Friday

a policeman wearing a fluorescent yellow safety vest over his rain gear directed a long stream of cars through the intersection. He looked as miserable as Raymond felt.

Two blocks ahead he could see the lights of the traffic on Interstate 95. Cars, trucks and RVs, headed north and south even this early on a cold, dreary morning. Not for the first time, or even the thousandth, Raymond was tempted to take an onramp and leave it all behind him. The shrewish wife whom he could never please, the kids who barely acknowledged his presence in the room, the dog, the job. All of it. North to Georgia or the Carolinas, south to the Keys. Which would be better? Did it really matter? Any place and anything would be better than this.

Later, much later, he would think about that moment and wonder what life would have been like if he had followed that urge.

A blaring horn behind him and the cop slapping the hood of the Nissan shook him from his reverie.

"Wake up! Come on, go!" The policeman pointed to the left and Raymond made his turn.

The parking lot was already crowded with cars, pickups, and SUVs and he didn't even try to find an empty space near the store. He parked at the outer edge of the lot and stepped out into a puddle, soaking his shoe and foot.

"Lovely. Just lovely." He shook his head with resignation and plodded across the pavement to the line of people waiting to get inside when the doors unlocked.

For the next 45 minutes Raymond stood in line, surprised to see the mood of the people around him. Seeming not to notice the weather at all, they were laughing and talking excitedly, as if they were all part of some big adventure.

"I just can't wait," a woman standing in front of him said. "I'm heading right for the electronics department to get in on those noise canceling headphones, and if I'm lucky I can grab one of the FunCenters, too. My son has the XM-1 but all his friends have the new Model 2. I don't know much about video games but he says it's the best thing on the market."

"Well I'm headed for Lawn and Garden," her companion told her. "Jerry's been wanting one of the new short-radius riding lawnmowers and they're featuring free delivery on Christmas Eve if I get it today."

"Do you think we'll have time to get to Greenfields when we're done here? Melissa Rodgers told me they're giving an additional 15%

off from seven to eight this morning only."

"We'll sure try. If not, we can..."

"Have you ever seen such a god-awful mess?"

It took Raymond a moment to realize the question was directed at him. He turned to see a slender, attractive woman standing behind him.

"I'm sorry?"

"Oh, don't be sorry, hon. They's enough sorry people in the world already."

"Huh?"

She laughed. "I just asked if you've ever seen such a sight? Two hundred people standin' in line in the rain to save twenty bucks on something they don't need. Nuts. They're all nuts! But what does that say about us? 'Cause we're standin' right here with them?"

Trying to cover his sour mood, Raymond smiled. "Yeah, what does that say?"

"Hey, aren't you the man from the grocery store?"

"Yes, I'm the manager at Palmetto Pantry."

"I thought so! I shop there all the time. I like the way you always have everything I need and nothing's ever out of stock."

"Well, I can't take all the credit," Raymond told her. "It's a team effort and I've got a lot of good people over there."

She offered him her hand and said "I'm Diane Rhodes."

"Raymond Winters."

In spite of the cold, her hand felt warm in his, and it almost felt like she left it there for just a second or two longer than necessary.

"So what brings you out here in this mess, Mr. Raymond Winters? 'Cause you seem a lot smarter than that."

He laughed, "What can I say? Somebody has to do it."

"I guess."

"So what about you?"

"Oh, don't even ask." She shook her head and the smile left her face.

"I'm sorry. Sounds like I hit a sore spot."

"No. Yeah. Oh hell, I don't know." She sighed. "Because I'm a crazy woman married to a loser?"

"I'm sorry, I didn't mean to pry."

Raymond had enough problems in his own life to want to spend time hearing about somebody else's. But apparently he was going to, like it or not.

Black Friday

"Ricky and me was supposed to be here together. But then he went and got himself drunk and never even showed up at his Mama's place for Thanksgiving dinner. So there I am with the stepkids, and his Mama starts in on me like it's my fault. Sayin' if I was a better wife he wouldn't be out drinkin' on Thanksgiving Day. That woman never had liked me and it was all I could do not to say somethin' back about how if she'd have raised him right in the first place, I wouldn't have to be doin' it. But all that would have done was start a big family fight, so I just sat there and took it, and as soon as we was done eating I left. Didn't even help to clean up or wash the dishes. Finally about ten o'clock Ricky come staggering in and passed out on the couch, and he was still sleeping it off when I left this morning to come here. Who even finds a bar open on Turkey Day?"

Before Raymond could say anything in reply there was a loud cheer from the front of the line as the doors opened and the crowd surged forward and he was carried along in the flow.

Black Friday

Chapter 2

Chaos greeted him inside the store as the crowd that had seemed so happy and excited while standing in line turned the place into a mob scene, pushing and shoving to get ahead, grappling over merchandise, and at times cursing and fighting. Two well dressed women who would have been taken for soccer moms in any other setting were struggling over a three foot tall doll, a hugely obese man dressed in dirty sweat pants and a too short shirt was pulling a box with a giant screen TV inside through the crowd with one hand and trying to hold his sagging drawers up with the other, and children and babies were crying everywhere.

By the time Raymond managed to get near enough to the display of tablet computers it was empty.

"Do you have more of these?"

"Huh?"

"The tablets you had advertised. Any more?" He had to shout to be heard above the bedlam and the disinterested young clerk just shrugged his shoulders.

"Can't hear you, man."

Somebody shoved Raymond from behind and he almost fell over the acne-faced young man, who took a step backward.

"The tablet computers that were on sale. Do you have any more of them? I need two."

"No. All sold out."

"Sold out? The store's only been open fifteen minutes."

"Sorry, man. You snooze, you lose."

"What about the Playstations?"

"Gone."

"Already? What about...."

But before he could say anything more he was swept away in the crowd, and by the time he was able to escape the flow, he was in the Houseware department. As he wandered around the huge store, sometimes under his own volition, but as often carried along in whichever direction the mass of shoppers was going until he could break free, he was amazed at how empty the store's shelves had become. He had seen television news footage of businesses that had been pillaged during riots and times of natural disaster that had looked no worse.

Finally, tired of the noise and the crassness around him, he made his way to the front of the store where a fresh faced young man asked, "Did you find everything you were looking for today, sir?"

"What? Are you kidding me? I didn't find anything I was looking for. How can everything be sold out fifteen minutes after you open?"

"Oh, we'll be restocking the shelves soon, sir."

"You will? So you have more of the tablets you had advertised for $149?"

"Well... not at that price. That was the Black Friday sale price."

"But you have them and it's still Black Friday, right? So why won't they be the same price? You lost me somewhere along the way."

The man came just short of rolling his eyes when he explained, "We put a predetermined number of items on the shelves for the sale, and once they're gone, they're gone."

"But they're not gone! You just told me you have more of them."

"Yes sir, but once the sale units are gone, we don't restock at that price."

"So everything sells out in minutes, and if I want to buy a tablet I have to wait until you restock them at the regular price?"

"That's correct, sir."

"Then why did I get up in the middle of the night to come here?"

"I assume to take advantage of our Black Friday bargains, sir."

"But you don't....." Raymond shook his head and said, "Never mind."

As he walked out the door the young man said, "Have a great day, sir. And thank you for shopping with us this morning."

***

The rain was still coming down, though not as hard, when he unlocked the Pathfinder's door.

"Well, hello again, Mr. Raymond Winters! Small world, isn't it."

He turned to see the same woman he had spoken to while standing in line earlier.

"Oh, hi. All done shopping?"

"I gave up. Too many people for me. I'm never doing that again."

"Me either. It's a madhouse in there."

"All that pushin' and shovin' and hollerin'...," she shuddered. "No thank you. Did you at least find what you was lookin' for?"

"No. I was supposed to get tablet computers for the kids, but they were gone by the time I got there."

"Figures. I think it's all a big come on to get you in there, and then everything's sold out anyways."

"I guess so," he said, just wanting to get in out of the rain but trying not to be rude. And to be honest, standing there in the rain talking to an attractive woman, even if she was a little rough around the edges, was still better than going home to face Sheila's wrath because he had failed to get the tablets she wanted for the kids.

"Hey, you said tablets? What kind?"

"I was supposed to get the new Samsungs. The guy at the door said they'll have some more out later at the regular price. I just dread going back in there again, ever."

"I bought three of them day before yesterday. One for Ricky, and he wanted me to get one for his Mama and sister, too. Do you want them?"

"What do you mean?"

"Well, I figure what the heck, why not? You can just pay me what I give for them and I'll go back when the store ain't so busy and replace them."

"That would be pretty inconvenient for you, wouldn't it?"

"No big deal. Right now I'm so mad at Ricky and that whole bunch that if they don't get nothin' at all for Christmas, it serves them right. Him and his fat ass Mama is sound asleep, and I'm the one that had to drag my butt out of bed in the middle of the night to get here for the other stuff on their list. They get toys like that, and do ya know what I got last Christmas? A pair of tennis shoes! And I'm not talkin' about Nikes either. No sir, I got a pair of cheap Chinese tennies that Ricky bought at the flea market down in Cocoa."

"You're kidding me."

"I wish I was. Do you want to see the tablets? I'm parked right over there, two spaces away."

He followed her to a beat up Chevrolet Astro minivan with faded red paint. She opened the side door, and the boxed tablets and some other merchandise were in plastic bags on the floor. Raymond had heard of scams where empty boxes were passed off as real merchandise and she must have read his thoughts.

"The receipts are right there in the bags. Listen, I'm about to catch my death standin' here in this rain. You want to go over there to the Denny's and get a cup of coffee and you're welcome to open them or whatever? Else I'm gonna head home and try to warm up."

Raymond figured he had nothing to lose but time, and that was just time he'd have to spend at home listening to Sheila complain about something anyway. And coffee did sound good, since he had not had any at home.

Chapter 3

The restaurant was busy but they managed to get a booth in the back, and when the waitress came to pour their coffee, Raymond realized that he was hungry.

"Have you had breakfast?"

"No, I was in a hurry to get to the store and skipped it."

"Let me buy you breakfast. It's the least I can do, with you being so nice about the tablets and all."

After the waitress left with their order, Diane asked, "Do you know how long it's been since somebody bought me breakfast? Or opened a door for me like you did? Whatever happened to manners in this country?"

"I think they are about as scarce as Black Friday deals," he said, and she laughed.

Raymond liked her laugh. It wasn't the forced kind some women used to acknowledge a joke, but a real laugh that made him smile, too. Diane looked to be in her early thirties, with what his mother had always called dishwater blonde hair that hung past her shoulders, and blue eyes that laughed with her. She was no different than a hundred women that had come and gone behind the registers at the grocery store he ran, or the thousands of shoppers over the years. Maybe it was the cold dreary day, or the prospect of the even colder reception he knew awaited him at home, but he found himself enjoying her company and was glad she had accepted the invitation to eat with him.

She half turned in her seat to watch the traffic on the interstate. "Did you ever wonder who all those people are and where they're goin'?"

"Sometimes."

"Me, too. All the time. I can't tell you how many times I wished I was right there with them, headin' off someplace new and different."

"I think about that all the time."

"Why is that? I mean, for me, I know why. 'Cause I got nothin' to hold me here but a lousy marriage that's headed down the drain anyway, and a job on the night shift at the 7-11. But you? You've got a good job runnin' that grocery store and you must make a good livin' and have a nice house and all. Why would you leave all that behind?"

"It's not nearly as nice as you make it all sound," he told her.

"Really? From where I sit it sure looks like the good life."

"Looks can be deceiving," he told her.

"I'm sorry," she said. "It sounds like I hit a sore spot this time."

He shook his head in dismissal. "No big deal. Life is what it is,"

"But why? *Why* is life just what it is?"

"What do you mean?"

"Look at all those folks out there on that highway goin' somewhere. Do you think they all feel the same way? Or are they excited to be headed off to wherever they're goin? I got to think they are. At least most of them. Otherwise, why do it?"

"I don't know. Maybe they'll be just as disappointed with wherever they end up as they were with wherever they left."

"Ya think so?"

"Maybe."

"So maybe the place ain't as important as just the goin'?"

"I don't know," Raymond admitted. "I'm a grocery store manager, not a philosopher."

"Are you happy?"

"Am I happy? I don't know. What's happy?"

"Are you happy with your life? I mean, you got this great job and you probably make a buttload of money and you probably have a fancy house. But does it make you happy? 'Cause I got to tell you, no offense, but you don't look very happy."

He wanted to tell her that the job was no more than a rut, that the pay barely stretched to make ends meet and pay for a few small comforts, and that he always felt like a stranger in his own home. But those weren't things he liked to admit even to himself. Sure, he vented to his neighbor Wayne after a couple of beers now and then, but was his life really any worse than the next guy's?"

"Well, are you? Happy?"

"Is anybody really happy?"

"I think I was, growin' up," she said. "My Daddy was in the Air Force and we got to live in some nice places and see a lot of things. But then..., I don't know. I hoped when I married Ricky life was goin' to be some kind of fairy tale. And it's not."

Black Friday

The waitress brought their meals and they ate in silence for a minute.

"It ain't like I expected to be driving some big fancy car and wearin' a ring on every finger. But it's like we're just roommates who don't even much like each other, not a husband and wife. Do you know when the last time we made love was? On his birthday, back in September. And as soon as he was done he got up and went in the other room and watched TV without a word. How do you think that makes a woman feel?"

A solitary tear rolled down her cheek and she brushed it away and looked back out the window at the highway.

Raymond wanted to tell her that he knew all about rejection. At least she *could* remember the last time she and her husband had sex. It had been so long with Sheila that he honestly did not know. There was always an excuse; she was too tired, she had a migraine, it was her time of the month, the kids would be home soon. He had finally stopped trying, and just stayed in his own bed. Sheila had insisted on twin beds because she said he tossed and turned too much to allow her any sleep if they shared the same bed. Over time, the distance between their two beds had widened to much more than mere feet, and lately Sheila had been talking about buying a different house with an extra bedroom so Raymond would not wake her up in the morning when he left for work or to go fishing on his days off.

Instead, he just said, "No offense, but your husband's an idiot."

She turned back to him and he wasn't sure what her pensive expression meant. "I've tried, I really have. For eight years now. There's nothing I won't do to please my man, but he just ain't interested. Maybe if I was better lookin' or had bigger boobs or... I don't know."

"Nonsense. You're a beautiful woman."

"Now don't you go lying to me to try to make me feel better. I don't need that. I have a mirror. I'm okay lookin' but I sure ain't beautiful. Not by a long shot."

"Okay, maybe you're no movie star, but you sure aren't a hag either. You're a very attractive woman and any man who can't see that is an idiot. And I bet Hollywood's not knocking on Ricky's door either."

She laughed and reached across the table to put her hand on his. "Thanks, I needed that." She squeezed his hand and said, "You're not so bad yourself."

"Now who's telling fibs?"

Raymond had a mirror of his own, and at forty, his hair was thinning noticeably and in spite of the time he spent unloading trucks and stocking shelves, the beginning of a potbelly was starting to show above his belt.

"Hush, now. I'll be honest. I find you very attractive, Raymond."

He realized she was still holding his hand, and though he knew he should pull away, he didn't.

"Do you really think I'm pretty?"

"I do."

The next thing he became aware of was her foot gently moving up the inside of his leg.

"Uh, Diane?"

She smiled but didn't say anything. The foot moved slowly upward. Meanwhile, her eyes never left his.

Raymond knew he should stop this, whatever it was, right then and there. He had had opportunities to cheat before. Any man who supervised a crew of women did, sooner or later. And it wasn't just company policy that prevented him from stepping over the line. His marriage may have been empty, but it was still a commitment that he had always honored. Growing up, he had been witness to the havoc infidelity could wreak on a family.

Maybe it was because he was still mad at Sheila for sending him out alone on such a dismal morning on a shopping expedition that she had planned. Maybe it was her recent announcement that they needed to buy a bigger home so that they could move their separate beds into separate rooms. Or maybe the opportunity simply arose because his resolve was weak. But whatever the reason, fifteen minutes later he was paying for a room at the TravelersRest Motel on the other side of the parking lot.

Chapter 4

He was so nervous that his hand shook when he slipped the plastic keycard into the slot in the door. He held it for her and she went in ahead of him, then turned and kissed him as soon as the door closed behind him. She had apparently used some sort of mouth spray because her mouth and tongue tasted of cinnamon, not coffee.

The kiss seemed to last forever, and any misgivings Raymond might have had were wiped away as his hands tentatively explored her body. She moaned into his mouth as he cupped her breast, then she drew back and looked him in the eye again before dropping to her knees and unzipping his pants.

Later it all seemed like a blurred dream to him, but at the same time it was crystal clear. Raymond had only been with two women in his life before her. The first had been a college girlfriend who was just as inexperienced as him, and between the fumbling and trying to get the condom on, it had been over almost before it began. They had been together three times after that, each one better than the last as they figured out what worked and how to make it happen. Then she had gone home for the summer and never returned. Her letter said that she was sorry, but she had reconnected with an old high school boyfriend and was not coming back to school.

Sheila had kept him at arm's length throughout their courtship and engagement, but had promised him that their wedding night would be one to remember. And it was; she had gotten drunk at their reception and thrown up in the elevator on the way up to their room and passed out on the bed, fully dressed. For the next two days and nights she was too sick and hung over from the alcohol to do more than lie in bed with a wet washcloth over her face. When they finally did consummate their marriage she had kept her face turned away from him, and afterward she was quiet and withdrawn for the remaining four days of their honeymoon.

Raymond had tried to excuse her by telling himself that things would change, that Sheila would draw closer to him if he was patient and gave her enough time. Instead she had only grown more and more distant and hostile. On the increasingly rare occasions when they did have sex, it was always the same. She had endured it but made it plain that it was not something she enjoyed.

For years Raymond had tried to talk to her about the problems in their marriage but his words fell on deaf ears. He had even suggested counseling, which had only resulted in yet another argument when Sheila insisted she did not have a problem, he did, for being an oversexed pervert. Many times Raymond had asked himself why he stayed. He wasn't happy and he knew his wife and children wouldn't notice his absence, except for his paycheck. But he had made a vow, and whether or not the marriage had been all that he had hoped for, he felt a responsibility to make it work. Or at least to endure.

Diane had been so different from either the college girlfriend or his wife that it amazed him. She obviously enjoyed sex and approached it with great enthusiasm, moaning, raking her fingernails across his back, and doing things to him that Raymond had only heard of. At one point as she rode him he had convinced himself that this was all a dream, and that soon enough he would wake up in his lonely bed and hear Sheila snoring across the room. But it wasn't a dream, and now they cuddled together in the motel bed, drowsing in the afterglow.

"What are you thinking?"

"I think I've died and gone to heaven. I think you're amazing. I think..."

"Do you think I'm some kind of slut? 'Cause I'm not. I mean, I ain't gonna lie and say that I don't like sex, 'cause it's obvious I do. But I've never done this before. Well, I've done *this* a lot, but not this. Not picking up some stranger and going to bed with them. And don't ask me why I did it with you. Maybe because I was so mad at Ricky, maybe because you're such a nice man, I don't know."

"There are a lot of nice men in the world."

"You couldn't prove it by me," she said. "The only two I've ever known are you and my Daddy. And no, that don't mean I've got some kind of kinky Daddy thing going on in my head!"

"Okay. So what kind of kinky things *do* you have going on in there?"

She reached under the sheet to touch him and asked, "Really? After twice?"

"What can I say? I've been saving up for a long time."

Black Friday

"Well then Mr. Raymond Winters, I guess I'd better take care of that for you right now, shouldn't I?"

And she did.

***

Before he knew where the time had gone it was 10:30 and his cell phone was ringing.

"Shit."

"I guess you better answer that, huh?"

He didn't want to. He wanted to stay there in that room with her forever. Or to take her and climb into the Pathfinder and get onto that interstate highway and just go. Leave it all behind him and start over somewhere.

"Go ahead. Answer it."

"No. It can go to voice mail."

"We can't stay here forever, can we?"

"I was just thinking that," he said. "Why can't we?"

"I wish we could, Raymond. I really do. But we both know this was a one time thing."

"Why?"

"Why? Because this ain't you and me. We're not the kind of people who do this."

"But we did."

"Yeah, we did. But that don't make it right."

"You said you've always wanted to get on the highway and just go. Let's do it!"

"And then what, Raymond? How are we gonna live? 'Cause my Daddy always said you can't live on love for very long."

"I can get a job. There are grocery stores everywhere."

She sat up, the sheet falling away from her breasts. "Raymond, I don't have much of an education but I'm not stupid. We don't even know each other. This was sex. Darned good sex, but just sex. You don't love me. And even if we did run off together, what then? What happens next? What happens when I'm an hour late getting home, or you are? Are we going to wonder what motel room the other one is in and who they're with? 'Cause that's how we started out."

"Can I see you again?"

"Do you really want to have an affair? Spend your time sneakin' around meeting in some motel room for an hour or two of screwin'? I think we're both better than that. Don't you?"

He knew she was right. As his father had often said, he was thinking with the little head instead of the big one.

"So what happens now?"

"Now you get dressed and go back to your life, and I take a long, hot shower and go back to mine."

"That's it?"

"Yeah, Raymond, that's it. We both know that's the way it has to be."

He started to reach for her, but she held up a hand to stop him. "Don't make this uncomfortable, Raymond. Don't ruin what can be a good memory for both of us, okay?"

After a long moment he got out of bed, dressed silently, looked at her still sitting in the bed, and went back out into the rain.

Chapter 5

"Where the hell have you been?" Sheila demanded as soon as he walked in the door.

"Where do you think I've been? Shopping."

"For six hours?"

"Do you have any idea how crazy it is out there?"

"Well, where are they?"

"Where is what?"

"The tablets, you idiot! Where are they?"

He realized he never had gotten the tablets from Diane. He silently cursed himself.

"Uh, they were sold out."

"Sold out? How could they be sold out? It's Black Friday!"

"Apparently they only put out a limited number of each item and once they're sold, that's it."

"Well did you get a rain check?"

"A rain check?"

"Yes, you numbskull, a rain check. Jesus, Raymond, how dumb are you? You have rain checks at the grocery store don't you, for when you run out of a sale product?"

"I guess it doesn't work that way with Black Friday sales."

"You guess? Did you even ask, Raymond?"

"I talked to a kid at the store. He said they only had a few on sale and that's it."

"A kid? You talked to a goddamned kid? When somebody has a problem at your store do they talk to a bag boy? No, they talk to you! That's what a manager is for. Did you even ask to talk to the manager, Raymond?"

He sighed. "No, I didn't ask to talk to a manager."

"Of course not. Because you're a spineless jellyfish! You don't care that your children won't have a Christmas at all, do you Raymond?"

"They'll have a fine Christmas. There will be plenty of tablets to buy between now and Christmas."

"And you know this because why, Raymond? Are you psychic? Can you predict the future?"

He didn't reply. He had learned from long experience that it only made things worse with Sheila.

"I'm not stupid, Raymond. I know where you've been all morning."

His felt his heart make a guilty lurch, but before he could say anything, she said, "You've been fishing, haven't you?"

"Fishing? Sheila, it's pouring rain. Who goes fishing in this kind of weather?"

"A man who doesn't care about his children, that's who. Raymond, I swear, you'd skip my funeral to go fishing."

He was tempted to say that he might get roaring drunk to celebrate her funeral if he ever outlived her, but instead he just shook his head and walked out of the room.

"Where are you going? I'm not done talking to you," she shouted.

"I'm going to get out of my wet clothes, take a shower, and then take a nap. I'm beat."

"Oh no you're *not*, buster! Did you even notice the sink full of dirty dishes you left this morning?"

"I'm not the only one who lives here," Raymond said. "Why is it my job to do the dishes?"

"Do you expect me to do it with my migraine?"

"What about those two?"

Fourteen year old Jason was sitting cross-legged on the floor playing a video game and Kimberly, two years older, was texting on her phone. Neither looked up or acknowledged his existence.

"You leave them out of this, Raymond. Don't you dare keep walking away when I'm talking to you!"

He ignored her and went into the bedroom, closing the door behind him. He stripped off his clothes and put them in the laundry hamper, then spent a long time in the shower, letting the hot water wash away the tension in his body as well as the lingering smell of sex with Diane. When the water hit his back he felt a slight sting where Diane had scratched his shoulder as she climaxed. Stepping out, he toweled himself dry and went to bed, falling asleep almost as soon as his head hit the pillow. His dreams were of driving down a long empty stretch of highway, with Diane at his side.

Black Friday
***

Raymond woke up three hours later, feeling sick. *"What have I done? Holy shit, what have I done?"* As bad as his marriage was, as bad as it had been right from the start, he had never strayed. It was the one thing he could be proud of. He had sworn a vow for better or worse, and though there had been a lot more worse than better, he had upheld that vow. Maybe because he really believed that a vow was sacred, maybe because in some way it made him feel noble for enduring all of his wife's abuse and remaining faithful, whatever the reason, he had honored his commitment. Until today. Now he was no better than...

No, he wouldn't allow himself to go there. He dressed and went into the living room. Both kids were in the same places he had last seen them. He wondered if they had moved at all.

"Where's your mother?"

Neither replied.

"Hello? Are you both deaf?"

When they continued to ignore him, Raymond picked up the remote control from the end of the couch and turned the TV off.

"Hey man, what's your problem?"

"I asked you where your mother is, Jason."

"I don't know. It's not my day to watch her."

"Kim? Kimberly?"

"What?"

"Do you know where your mother is?"

"No. Probably back in bed."

"I just came from the bedroom, she's not there."

"Then how the hell should I know? She's your wife!"

All the while, she had never looked up from her phone. He was tempted to take it away from her and throw it on the floor and stomp on it. Instead, he just shook his head and left the room. He opened the door between the kitchen and the attached garage. The Pathfinder was gone.

Back in the living room, he asked, "Did your mom say anything about going to Grandma's or Aunt Lila's? " He did not expect a response and didn't get one. He knew it would be a waste of time to ask again, so he shook his head in resignation and walked outside.

The rain had stopped but the air was still heavy with moisture. Raymond walked across the street and knocked on the door of a house that looked very much like his own, and every other house in their cul-de-sac.

Wayne Lamb opened the door with a bottle of Heineken in each hand, offering one to Raymond.

"How did you know I was going to need this?"

"Because your wife was over here telling me all about your latest sins an hour ago. You really stepped on your dick this time, buddy."

He felt his heart make that same guilty lurch again, but did not let it show. There was no way Sheila could know, and if she *had* found out about his tryst, she would have been busy dismembering him by now.

"What did she say?" he asked, not meeting Wayne's eyes.

"That you're a no good son-of-a-bitch who doesn't care about his precious children and who can't do one simple thing like going to a sale without screwing it up. So now your kids aren't going to have anything under the Christmas tree and you don't give a shit. I also think there was something about kicking puppies or pulling the wings off butterflies or some such. I kind of lost track and spaced out somewhere along the way."

Raymond had been a loner much of his life and Wayne was about the only real friend he had ever had. From the time he had bought the house across the street they had connected, though they were different in many ways. While Raymond was by nature quiet and somewhat reserved, Wayne was gregarious and had never met a stranger. Raymond was never happier than when he was alone on his boat, away from his wife's nagging and the pressures of his job. Wayne enjoyed the neighborhood backyard barbecues and was on softball and bowling leagues. Raymond could tear down and rebuild an outboard engine with ease, or look at the surface of the Indian River or Mosquito Lagoon and tell you where the redfish were hiding, but hooking up a DVD player or setting up a computer printer left him lost in a tangle of wires and cables. Fortunately, Wayne was a techno-geek who kept their computers, TVs, and other electronic gadgets up to date and working perfectly.

And while Raymond was trapped in a loveless marriage and was unappreciated by his teenaged children, Wayne was a carefree bachelor who never seemed to have a care in the world. He never dated, and when he first moved into the neighborhood there was some speculation that he might be gay, since he never hit on any of the divorced soccer moms, of which there were several in the community. Raymond didn't really care one way or the other. He had more than enough problems in his own life to waste any energy worrying about how anybody else lived theirs."

Wayne motioned him toward the living room sofa and dropped into his recliner, then tipped the neck of his beer bottle in salute before taking a drink.

"So tell me, Raymond, why do you go so far out of your way to make your poor wife miserable?"

"What can I say? Some men collect stamps, some climb mountains. Me? I just get up in the morning."

Wayne laughed and shook his head. "Every once in a while I get tired of eating my own cooking and think I should get me a wife and settle down, but then I look at your life and decide I'll just order pizza instead."

"You're a wise man, Wayne."

"Well, yeah, I assumed you already knew that."

They laughed and then Raymond asked, "Did Sheila happen to say where she was going? I couldn't find her at home."

"Why did you even look, man?"

"Beats me. I guess I'm a glutton for punishment."

"Well, there you go," Wayne said, draining his beer and getting up to fetch two more from the kitchen. He handed one to Raymond and sat back down, then said, "She said she was going to her sister's. She wanted me to go along, said something about Lila needing something done to her laptop, but I passed. Your wife's attempts at matchmaking are rather transparent."

"You're missing the boat there," Raymond told him. "You should hook up with Lila. Then you could be as happy as I am."

"Yeah, I think I'm going to pass on that, buddy. But thanks just the same."

Two hours and three beers each later, they had solved most of the problems of the world and Raymond walked back across the street, noticing that the garage door was open and Sheila's Pathfinder was parked inside, next to his Ford pickup. The interrogation began as soon as he walked in the door.

"Raymond, don't you even know that you have a family?"

"Of course I know."

"You couldn't prove it by me! You leave your children here all alone with nothing to eat while you sit over there at Wayne's place getting drunk. Some father you are!"

Normally Raymond would have let it drop because he knew there was nothing to be gained by arguing with his wife, but the alcohol had loosened his tongue. "Knock it off, Sheila. It's only a little past six. Nobody's starved to death. Besides, they have a freezer full of food and a microwave. And if you were so damned worried about them why did you take off without fixing something?"

"Don't you dare speak to me that way! My sister needed me, and I care about my family, Raymond. But I know that's a concept you don't understand because you're so selfish."

"Whatever."

"You'd better shape up, Raymond. You're living on borrowed time. I'm not going to take this forever. One of these days you're going to have to be a man and accept some responsibility for this family."

"Yeah, okay, I'll get right on that."

He left her in the kitchen and went into the living room. He tried to get into a movie Jason was watching, something with a weak plot that was supplemented with a lot of car chases and violence. From the kitchen Sheila continued to complain as she rattled things around, eventually summoning Jason and Kimberly for dinner, pointedly ignoring him.

The meal was typical Sheila fare, fish sticks and tater tots, and typical of any meal the family shared together, nobody spoke much, except for Sheila, who complained that Raymond had done a sloppy job of making his bed that morning.

"That was probably because I made it in the dark. What do you expect?

"Nothing, Raymond," she hissed. "I expect nothing from you. And that's what I get every day. Nothing!"

The rest of dinner was silent, and by the time they had finished, Sheila's migraine had returned and she retired to the bedroom. The kids returned to whatever they had been doing while Raymond washed the dishes and cleaned up the kitchen. When he went to bed a little after ten, Sheila was snoring.

Chapter 6

Mike Rosemont, the usual weekend manager, had taken a few days off to go St. Petersburg for Thanksgiving with his family and Raymond was filling in for him Saturday morning. He didn't mind. Mike was a good guy who pulled his weight at work, and to be honest, Raymond would prefer being in the store over being at home most days. While he wasn't a slap the back kind of manager, and kept his relationship with his staff strictly professional, he had a good team and they worked well together.

He was in the produce department explaining to a stock boy named Patrick Meyers why it was important to rotate the tomatoes and check for soft spots when two men in slacks with loose fitting shirts that were not tucked into their waists approached him.

"Mr. Winters? Raymond Winters?"

"Yes. How can I help you?"

One of the men was about thirty, good looking, with carefully styled hair, manicured nails, perfect teeth, and a tan that Raymond thought came from a booth, not the sun. The other was a short, stocky Cuban with a thin mustache and a diamond stud in his earlobe. He flashed a badge and asked, "Is there someplace we can talk in private?"

"Uh, sure. I'll be right back, Patrick."

He led them to the office, a small crowded room elevated a few steps above floor level, with two desks, boxes of sales flyers stacked along one wall, and a large safe. Norma Swirensky, his assistant manager, was at her desk checking a bill of lading against the delivery sheet.

"Norma, can you excuse us for a few minutes?"

She looked at the two men with curiosity, but didn't ask any questions, which was fortunate, because Norma could be pushy at times. "Sure, I need to go in back and do a count anyway. It looks like Coral Beverages shorted us again."

When she left, Raymond turned to the men and said, "I'm sorry, I didn't get your names."

"Detectives Harrison and Acosta," the tanned one told him.

"Is this about the counterfeit money?"

Fake $20 bills had been floating around the county, and the Palmetto Pantry had been hit three times in the hectic shopping days before Thanksgiving.

"No, sir, it's not. Do you know a woman named Holly Coulter?"

"No, not that I can recall. Is she a customer here?"

"I wouldn't know about that."

"The name doesn't ring a bell."

"Are you sure, Mr. Winters?"

"Pretty sure," Raymond said. "A lot of people come through here every week and it's impossible to know them all by name."

"Think about it, Mr. Winters. Think real hard. Holly Coulter."

"What's this about?"

"We'll ask the questions."

Raymond did not like the man's attitude and turned toward his partner, who seemed content to lean on the edge of Norma's desk with his arms folded across his chest and let Detective Harrison do the talking. His face was impassive.

"Mr. Winters, I'm going to ask you one last time, what can you tell me about Holly Coulter?"

"I told you, I don't know who she is."

"So you're denying you have a relationship with her?"

"Relationship? How can I have a relationship with somebody I've never even heard of?"

"Where were you yesterday, Mr. Winters?"

"Yesterday? I was home."

"All day long?"

"Yes. No, I went to one of those Black Friday sales in the morning."

"Which is it, sir, yes or no?"

"I went to Merchants in the morning. My wife wanted me to get a couple of tablet computers for our kids."

"And you were home the rest of the day?"

"Yes."

"You came home and never left the house until you came to work this morning?"

"Yes. What's going on?"

"Can anybody confirm that you never left the house after you came home from shopping?"

"My wife was there part of the time, and my kids were there."

"And they'll tell us the same story? That you never left the house?"

"Yes! Wait, I did leave the house. I went across the street to my neighbor's place for a couple of hours."

"You seem to have a problem with your memory, Mr. Winters. First you say you never left the house, then you say you went shopping and came home and stayed there all day and night. Now you're saying you were at a neighbor's for a couple of hours. Is your memory always this bad?"

"My memory's fine."

"Really? Then if your memory is fine, are you lying to us, Mr. Winters?"

"No! I just got confused there for a minute."

"You got confused at least twice. You forgot going shopping and you forgot going to your neighbor's house. Do you get confused often, sir?"

"No, I don't. What's this all about?"

"It's about Holly Coulter, Mr. Winters."

"I told you, I don't know her."

"Are you sure about that? Or maybe you're *confused* again?"

"I don't appreciate your sarcasm," Raymond said.

"Mr. Winters, how would you feel about taking a ride down to the station with us?"

"What for?"

"To answer some more questions."

"Am I under arrest?"

"Have you done something to be arrested for, sir?"

"Of course not!"

"Then you're not under arrest."

"Then I don't have to go anywhere with you, right?"

"That's correct, sir. But then I might have to arrest you. Would you prefer to walk out of here under your own power or to do it in handcuffs?"

"So I am under arrest?"

"That's entirely up to you at this point, Mr. Winters. We'd prefer that you tell your assistant manager that you have to step out for a while, rather than make a scene."

"One way or another, it looks like I don't have much choice in the matter."

"Which is it going to be, sir?"

Raymond shook his head in resignation, leaned over his desk to push the intercom button, and said, "Norma, can you come to the office please?"

***

The ride to the police station on the south side of Titusville was silent. Detective Acosta drove and Harrison ignored him. Raymond, who was quiet by nature, didn't say anything, though his mind was racing, trying to make sense of what was happening.

At the station they led him inside and down a hallway to a small room furnished with just a table and four chairs, and left him there for what seemed like a very long time but was probably no more than fifteen minutes. When they returned, Harrison pointed at a chair and when Raymond sat down, he and Acosta sat across the table from him. Harrison pushed a button on the table, said his name and the date, and that the other two people present were Detective Luis Acosta and Raymond Winters. Then he sat back and stared at Raymond for a long moment that stretched out uncomfortably. For his part, Acosta was just as impassive as he had been at the supermarket. Finally, Raymond broke the silence.

"Can you please tell me what this is all about?"

"I already did," Harrison replied. "Holly Coulter."

"Look, I don't know any Holly Coulter. Or anybody named Holly or Coulter, as far as I know."

"But you do seem to have these moments of *confusion*, right? So maybe you just forgot. Like you forgot that you *did* leave your house yesterday to go shopping, And that you left it *again* to go to your neighbor's house, after first telling us that you were home all day long. Could that be what's happening here, Mr. Winters?"

"Why are you baiting me, Detective Harrison?"

"Why aren't you telling us the truth, Mr. Winters?"

"I am telling you the truth! I don't know this woman you keep asking me about. How many times do I have to tell you that?"

"You don't know her? So then I guess you're going to say that you weren't with her yesterday?"

"No! I wasn't with anybody yesterday."

The moment those words were out of his mouth, Raymond regretted

Black Friday

them. But before he could say anything else, Harrison said, "Either you're lying to us or you're confused again, Mr. Winters. We know you were with her at the TravelersRest Motel on Cheney Highway yesterday. We've got your signature on the registration card, and the security video shows you registering, with Ms. Coulter standing just few feet away."

"Okay, yes I was there with a woman yesterday," Raymond admitted. "But her name wasn't Holly Coulter, it was Diane Rhodes."

"I see. So did you forget all about that because you were confused again, Mr. Winters?"

Raymond didn't say anything.

"Can you describe this Diane Rhodes?"

"Ah... mid-30s maybe. Blonde hair, nice looking. Not beautiful, but pretty. Maybe 5'3 or so. Talks with a southern accent."

Harrison opened a file folder and put a Florida drivers license on the table.

"Is this the woman you call Diane Rhodes?"

Raymond looked at her picture and said, "Yes, that's her."

"Well, as you can see by her license, that woman is Holly Coulter."

"That's not the name she gave me. What's going on here? Did she say I did something to her?"

"*Did* you do something to her, Mr. Winters?"

"No!"

"So what, you took her to a motel room to just stare at each other?"

"No, of course not. We... we had sex."

"What kind of sex?"

"Just sex."

"Did you pay her for that sex, Mr. Winters?"

"No! She's not a hooker. She's just a nice woman I met and we got to talking and one thing led to another and we caught up in the moment. Why? What's she saying?"

"She's not saying anything," Harrison said. "She's dead, Mr. Winters."

Black Friday

Chapter 7

Raymond just stared at the detectives, not aware that his mouth was hanging open. How could Diane be dead? Or Holly? Or whatever her name was? And why had she lied about who she was in the first place?

"Now, how about telling us how you two ended up in that room and what happened in there, Mr. Winters? And try not to get confused this time around, okay?"

Raymond went through the whole story, start to finish, from the time Diane, or Holly, had first spoken to him in line outside the store to when they had met again in the parking lot and she had offered to sell him the two tablets, to them having breakfast together and then going to the motel.

"How long have you known this woman?"

"I never met her before yesterday."

"Are you in the habit of picking up strange women, Mr. Winters?"

"No. And I didn't pick her up. If anything, she picked me up."

"I see. How old are you, Mr. Winters?"

"I'll be 41 next month."

"And do younger women pick you up often?"

"No. Never."

"But it happened this time?"

"Yes. But it wasn't a pickup. We're both married."

"I see. So that makes it okay?"

"No, it doesn't. It was out of character for both of us. It just happened."

"I see. So you two meet, you hit it off, you go to a room and screw like bunnies, and then what?"

"And then I left."

"And was Ms. Coulter alive when you left?"

"Of course she was! What happened to her anyway? She didn't seem like anything was wrong with her."

"She was murdered, Mr. Winters."

If the news that Diane was dead had stunned him, the news that somebody had killed her hit him like a sledgehammer. He gasped for breath and felt the room spinning.

"Are you alright, Mr. Winters?"

He couldn't reply. Acosta slipped out of the room and returned in a moment with a bottle of water, which he handed to Raymond. With shaking hands he managed to twist the cap off and took a drink, then had to fight to keep it down. Acosta sat back down, folded his arms across his chest again, and stared at him.

When he could finally speak, Raymond said, "You can't think I had anything to do with this."

"Did you?"

"No! I swear to God! No!"

"Are you sure about that?"

"Of course I'm sure!"

"Okay, I'm just asking because sometimes you get confused, right?"

"Stop it. I didn't kill anybody. I could never hurt anybody."

"Did you and Ms. Coulter have a fight at some point?"

"No. We got along fine."

"She didn't say anything that made you mad?"

"No."

"Look, we're all guys here, okay? Maybe you asked her for something kinky that she didn't want to do and she got pissed off. Is that what happened?"

"No!"

"How about rough sex? Was that it? Because some women go for that. Maybe rough sex that got out of hand?"

"No!"

"Did you hit her, Mr. Winters?"

"No, I didn't."

"Did you choke her?"

"No!"

"So you had sex with her and when it was done you just got up and left without saying a word? That's kind of cold, man."

It was the first thing Acosta had said since they had approached him at the supermarket.

"No. We talked for a while."

"What about?"

"I... asked her to run away with me. I know that sounds crazy, but

I did."

"What did she say?"

"She said no, that we needed to be realistic."

"Did you argue about that?"

"No."

"What else did you talk about?"

"I told her I wanted to see her again."

"And did you make plans to get together again?"

"No. She was more sensible than I was, I guess. She said neither one of us was the kind of person who has an affair. And she was right."

"How did that make you feel? Mad? Rejected? Frustrated?"

"I don't know. Disappointed, I guess. But I knew she was right."

"Did you try to press the issue? Maybe try to convince her to see you again?"

"I'm not the kind of guy who presses issues."

"So there was no rough sex, no fight, nothing like that?"

"No. Not at all."

"Did she leave the room with you?"

"No, she was still there when I left."

"Was she awake? Dressed?"

"No, she was still in bed."

"What was she wearing?"

"Nothing."

"So you have sex with this good looking younger woman. You ask her to run away with you and she says no. You ask to see her again and she says no. So you just leave her there, naked?"

"That's right."

"Maybe you started to leave and got out in the parking lot and decided to go back to give it one last try. Or maybe you got to thinking about her there still naked and went back for one more taste of honey?"

"No. I kissed her goodbye and left."

"And she was alive when you last saw her?"

"Yes."

Harrison had remained silent while Acosta questioned him, but now he asked, "Do you mind taking your shirt off, Mr. Winters?"

"My shirt?"

"Yes, please."

Raymond stood up and took off his shirt.

"Turn around please."

He did, and the detective asked him where the scratches on his shoulder had come from.

"From Diane."

"When you say Diane, you mean Holly Coulter?"

"Yes."

"Why did she scratch you, Mr. Winters?"

"She got kind of carried away when..."

"When what, sir?"

"When she came."

"You must be quite the stud," Acosta said. "It's been a while since I've had that kind of reaction from a woman."

Raymond felt his face redden but didn't reply.

"Was Ms. Coulter, shall we say, an enthusiastic lover?" Harrison asked.

In fact, she had been very passionate in bed, but Raymond didn't want to discuss that with them. He had never felt comfortable with locker room talk, and felt like it would be some kind of a betrayal.

"Well, was she?" Harrison prompted.

"I think she enjoyed it as much as I did."

"Because you're such a stallion, right?" Acosta was grinning like they were two buddies sitting on barstools swapping stories of their conquests, but Raymond ignored him.

"Let me ask you something," Acosta said. "Why do you think this good looking woman you never met before picked you up, took you to a room, and did the nasty? I mean, no disrespect, but Detective Harrison and me, we're both younger and we're in pretty good shape, and not too bad looking, if I do say so myself. But that's never happened to me. Has it happened to you, Detective Harrison?"

"Never."

Raymond did not respond.

Harrison picked up a digital camera and took three photographs of the scratches on Raymond's back, then examined his hands and arms. He pointed to a small scrape on the side of his right hand. "What happened there?"

"I don't know," Raymond told him.

"You don't know?"

"I'm always scraping and scratching myself moving stock around in the store or else out on my boat. I think I got this the other day when I was replacing a couple of metal shelves in the store, but I can't remember, to be honest."

"You can't remember? Are you getting confused again, Mr. Winters?"

He wanted to tell the smug detective to shut up, to either charge him with something or else let him go, but he was afraid that if he did that, they might actually charge him with Diane's death. So instead, he just repeated, "I don't remember."

"Did you pay her for sex?"

"No. I told you, she wasn't a hooker. She told me she was married."

"According to you, she also told you her name was Diane Rhodes."

Acosta was looking through papers in the file folder and asked, "What kind of car did she have?"

"I don't know. A minivan of some kind. Red, I think."

"You think?"

"Yes, it was red."

"Did she drive it to the motel?"

"No, we left both of our vehicles at the Denny's and walked over to the motel."

"You said something about her offering to sell you two tablet computers, is that right?"

"Yes."

"How did you pay her? Cash, a check?"

"Neither," Raymond said.

"What do you mean?"

"I guess we both forgot about them. I didn't realize until I was home that I forgot to get them from her."

Acosta pulled a sheet of paper out of the folder and handed it to Raymond.

This is an inventory of the contents of the Chevrolet Astro van registered to Holly Coulter that was parked at Denny's. Can you read it to me, please?"

"Black plastic case with five music CDs, twelve volt cell phone charger, 97 cents in change, a SunPass transponder, and a receipt from the WalMart gas station."

"I don't see any tablet computers listed there, do you?"

"No, but there were three of them and some other stuff in plastic bags on the floor behind the passenger seat."

"Then where are they?"

"I don't know. Maybe somebody broke in and stole them."

"According to the officers who found the van, it was locked and the keys were in the motel room with the victim."

"Then I don't know what to tell you."

"Let's get to the point," Harrison said. "Did you kill Holly Coulter?"

"No!"

"Did you hit her or choke her?"

"No. I told you. We had sex, we talked, and I left."

"And that's it?"

"That's it."

"Look at it from our point of view, Mr. Winters. You said you didn't know the victim, you said she offered to sell you two tablets, you said you went right home after shopping yesterday morning and never left the house again. Then later you admit that you did know her, that you did go to a motel room with her and that you had sex with her more than once before you went home, that you left the house at least once for a couple of hours that evening, and the inventory of her car did not include these tablets that you told us about. Can you understand why your credibility might be a bit questionable?"

"Look, I know this doesn't look good," Raymond said.

"No sir, it doesn't."

"I can explain."

"Okay, I'd appreciate that." Harrison sat back and mimicked Acosta's pose, with his arms folded across his chest.

"I didn't know her name was Holly. She told me it was Diane. So when you kept asking me if I knew this Holly person, I kept saying no, because I didn't."

Neither detective said anything, they just continued to stare at him. The only sound was the large round clock on the wall ticking off the seconds.

"And yes, I did go to that room with her. But put yourself in my place, guys. I'm a married man. I screwed up and shouldn't have been there with her in the first place. So yes, I lied about that. I know that was wrong. I'm sorry. And as for going across the street to my neighbor's place for a couple of beers, I guess it's almost home to me. I thought you meant did I leave the neighborhood or something."

Still nothing. They just sat there staring at him like he was some specimen under a microscope.

"I didn't kill her!"

He couldn't read their faces and found himself rambling on. "I know all of this probably sounds like some kind of fantasy gone bad, but that's the way it happened. We started talking in line outside the store, we bumped into each other again in the parking lot, we went to Denny's for breakfast, and the next thing I knew we were in the motel room. It's never happened to me before, and I even remember laying there in bed with her and thinking I was dreaming. That's it. That's all that happened."

He ran out of things to say and finally stopped talking. Raymond felt sick to his stomach and his mind was racing. What if Sheila found out about all of this? How could she *not* find out? What about Mr. Duncan? The owner of the Palmetto Pantry grocery chain was a devout Christian who held family values dear and had no tolerance for those who might do anything to make the business look bad in the eyes of the public. What if they actually arrested him? Raymond's life may not have been perfect, in fact it was far from perfect, and more than once he had fantasized about running away and getting a new start someplace, but would he ever do it? If Diane or Holly or whoever she was had actually agreed to leave with him, would he really have gone? He didn't know, but suddenly the thought of going to jail made him long for his home, with his cold, often hostile wife and indifferent teenagers.

Finally, Harrison broke the silence. "You said something about thinking it was all a dream. Do you ever have incidents where you confuse dreams and reality, Mr. Winters?"

"No! I'm not crazy, and I didn't hurt that woman in some blackout or whatever you're implying."

"So that's it? That's your story? You met a stranger, had breakfast with her, went to a motel with her, had sex and left, and never saw her again?"

"That's what happened."

Harrison set a lined tablet and an ink pen in front of him and said, "Write it all down, Mr. Winters, from the time you first met Ms. Coulter standing in line until we came to your store this afternoon. And try not to get *confused* and leave anything out, okay?"

Black Friday

Chapter 8

A uniformed police officer drove Raymond back to the supermarket, and he was just as quiet as the detectives had been on the ride to the police station. But that was fine with Raymond because the last thing he wanted to do was talk to anyone else that day. Maybe not ever. He already felt like he had said too much, but other than his tryst with Holly, as he now thought of her, he had nothing else to hide. He had not objected when they asked to swab his mouth to take a DNA sample, thinking that the sooner they eliminated him as a suspect, the sooner they could find her killer, and the sooner this would all be over.

Raymond was trying to understand all that had happened, but the more questions he asked himself, the more confused he became. Why had Holly Coulter given him a false name? Because she was married and knew their encounter was a one-time thing and did not want him to be able to contact her again? That made sense, and he mentally kicked himself for using his own name when he had checked into the motel. But it wasn't like philandering was a way of life for him and it had all happened so fast, from their first conversation to meeting up again in the parking lot when he left the store, to feeling the woman's foot seductively caressing his thigh under the table.

And why him? The detectives had asked him why an attractive younger woman had chosen him to pick up. He didn't have an answer then, and he still didn't. And most of all, who had killed her, and why? Had her husband followed her and gone to the room after Raymond left and done it in a fit of rage and jealousy? Was he going to be the next target of her husband? *If* it was her husband. But who else could it be? What were the odds of some random madman finding *that* woman in *that* motel room on *that* day?

While he struggled to make sense of it all, he was also trying to assess his own feelings about the woman he had met so briefly. Did he feel a sense of loss? He wasn't sure. When she had told him that running away together was a dream, he had known on a practical level that she was right. And he had awakened that morning disgusted over his weakness in being with her in the first place. As good as the sex had been, and it was incredible, and as much as he wanted more, in the clear light of day he had been grateful that she had been firm in not giving him her telephone number or agreeing to meet him again. Because Raymond knew that she had uncovered a weakness within him that he could not deny, as much as he wanted to.

"Sir?"

The policeman's voice startled him out of his reverie.

"Huh?"

"We're here, sir. Back at your store."

Raymond had not realized that they were stopped in front of the Palmetto Pantry. The officer opened the rear door of the car and Raymond stepped out.

"Thanks."

"Have a good day, sir," the officer said, as he got back behind the wheel and drove way.

It had not been so far, that was for sure. And Raymond had a terrible feeling that it would be a long time before he ever had a good day again.

***

"Where have you been?" Norma asked as soon as Raymond walked into the office. "You just left with those two cops and not a word from you for over two hours. Did somebody die or something?"

She saw the stricken look on his face and said, "Oh God, somebody *did* die! Who, Raymond?"

"Nobody you know," he told her. "Just.... just a friend."

"I'm so sorry. Here, sit down."

He sat behind his desk and she hovered over him. "Do you need anything, Raymond? Some water? Or coffee, maybe?"

He shook his head. "No, I'm fine."

"Are you sure?"

No, he wasn't sure, but he didn't want to make things worse, so he just said, "Really, I'm okay."

Norma looked at him skeptically. "Are you sure? Maybe you should go home and get some rest. I can hold down the fort until Andy gets here."

Andy Tyson was the store's night manager and was due in at 6, but

Black Friday

the last thing Raymond wanted was to go home. He didn't know if the police would have contacted Sheila yet to ask about where he had been the day before, but he knew if they did, there would be hell to pay. And even if they had believed his story, she was sure to have something to complain about. She always did. Raymond's mind flashed back to the moment when he had been sitting on Cheney Highway waiting while the cop directed traffic, and saw the traffic on Interstate 95 and thought about getting on it and just driving away from it all. Where would he be right this minute? Wherever it was, it would be better than the situation he found himself in right now.

"Raymond?"

"Huh?"

"I said, why don't you go home? I'll be fine here until Andy comes in."

"Oh. No. No, I'm fine Norma. Thank you, though. I think I'll do a walk around."

She watched him get up and studied his face carefully. He thought she would try to convince him to go home, but all she said was, "Alright then, if you're sure."

He managed a smile and said, "I'm sure."

No matter how busy or how slow it was in their stores, Palmetto Pantry required a manager or assistant manager to walk the floor once every hour in each location. While some of the managers groused about the policy, Raymond believed it made sense. It allowed managers to be out among their customers putting a human face to the company, and gave them the opportunity to be sure that shelves were stocked properly, spills were cleaned up quickly, and that the stores met company standards.

He ran a tight ship and it showed, both in the look of the store and in employee morale. Raymond was one of the few store managers who shared his quarterly productivity bonuses with his staff, and though it wasn't a lot of money by the time it was divided equally, an extra $25 or $50 was always welcome. And as much as the crew appreciated the money, their manager's willingness to share equally was even more important to them.

Of course Sheila didn't know about the bonuses, and since she always seemed to develop one of her migraines whenever a company dinner or the annual Christmas party was held, she probably never would. For his part, Raymond quietly invested the bonuses in a separate account, and while it was not enough to retire on, it had grown considerably over the years. He thought of it as his escape fund, though in reality he knew that escape was not an option. He expected to live and die in the same rut he had been in for what seemed like forever. But it was always fun to dream. And sometimes those dreams were the only thing that made it possible for him to tolerate the reality of his life.

He went through the motions for the rest of the day, and when he got home he was relieved to find that Sheila wasn't there. Jason was in his usual position on the floor, playing a video game that seemed to involve blowing things and people up with vivid red graphics, and music was blasting from his daughter's bedroom. When he went down the hall and knocked on the door, nobody opened it. Raymond knocked again, and then pounded with his fist. Kimberly jerked the door open and demanded, "What?"

"Turn it down."

"Why?"

"Because it's too loud, that's why. I could hear it halfway down the street."

She rolled her eyes at him and slammed the door. The volume did not go down and he pounded on the door again. When she didn't answer, Raymond opened the door. His daughter and two of her friends, a girl named Kyra and another, whose name he could not remember, were lounging on the bed and floor, and Kimberly shouted, "What the hell? You can't just open the door like that!"

"Well, I just did. Turn the damn music down. Now!"

She stared at him, arms folded defiantly. "Get out of my room!"

"Turn it down!"

"Out!"

The other girls ignored the confrontation, and Raymond suspected they had had the same kind of conversations with their parents more than once. He crossed the room and turned the stereo off.

"You can't do that!"

"I just did."

He walked out of the room and she slammed the door behind him. A moment later the music came back on, even louder this time.

Raymond stopped and clenched his fists, then shook his head and went through the kitchen and out to the garage. He opened the circuit breaker box and found the one marked "Bedroom 2" and turned it off. Immediately the music stopped.

Kimberly met him in the kitchen. "What did you do?"

"I turned off the music."

"Turn it back on!"

"Nope."

"I have a right to listen to my music."

"Not when it's that loud. Your rights end where my rights begin, young lady."

"It's a free country!"

"Yes, it is. But electricity isn't free, and as long as I'm paying the bills, we'll do it my way."

"I hate you!" She turned her back on him and stomped back to her room, slamming the door so hard a photograph hanging on a wall in the hallway fell to the floor.

Ignoring the verbal battle around him, Jason had continued to slay dragons and space monsters through it all.

"Jason?"

The boy was absorbed in his game and didn't answer.

"Jason?"

Raymond looked for the TV remote control, and not finding it, he stepped in front of the screen, blocking his son's view.

"Hey!"

"Why don't you ever answer me when I'm talking to you?"

"Because I'm busy. And besides, you never say anything worth listening to anyway."

"Where's your mother?"

"Don't you remember? She went with Grandma and Aunt Lila to Orlando today to go shopping. I guess she's right, you never do listen."

Raymond remembered that somewhere in her nagging the evening before his wife had mentioned the shopping trip. It was amazing that Sheila never had a migraine when she wanted to spend time with her mother and sister.

"Did anybody come here looking for me today?"

"Yeah, two guys. I told them you were working."

"Did they leave a card or anything?"

"No. They just said they'd go see you at the store. Who were they, anyway?"

"Just a couple of friends of mine."

"You have friends? I never knew that."

In the coming days Raymond was to find out just how rare true friends were.

***

The story headlined the evening news. Under a graphic that showed a pistol, an anchorwoman with lacquered hair reported that on Saturday morning a housekeeper at the TravelersRest Motel on Cheney Highway discovered the body of a murder victim later identified as Holly Lynn Coulter, age 32, of Titusville, in one of the motel's rooms. "Details are sketchy at this time," the reporter said, "and while police declined to say how the woman was killed, they do say they spoke to a person of interest in the case, but that no arrests have been made as of this time."

Turning to her co-anchor, she said, "Such sad news at what is supposed to be a happy time of year."

"Yes it is, Laura. However, merchants here in Brevard County have reason to be happy. Early reports say that yesterday's Black Friday sales numbers were up nearly double from last year, and they expect the trend to continue through the holiday shopping season. Let's go to Staci, who is at Cocoa Square Mall today, for her report on what's topping Christmas shopping lists this fall."

Raymond stared at the television screen in confusion. Neither of the detectives had mentioned anything about Holly being shot. They had asked if he had hit her or choked her, but never mentioned a gun or wanted to know if he owned one. Was the pistol just a generic graphic the television station used for all crime stories? And was *he* the person of interest the news story had referred to?

He went to bed with a feeling of doom. He was sure that if the detectives had felt he was responsible for Holly's death they would have already arrested him. But even so, he had a terrible feeling that sooner or later, his involvement with the dead woman was going to be revealed.

Chapter 9

Sunday morning Raymond hitched his boat trailer to his pickup in the predawn light and drove to the Parrish Park launch under the A. Max Brewer Bridge. The wide Indian River was flat and calm, and Raymond nodded to a couple of other fishermen he saw frequently as he waited his turn to put his boat in the water. He unhooked the safety straps

Once he backed the trailer into the water and released the winch hook, he pushed the boat off the trailer and used the bow and stern lines to secure it to cleats on the dock, then quickly parked the truck and trailer. Five minutes later he was on the water, trolling slowly southward.

He rigged a red and white jig to one rod and dropped it overboard, then baited another with a live shrimp and cast off to the side, then retrieved it. On the second cast the rod tip bent sharply and he pulled hard to set the hook, then reached over to move the gearshift into neutral. He boated the nice spotted seatrout, carefully removed the hook, and dropped it overboard.

Raymond worked the large sea grass flats that cover the shallows of the Indian River Lagoon, catching and releasing several more seatrout and three redfish. He seldom brought any of his catch home since Sheila complained about the smell of cooking them and the kids did not like any fish that did not come from the frozen foods section of the supermarket. Occasionally he'd take a nice one or two to Wayne, but since his neighbor's job as a pharmaceutical representative kept him on the road a lot, he did not eat at home all that often.

But for Raymond, just being alone out on the water was good enough, whether he caught anything or not. He had tried to interest Sheila and his kids in the sport, but she wanted nothing to do with it, and both times he had enticed Jason to go with him the boy had complained about being bored from the time they left the dock until they were back home.

The boat itself, an eighteen foot Key West bay boat, had been a major bone of contention between Raymond and his wife. She had resented the battered old V-bottom aluminum fishing boat he had picked up at a yard sale and used for over ten years, and when it finally sprung a leak he could not repair Sheila had hoped he'd give up fishing and stay home to help her with the house and to watch the kids while she spent some quality time with her mother and sister. Because Lord knows, there was nothing quality about being stuck at home with Raymond. But fishing was his one escape from the pressures at work and home, and in a rare moment of defiance he had bought the new boat and trailer over her objections. Mornings like this made it worth the three weeks he had spent sleeping on the couch after the purchase.

In those frequent moments when Raymond dreamed of escaping the dull routine of his life, he had never really given much thought to where he would like to actually escape to, only that it would have to be someplace on the water. His brief interlude with Holly aside, he had not fantasized about a woman in the new life he envisioned for himself. His thoughts went to maybe a nice Mako center console in the 22 to 25 foot range with twin Mercury outboards. Nor had he given any thought to how he would earn a living. Sure, he'd love to be a fishing guide someplace, maybe the Keys or down on Lake Okeechobee, but how realistic was that? Then again, how realistic is any fantasy?

And then there was the whole sordid mess with Holly. Whatever had possessed him to even agree to have coffee with her in the first place, let alone everything that had followed?

"Thinking with the little head instead of the big one," Royce would say with a chuckle. *"A chip off the old block, that's my boy!"*

But he wasn't like his father. He would never be like his father!

Royce Winters was an old school rake, a skirt chaser who had been involved in one affair after another throughout his marriage to Raymond's mother. And even while enamored with his latest conquest, he still divided his attention among one night stands and backseat quickies with what seemed to be an endless stream of vapid women attracted to his good looks and witty charm.

Raymond was only nine when the marriage broke up, and though he never knew details of the scandal, whatever it was created enough discord that his mother had moved him and his sister across the state and spent the rest of her life as a bitter man-hating woman who directed much of her animosity for her ex-husband onto her son. He could not begin to count the times that she told him, *"You're just like your father, Raymond, and you're going to end up just like him"* for some infraction, no matter how small it might be. If he forgot to wipe his shoes before coming inside on a rainy day, if he failed to take out the trash or mow the lawn, if he was two minutes late to the dinner table, it was always the same thing. *"You're just like your father, Raymond."* He had determined at an early age *not* to be like his father, in spite of his mother's forewarning. And yet, look at him now. *Was* he just like Royce?

"Gettin' any?"

He had been so absorbed in his own thoughts that he had not noticed the Hobie Mirage until the man in the kayak called out to him.

"Some trout and a couple of reds."

"The snapper were biting on live shrimp by the marina yesterday."

"Good eating," Raymond said, and the kayak fisherman nodded and paddled away. Fifty yards from Raymond's boat he hooked onto something big, and Raymond watched while he battled a nice sized redfish into the kayak.

He stayed on the water until almost noon, past the time the fish had stopped biting, using the foot control for the Minn Kota trolling motor to move slowly along the flats. When the alarm on his cell phone buzzed he reluctantly stowed his fishing rods away in the boat's rod holders, tilted the trolling motor up and started the outboard. He kept it at mid-throttle and his trip back to Parrish Park was quicker.

With nobody ahead of him, it was a simple matter to remove the scupper plugs, load the boat back onto its trailer, make sure everything was secure, and he was home within a half hour. He backed the boat up beside Wayne's garage, since Sheila had refused to allow him to keep it at their house, and unhooked the trailer. Using a garden hose hanging on the side of the garage, he flushed the engine, washed the boat down, and patted it lovingly on the bow before he went across the street to clean up for his Sunday afternoon ritual.

***

"She's having a good day," the young nurse aide said as Raymond signed in at Whispering Palms Nursing Home. "She just finished lunch and is back in her room. Have a nice visit."

Visits with his mother were seldom nice. On the days when she was coherent she spent the hours chastising Raymond because he didn't visit often enough, or because Sheila and the kids never came with him, or else reminding him that he was just like his father. Other days she did not know who he was and either demanded to know why he was in her room, or else prattled endlessly about nonsensical things he didn't understand. He was never sure which was worse and was always relieved when his self-imposed hour was up and he could leave.

Alice Winters was sitting in the rocking chair in her room watching an infomercial on television, and scowled when he knocked on her door and opened it.

"Hello, Mother, how are you today?"

She allowed him to kiss her cheek, but otherwise did not acknowledge his presence. Raymond sat in the room's other chair, a straight-back affair with no padding. "What are you watching?"

Nothing.

"You're looking nice today."

She sighed and pushed the remote control to turn off the television.

"Why do you only visit when I'm in the middle of something, Raymond? It's very inconsiderate."

"Mother, it was an advertisement for home exercise equipment, not *Gone With The Wind.*"

"That's not the point, Raymond. I don't see you for weeks at a time and then you just show up out of the blue and I'm supposed to drop whatever I'm doing to give you my full attention."

"I'm here every Sunday afternoon, Mother."

"Where are Sheila and my grandchildren? They must be too busy for me. I guess I'm just an old woman and don't matter."

"I'm sorry, Mother. They had other plans today."

"They always seem to have other plans that don't involve their family obligations."

"I'm sorry."

"Don't be redundant, Raymond. You've already said that."

"I'm.... anyway, how are you today?"

"How am I? What kind of question is that? I'm 71 years old and fading fast. Not that it matters to anybody."

"You're not fading, Mother. The doctor says you are in very good health for a woman your age."

"And you believe him over your own mother? I know how I feel!"

"Yes, Mother."

"Have you even thought about what we talked about last week, Raymond?"

On his last visit his mother had not known who he was and spent the hour talking about some obscure television soap opera that had been off the air for twenty years.

"I forgot, what did we talk about?"

"You forgot? That's so typical of you, Raymond. Just like your father. We talked about your future, Raymond. Do you expect to be a bag boy at the grocery store forever?"

That conversation again.

"Mother, we have talked about this dozens of times. I'm not a bag boy. I'm the manager of the store."

"So you're a glorified bag boy. Your sister's married to an attorney, Raymond. How does that make you feel?"

"Good for her. Maybe I should have married one, too."

"Don't be snippy with me, Raymond! You're just like your father."

And so it went for the rest of his visit. He was a failure as a son and as a man, he had no drive or initiative, and he was doomed to end up just like his father. She would not allow him to kiss her cheek when he left, telling him she was sure he was in a hurry to leave so he could go find a whore just like his father had.

As they did often after his weekly visit to his mother, Raymond's hands shook so badly that he had to make two attempts to get the key in the ignition of his truck, and he had to sit for a few minutes before he trusted himself to start the engine and drive out of the parking lot.

Chapter 10

Raymond was just pulling out of his driveway Monday morning when the white Chevrolet Caprice pulled across his path and blocked him.

"What the hell?"

Detectives Harrison and Acosta exited the car and approached his truck. While neither man displayed a gun, it was obvious this wasn't a social call, and Raymond had a feeling it was not going to be a pleasant encounter.

"Mr. Winters, we need you to come with us."

"What's going on?"

"Please shut the truck off and come with us, sir."

"Am I under arrest?"

"Mr. Winters, as a courtesy, we are trying to keep this low key for the sake of your family. Now you can either do as we say or we can do it the hard way."

Raymond did as he was instructed, and as he got into the back of the unmarked police car he saw Wayne standing in his driveway across the street watching. He wondered how many other neighbors had witnessed the encounter.

As it had been on Saturday, the drive to the police station was quiet, neither the detectives nor Raymond saying anything. They led him down the hallway to the same room, where a stern-faced woman awaited them.

Harrison indicated the same seat he had on Saturday, and when Raymond sat down the woman said, "Mr. Winters, I'm Janet Morrison with the Brevard County Attorney's Office."

It did not feel like a greeting that required a response, and before he could offer one, she said, "Mr. Winters, before I invest any time in this conversation, are you prepared to be honest with us today?"

"Am I under arrest?"

"Not at this time, but that is subject to change."

"Based upon what?"

"Based upon how this conversation goes."

"Do I need an attorney?"

"That is certainly your right. Do you wish to have an attorney here?"

"What happens if I say yes?"

"Then this turns from a conversation to an adversarial situation, and I assume you have something to hide."

"I don't have anything to hide."

"Sure you do, Mr. Winters. You wouldn't want your wife or your coworkers or supervisors at Palmetto Pantry to know about your affair with Holly Coulter, would you?"

"It wasn't an affair, it was a one-time thing."

"So you don't mind if word gets out about it?"

"I wouldn't want that to happen."

"So you *do* have something to hide."

"Yeah, I guess I do."

She smiled, but there was no warmth in it, and she folded her hands on the table and said, "Let's talk about what else you have to hide."

Raymond was irritated with her attitude and was debating with himself about whether he should have an attorney there, but she did not give him time to consider it for very long.

"Mr. Winters, let me make it perfectly clear to you that your best option is total honesty. I'm more than willing to hear your side of things, but I'm a very busy woman. So if you plan on playing games with me, let's just end this right here. These officers will take you into custody, we'll book you for the murder of Holly Coulter, and life as you know it ends today. Is that what you want to happen?"

"No! And I didn't kill anybody!"

"So that's the route you're going to take?"

He felt himself panicking. It was like the room was closing in on him and he wanted out of there more than he had wanted anything in his life.

"It's the truth!"

"Really?"

"Yes, really!"

"There's no reason to raise your voice, Mr. Winters."

He had not realized he had shouted. "I'm sorry. But I didn't do it."

"Do you lose your temper like that often, Mr. Winters?"

"No. And I didn't lose my temper. I just got a little loud."

Black Friday

"I see. Did you lose your temper with Holly Coulter Friday in that room at the TravelersRest Motel?"

"No! Look, I keep telling you. I didn't do it. She was alive when I left her in that room."

"How about we start right from the top, Mr. Winters? Tell me everything that happened that day."

So he repeated the story again, from meeting the woman who told him her name was Diane Rhodes while standing in line in the rain, to having breakfast with her and then going to the motel room, and from there back home. He made sure to include his visit with Wayne Lamb after his nap.

"And that's the first time you ever met Holly Coulter?"

"Yes. I had never seen her before that."

Janet Morrison shook her head. "BZZZZZT! Wrong answer. Do you want to try that again, Mr. Winters?"

"What do you mean wrong answer? It's the truth!"

"I thought you were going to be honest with me."

"I am being honest! I never met her before Friday morning."

"Well, so much for honesty, Mr. Winters."

"I am being..."

Detective Harrison slapped the tabletop and said, "Cut the bullshit, Mr. Winters! We know that you and Holly Coulter have been having an ongoing affair."

"No! I told you, I never saw her before Friday morning."

"Stop lying to us."

"I'm not lying!"

"This is going nowhere. Let me just lock him up right now," Harrison said, but Janet Morrison shook her head.

"No, for his own sake, let's give him the opportunity to do the right thing."

"Look, I've told you everything there is to tell," Raymond protested. "I met her just that one time. And at this point, I wish I'd never seen her in the first place."

"Mr. Winters, we know for a fact that Holly Coulter told her sister that she was seeing a married man. That she had been involved with him for several months. And she said she was meeting him at the TravelersRest Friday morning. The same morning that you were there with her. The same motel where she was murdered."

"It wasn't me!"

"So what are you saying, Mr. Winters? That it's all a big coincidence? Maybe her boyfriend stood her up so she went to a store to stand in line in the cold and the rain in the hope of meeting somebody else? And that somebody just happened to be you?"

"I don't know. I know it sounds crazy. But if she was having an affair, it wasn't with me."

His cell phone rang.

"Can I answer that?"

"Of course. You're not under arrest. Yet."

It was Norma. "Raymond? Where are you?"

He was never late for work. Never. He always made it a point to be at the store at least thirty minutes before his shift began. He didn't know how to explain his absence.

"Ahh, something came up. Can you cover for me for a little while?"

"Are you sick? Do you need to take the day off? I can call Mike in."

"No, don't do that. I'll be in."

"Are you having car trouble? Do you need a ride? I can send somebody to pick you up."

"No. No, I'll be in. Just... just cover for me for a little while, okay?"

"Alright, but..."

"Look, I have to go, Norma. I'll be there as soon as possible. Thanks."

He hit the button to end the call before she could say anything else.

The room was silent for a moment and he knew they were all waiting for him to speak.

"Listen, Mrs. Morrison..."

"It's Ms. Morrison."

"Sorry. Listen, Ms. Morrison, I'm telling you the truth. I never met Holly Coulter before Friday morning. Look at me, I'm not the kind of guy who picks up good looking younger women and takes them to motel rooms."

"But you did."

"If anybody picked anybody up, it was her picking me up."

"Either way, you both ended up in that room together."

"Yes, we did."

"And only one of you walked out alive."

"I keep telling you, I didn't kill her."

"Did you hit her?"

"No! I've never hit a woman in my life."

"Really, Mr. Winters?" She opened a folder and looked at a piece of paper. "Because according to this, you have assaulted at least one other woman. Your wife, right?"

She sat a police report in front of him on the table and Raymond felt his stomach fall.

"Is Raymond Alan Winters you or not?"

"It's me."

"And were you not cited for domestic violence on January 2, 2002?"

He closed his eyes.

"Mr. Winters?"

"Yes, I was."

Black Friday

Black Friday 57

Chapter 11

It had all been a mistake and Raymond had regretted it every day since. It was a Thursday and he had been nursing an impacted wisdom tooth for three days, waiting for an appointment the next morning with his dentist, who had been closed for the holidays. Finally giving in to the pain, Raymond had come home from work early to find their rented mobile home a mess. The usual dirty dishes piled up in the sink and Jason, who was going through the Terrible Twos at the time, was throwing a tantrum about something.

"What are you doing home two hours early?"

"My tooth is killing me."

"God, you are such a baby, Raymond! You skipped work because you had a toothache?"

"I didn't skip work, Sheila. I came home early."

"And how are we supposed to pay our bills if you just walk off the job anytime you want to?"

"I didn't walk off the job. Bernie saw I was hurting and told me to go home early. And I'm the assistant manager, so I'm on salary. Don't worry, I'll still get paid."

"So your manager sent you home? How's that going to look on a résumé, Raymond?"

"Give me a break, Sheila. Christ, I never miss work."

"No, you just get sent home! My mother is on her way over here. How's it going to look to her when she finds you here sitting on your butt in the middle of the day?"

"Do you think I give a damn what your mother thinks?"

"No, Raymond, I already know you don't. You don't care what anybody thinks. You're too selfish to care."

He shook his head in disgust and went into the bedroom to lie down, almost tripping over the crying toddler when he turned. Ten minutes later Sheila marched into the room and said, "Here, since you're home, you can watch this screaming brat. My mother's here and we're going to pick up Kimberly at daycare."

She had plopped Jason down on his stomach and left the room. "Damn it!"

He followed her down the hallway. "Can't you take him with you? I told you, my tooth is killing me."

"Oh, stop it Raymond. You get to get out of here every day and go to the store. I never get a day off."

"A day off? Every day is a day off for you. You don't clean the house, you don't take care of the kids, all you do is..."

And Sheila had slapped him, "Don't you ever say I don't do anything around here! I work my fingers to the bone taking care of your children!"

But Raymond wasn't listening to her. The blow sent the pain from his sore tooth shooting through his jaw and across the top of his head. It was so intense that he thought he would throw up, and he started back down the hallway to the bedroom.

Sheila had grabbed his arm and blocked his path, "You're not going to bed, you're going to take some responsibility and watch your son!"

In his pain and frustration, he had blindly shoved her aside, not realizing that Jason had followed him out into the living room. Sheila took a step backward from the shove and fell over the boy, and both of them had screamed as they hit the floor.

"You bastard," his mother-in-law had screamed. "Look what you did!"

"I'm sorry," Raymond had said, shocked at his actions. "I didn't mean to. I just..."

Sheila had scrambled to her feet, snatched up the boy, and screamed a long line of invective at him as she and her mother fled. Raymond stood staring at the door they had slammed in their exit, dumbfounded by what he had done. He had never raised a hand to anyone, man or woman. Even as a schoolboy, he had walked away from fights and tolerated the abuse of bullies rather than defend himself.

He didn't have long to think, because within minutes he heard sirens outside and two police officers were pounding on the door. Raymond had expected to go to jail and knew he deserved to, but after listening to his story and interviewing his wife and her mother, both officers had agreed that the shove had been more of an accident than an assault. The fact that his face was swollen from the tooth and that he was in obvious pain, and that his face still had the lingering red imprint from the slap, had played a factor in their decision to issue a citation to both he and Sheila rather than arrest anyone.

Sheila had spent the weekend at her mother's house, and by Monday morning had come to realize that a conviction for domestic violence could cost her husband his job, and she might have to go to work herself. And that since she, too, had been cited, she also faced whatever punishment he might receive. Monday morning they had gone to the courthouse together, told the judge that it had been no more than a misunderstanding and that nobody had actually been assaulted. The judge had read the police report, taken into consideration Raymond's promising position in a well established company and how much damage a conviction could do to a family with two young children and had dismissed the charges after giving them both a stern lecture.

***

"Mr. Winters?"

Janet Morrison's voice brought him back to the present.

He shook his head. "It wasn't like that. Did you read the report?"

"Yes I did. You assaulted your wife and young son. That's pretty despicable to me. And it makes me think that a man who would do that would do anything."

"Did you read the whole report, Ms. Morrison?"

"I'm not the one being interrogated here, Mr. Winters."

"Oh, so this is an interrogation now? When did it stop being a conversation?"

"Why don't you just admit it, Mr. Winters? You killed that woman. You know it, I know it, and these two detectives know it."

"I didn't kill anybody!"

"You never hit a woman either, right? This police report is all fiction?"

"Where does it say I hit anybody? I was the one who got hit. Yes, I shoved my wife. That was wrong. I admitted it then, and I admit it now. But that doesn't make me a murderer."

"I think it does."

"Then I think it's time I have an attorney here."

Since the only attorney he knew was his brother-in-law, and he didn't know Brian's telephone number, he had called Julia. They were at the police station in just over a half hour; a long half hour because both detectives had sat in the room with him and nobody had spoken for the entire time. Eventually there had been a knock on the door and Detective Acosta had gone out into the hallway. A moment later he had returned and said, "Your attorney's here." The detectives had left them alone and Raymond told his sister and her husband why he was there.

When he was done, Brian had then opened the door and asked, "Is Mr. Winters under arrest?"

"Not at this time," Detective Harrison had told him.

Brian had then said, "Let's go, Raymond," and a moment later they were out in the parking lot.

***

"Jesus Christ, Raymond, do you know how this makes me look?"

"You? What does this have to do with you, Julia?"

His sister was livid, and stopped to look at him like he was some alien life form that had appeared in front of her. "What does it have to do with me? I'm the Vice President of the Art League, I'm on the board of directors of the Beautiful Brevard Foundation, and I'm being considered for nomination to the Coastal Arts Guild. Do you have any idea how difficult it is to even get noticed by that crowd? Of course you don't, you sell grapes for a living!"

"Whatever. I'm sorry I called Brian, but he's the only lawyer I know."

"He doesn't deal with criminals. He's a corporate attorney, you idiot. Or at least he *was*. Once word of this gets out we'll probably have to leave town in the middle of the night."

"I'm not a criminal. I didn't do anything."

"Really, Raymond? You didn't do anything? Then why did the police arrest you? Do you think they just go around arresting people for nothing?"

"I wasn't arrested. I was questioned."

"And that makes it alright? If you weren't running around like Royce sticking your dick in anything that moves, none of us would be in this mess."

"*We* aren't in this mess, Julia. I'm in it."

"Oh really? Then please explain why Brian and I are standing here in front of the police station?"

"Julia, I shouldn't have called. I just..."

"Oh, shut up, Raymond! This is going to kill Mother. It's absolutely going to kill her."

"Listen, how about we get out of here?" Brian Rutledge said. "I've got an appointment this afternoon that I'm barely going to have time to get to as it is."

"Fine," Julia said, "This whole sordid thing is making me sick."

"Listen Raymond, I'm glad I could help you out, but this really isn't my area of expertise. I strongly advise you to hire yourself a good criminal defense attorney."

"Can you recommend anybody?"

"No, we're done with this," Julia said before her husband could reply. "Look in the phone book, Raymond. And while you're at it, lose our number."

She turned on her heel and stalked away. Brian stood there a moment longer, looking uncomfortable. Though they had been related by marriage for over twenty years, the two men had nothing in common and had never been close. Finally, Brian said, "Call William DeLeon in Cocoa and tell him I sent you. He's not cheap, but he's good. And you're going to need somebody good."

"Thanks, Brian, I do appreciate it."

"Yeah, no problem. Look, I've got to go. And Julia is right. It's probably better if you don't contact us for a while."

He left Raymond standing in front of the police station alone, and only after he watched his sister's Jaguar pull out of the parking lot did he realize that he didn't have a ride home.

Black Friday

Chapter 12

Raymond turned on his phone and looked at the screen. Eleven missed calls. Six were from Norma, each increasingly more concerned and wondering where he was, if he was alright, why he wasn't returning her calls, and asking what she was supposed to say to Mr. Kirtidge from the main office, who had called twice for him. Four more were from Sheila, the first asking why his truck was still in the driveway and the rest demanding to know where he was and why he wasn't at the store. By the last call she was screaming so loud that her words were distorted and it ended with a thumping sound as she had thrown her telephone across the room in frustration. The other call was from Wayne Lamb, asking if he was okay and telling Raymond to call him if he needed anything.

Wayne answered on the third ring. "Where are you, buddy?"

"I'm at the police station. Can you come pick me up?"

"I'm on my way."

That was Wayne. As steady as a rock and as faithful as an old yellow dog. It was past noon and he braced himself for the next call.

"Where are you, Raymond? My God, everybody's worried sick about you!"

"I'm sorry. Norma. Something crazy has come up that I need to take care of. I don't know if I'm going to make it in today or not."

"Your wife has called over and over and I don't know what to tell her, and Mr. Kirtidge wants you to call him immediately. He's really hot under the collar. What's going on Raymond? It's not like you to just drop out of sight like this."

Raymond's head was pounding and he wanted nothing more than to crawl into a hot shower and stand there for an hour and then go to bed and sleep forever.

"It's... it's crazy, Norma. I wish I could explain it, but I can't right now."

"But, I don't understand. What am I supposed to tell the crew?

What am I supposed to tell Mr. Kirtridge?"

"I don't understand it all either," Raymond said.

"Are you sick, Raymond? Is there..."

"Look, I'll try to get in there as soon as possible okay? Just hold down the fort. Can you do that for me, Norma?"

"What about Mr. Kirtridge?"

"I'll call him right now. Please, Norma, I just need a little time to get things straightened out. Can you cover for me?"

"Yea, Raymond, I'll do whatever you need. But I just...."

"I've got to call Stan. Just tell the crew I had a personal issue that came up, okay?"

"Okay. Raymond. I hope you know that whatever's going on, I'm your friend. You can talk to me."

"I know, Norma. And I appreciate that. I do. Now let me call Kirtridge."

Before she could say anything else, he ended the call and took a deep breath. Norma was an excellent assistant manager, and he had always known he could depend on her to keep things going smoothly at the store. No manager built a winning crew on their own, and he gave Norma a lot of the credit for his own success in the company. But he still clung to some tiny shred of hope that he could keep all of this from becoming public. Now for the next call.

"Raymond? Where are you? You just vanished!"

"I'm sorry, Stan. I... I had a personal problem come up and it kind of threw me for a loop. I should have called sooner, but things just got away from me."

"I understand, those things happen. But you don't just drop off the radar for hours like this,"

"I'm sorry."

"Sorry doesn't keep the shelves stocked, Raymond. Sorry doesn't make sure the floors are mopped and the deposits get made."

"I know, Stan."

"This isn't like you, Raymond. We've always known we could depend on you."

"You can depend on me."

"Can I, Raymond?"

"Yes, I promise, this was just a hiccup. I just need a little bit of time is all. I have some vacation time coming. You can charge it against that."

"Raymond, I like to think that we're all friends here at Palmetto

Pantry. If something's going on, you can talk to me about it."

"I know, Stan. Thanks."

"Is it alcohol, Raymond. Or drugs?"

"No! No, it's nothing like that, Stan. I swear."

"Does this have anything to do with the police coming to the store on Saturday?"

Raymond's stomach lurched. He should have known that his departure in the company of the two detectives was not going to go unnoticed.

"Norma said there had been a death. Somebody close to you died."

"Yes. A friend."

"I'm, sorry, Raymond. I really am. But you can't just...."

"I know, Stan, I know. There were just some last minute arrangements that I needed to tend to. I handled it wrong. I'm sorry."

There was silence on the other end for a moment, and then Kirtridge said, "Look, Raymond, you're a good man and a fine manager. So I'm going to give you the benefit of the doubt on this one, okay? But don't leave us all hanging like this, Raymond. If you need some time off, we can arrange that, okay?"

"Thank you, Stan. I'll try to get to the store this afternoon. And I'll be there in the morning for sure. I promise."

"Alright. You let me know if you need anything, Raymond. I'm just a phone call away."

Wayne's blue Toyota Camry pulled up in front of him and Raymond ended the call with a promise to get things back on track at the store. He crawled into the car and closed his eyes, sinking back into the seat.

"You okay, buddy?"

Raymond couldn't trust himself to talk and just shook his head. Wayne looked at him with concern, but didn't say anything else, just shifted into gear and drove out of the parking lot. They were silent as they drove down Highway 1, which was called Washington Street as it traveled through town past restaurants, hotels, the Moose lodge, and empty storefronts that were victims of the downturn in the local economy after the shutdown of the Space Shuttle program.

Wayne made a right turn onto the A. Max Brewer Bridge and out onto the causeway that led to the Merritt Island National Wildlife Refuge. He parked the car and they sat watching the river and the scattered boats out on the water. Raymond found it hard to believe that just the day before, he had been out there on his boat.

"I'm in some deep shit, Wayne."

"Talk to me."

Raymond told him the whole story, everything from meeting Holly standing in line at the Black Friday sale, how they had started talking and eventually ended up in the motel room, about the visit from the detectives on Saturday and them coming to his house that morning, and the long interrogation that followed.

When he was finished, Wayne didn't make a crude joke about his dalliance with Holly, or tell him what a mistake he had made, or even ask him if he had harmed the woman. He simply said, "Whatever you need, Raymond, I've got your back."

And then the tears had come. Raymond had never considered himself an overly emotional person, and he could not remember the last time he had shed tears, but they poured out of his eyes and he felt his chest heaving with deep sobs. Wayne put a hand on his arm and squeezed, but did not say anything, just let him get it all out.

Finally Raymond managed to get control of himself and wiped his face. He was surprised that he did not feel ashamed for the breakdown in front of his friend, but he knew that Wayne was not the kind of man who judged others.

"So what are you going to do now?"

"I've got the name of an attorney down in Cocoa that Brian told me to call. I need to get to the store while I've still got a job."

"And then there's Sheila."

"Yeah, and then there's Sheila."

"She called this morning asking why your truck was in the driveway and I gave her some bullshit excuse about how it wouldn't start this morning so I gave you a ride to work. But I guess that was a mistake because later on she came over and said she'd called the store and you weren't there and nobody had seen you. So I guess I just made things worse. I'm sorry."

"That's okay," Raymond said. "I appreciate you trying to cover for me."

Then a thought hit him and he said, "Do you think any of the other neighbors saw me getting into the police car?"

"I don't think so," Wayne said. "After they drove away with you I stood out there for a while wondering what the hell was happening and nobody came out to say anything. And you can bet your ass that if Penny Odell had seen anything she'd have been out there in the yard asking

Black Friday

if I knew what was going on. And apparently nobody said anything to Sheila about it, because she didn't mention it."

Raymond was relieved to know that apparently nobody had seen him going away in the back of the police car, or if they had, at least they hadn't said anything to Sheila about it. Then again, his wife wasn't the most popular woman in the cul-de-sac, and she had been involved in feuds and arguments with most of the neighbors at one time or another. The one exception seemed to be Wayne, whom she adored and was always talking about trying to fix up with some woman or another.

"Listen, instead of going home and facing the wrath of Sheila right now, why don't you drop me off a block or so from the house and take my car to go to the store or whatever you need to do."

"Thank you," Raymond said. "Are you really sure you want to do that? I mean, she's always mad at me. No reason for you to get on her bad side, too."

Wayne laughed and asked, "What do I have to lose? Do you suppose she'll stop trying to fix me up with her sister?"

"You should be so lucky," Raymond said. Then he added, "Seriously Wayne, this could all get real ugly. It's not fair for you to get yourself dragged into the middle of my problems."

"You let me worry about me, okay? You're my friend and that's all that matters. Like I said, whatever you need, I've got your back."

Raymond felt a tremendous sense of gratitude and didn't know what to say, so he just nodded his head.

Black Friday

Chapter 13

Several employees stared at him as he walked through the store, curiosity evident on their faces. Raymond nodded to some of them, said hello to a couple, but didn't stop to talk. When he entered the office, Norma jumped up from her desk and hugged him. Raymond stood stiffly, not sure how to react and uncomfortable with the physical contact.

"I am so glad you're okay! *Are* you okay, Raymond?"

"Yeah, I'm fine. Thanks Norma. He did not know how to gracefully extricate himself from her embrace, but fortunately she let go of him and stepped back.

She eyed him critically and said, "You look like you've had a really rough time. What in the world is going on, Raymond?"

He liked working with Norma, and he trusted her as much as he trusted anybody, except possibly Wayne, but he didn't want to involve her in this situation. The more people that knew about Holly and his conversations with the police, the more likely it was that word would get out and eventually make its way to the main office. If that happened, Raymond knew his career was over.

"It's complicated," Raymond told her. "I really wish I could explain it to you right now, but I can't."

She stared at him for a long moment, and he was sure she was going to continue to question him but his cell phone rang. He looked at the number and answered it.

"Hello?"

"Mr. Winters?"

"Yes, this is Raymond Winters."

"This is Miranda Fernandez from Mr. DeLeon's office. I gave him your message and told him that Mr. Rutledge had referred you. Can you be here at 3 o'clock?"

Raymond looked at his watch. It was just after 2 and it was 24 miles to Cocoa. He'd have to hustle, but he could make it. "I'll be there."

He quickly hung up and said, "Look, Norma, I hate to do this, but

I've got to go."

"Go? Go where? You just got here!"

"I know, and I'm sorry. But I have to go."

"Raymond, you know I've always been here for you and you know you can depend on me. But you're asking me to operate in a vacuum. What am I supposed to tell the crew, or Andy when he comes on, or Mr. Kirtridge if he calls back?"

"Just.... I don't know, Norma. Just bear with me. Please?"

He didn't give her time to answer, he just left the store and headed south on Interstate 95.

***

William DeLeon was a heavyset bald man who got right to the point. "If we are going to work together, we need to set some ground rules, Raymond. I need total honesty. I don't care if you rob banks for a living and peep into old ladies windows at night. It's not my job to judge you, it's my job to defend you, and I can't do that unless you're absolutely straight with me. Got it?"

Raymond nodded.

"Okay. Let's talk about money. I usually charge $175 an hour, but because you're Brian's brother-in-law, I'll take your case for $150 an hour. And I need a $2000 retainer. Can you cover that?"

"Yeah," Raymond said. "I don't have anything on me but I can go to the bank and get it and come back."

DeLeon waved a hand dismissively, "I don't need it right this minute. How much *do* you have on you?"

Raymond opened his wallet. There was a $20 bill, two tens, and a five.

"Give me the twenty and sign this," DeLeon said, pushing a piece of paper across the desk to Raymond. "This is a power of attorney that gives me the right to represent you, and the money is a deposit on retainer that officially makes me your attorney. So from this minute forward, anything you say to me is privileged information. You got that?"

Raymond nodded, signed the form and handed him the money. DeLeon didn't look at either one, just slid them to the side of his desk and said, "Start at the beginning."

***

When he was done telling his story, DeLeon sat with his elbows on his desk and his hands steepled and was silent for several minutes. Then he said, "Okay, here's what's going to happen. They're going to arrest you. Maybe tonight, maybe tomorrow, Wednesday by the latest. When they do, don't say a thing. You've already said way too much. Tell them I'm your attorney and that you want me present, and not another word. Got it?"

Raymond nodded his head, feeling sick to his stomach. He had known this might happen, had actually been surprised they hadn't arrested him earlier in the day when he said he wanted an attorney. But he had clung to some small hope that the real killer would be found and he'd be off the hook before things got this far. He nodded around the lump in his throat.

"I'm not going to lie to you Raymond. This looks really bad."

"But I didn't do it!"

"It doesn't matter whether you did it or not. What matters is that they think you did it. Now it's all about damage control."

"What do you mean?"

"Raymond, you need to understand that life as you know it is over. I know. You say you're innocent, and I believe you. I really do. But the cops are convinced you're the man they're looking for. And put yourself in their place; there's no question you were in that room with the victim. They've got your name on the motel register, they've got video of you checking in, they've got your DNA, which is going to match evidence found in the room and on the victim's body. They've got a statement she made that she was meeting a married guy at a motel that morning. How can they *not* think you're the person they're looking for?"

"But I didn't...."

"Yeah, I know. You didn't do it. You can say that until the cows come home and it's not going to change a thing. You *are* going to be arrested, you will be charged with homicide, you are going to lose your job, and very possibly your family, your house, and everything you own. I guess you can call it the screwing you get for the screwing you got."

At that moment Raymond just wanted to curl up in a ball in the corner of the attorney's office and die.

"I'm sorry, but that's the way it is," DeLeon continued. "And as bad as all that sounds, and is, that's the least of your worries. If they convict you, you're looking at life without parole at best. And there's a very real chance they'll take you to Raiford and stick a needle in your arm."

Raymond felt the room begin to spin. He couldn't focus, and it seemed like the attorney was speaking to him from a mile away. DeLeon looked at him with concern and asked, "Are you okay, Raymond?"

Miranda Fernandez, DeLeon's assistant, who had been sitting off to the side taking notes, quickly rose and left the room and came back with a glass of water for him. Raymond took a drink, choked, and began coughing. When he managed to stop and catch his breath, DeLeon asked again, "Are you all right?"

Raymond nodded his head, although he wasn't sure he would ever be all right again.

"I'm not telling you all this to scare you, Raymond. But you need to understand just how serious your situation is. I know it's not fair, but there are a lot of innocent men sitting in prison. Not that there aren't a lot of people that belong there, too. What we have to do is keep you from becoming one of them."

"How do we do that?"

"You're absolutely sure you had never met this woman before?"

"Absolutely."

"Okay, then we have to figure out who this married man is that she talked about meeting that morning. We need to find out everything we can about her, where she came from, why she gave you a fake name, why she picked you up in the first place, and how she ended up dead."

"So what do I do now? Just go home and wait for them to arrest me?"

"From what you've told me so far, your marriage isn't all that great."

Raymond shook his head.

"How much money do you and your wife have in the bank?"

"Maybe $1200 or so in checking, a couple thousand in savings, and two CDs that total about $30,000. I've also got a separate account that my wife doesn't know about, where I've been stashing my bonus money for a while."

"How much is in this bonus account?"

"About $11,000."

"Anything else? How much equity do you have in your house? What kind of vehicles do you have?"

"You know what the housing market has been up in Titusville. We owe $85,000 on a house that would probably bring fifty if I was lucky. We've got an SUV and a pickup that we're making payments on, and

Black Friday

I've got an eighteen foot boat that's financed." Saying this out loud, it didn't sound like very much for a lifetime of hard work.

"If I were you, I'd go to the bank right now and transfer half of the money and CDs into that separate account of yours."

"I don't want to leave my wife and kids hanging," Raymond said.

"Well, without sounding judgmental, you should've thought of that before you ever went into that room with the victim."

"I wish I'd never seen her, or that room."

"Woulda, coulda, shoulda. The fact is that you did, and we can't go back and rewrite history. What we can do is make sure you have a future."

"Okay. So what happens after I'm arrested?" It felt like he was asking a surgeon what would happen after a heart or lung transplant.

"Once you are booked you'll get a phone call. Call me immediately. Don't talk to anybody. Not the police, not your cellmates, nobody. Don't even talk to yourself until I get there. With any luck, given the fact that you're an established member of the community and have a job, I might be able to get you released on bail. That's why I asked you about assets. You're going to need something to put up to secure bail. Usually 10% of whatever the judge sets. I work with a couple of good bail bondsman here in town and I'll be talking to them as soon as we're done here, to have everything in place. And I've got a private detective I'm going to put on the trail of the victim to see what we can find out about her. So go ahead and get out of here, and whatever you do, keep your mouth shut. And do not talk to any reporters. Because if you do get released on bail, they're going to be everywhere pointing cameras and microphones at you."

Raymond left the attorney's office and drove to the nearest branch of their bank, where he withdrew $1500 from the checking and savings accounts he and Sheila shared. When he tried to transfer one of the CDs into his name alone he ran into a roadblock.

"I'm sorry, but I'm afraid we will need Mrs. Winters approval to do that, since both names are on the CDs," the young assistant manager at the bank told him. "Can she come in? If not, I can give you a form that you can have her sign in front of a notary."

"Thank you," Raymond said, knowing that there was no way Sheila was going to sign off on one cent of their joint assets.

He left the bank and drove three blocks to a different bank, the one where he had his secret account, and withdrew an additional $500, which he dropped off at DeLeon's office on his way out of town.

He didn't know where to go from there so he drove back home, knowing it might well be the last time he would ever call the house in the cul-de-sac home.

Chapter 14

If Raymond wondered what kind of reception awaited him at home after his disappearing act, he forgot all about it when he turned onto his street. Two marked police cars and the white Caprice were parked in front of his house. A horn beeped behind him and he looked in the rearview mirror to see a television news van.

Raymond felt his stomach churn and was tempted to turn the car around and drive away and keep on driving as far as he could. But he knew that would only make his situation worse. He parked the Camry in Wayne's driveway and walked across the street as the news crew got out and pointed a camera at the house.

A uniformed officer met him at the door and said, "I'm sorry, you can't go in there."

"It's my house," Raymond said.

"Are you Raymond Winters?"

"Yes."

The officer pushed a button on the microphone attached to his shirt and said, "Mr. Winters is out here now."

A moment later Detective Acosta came to the door and said, "Mr. Winters, we are executing search warrants on your house, your vehicles, and your office at work. I also have a warrant for your cell phone. May I have it, please?" He handed Raymond copies of the warrants.

"I think I need to call my attorney."

"You can do whatever you want, sir."

"Can I use my phone for that, before I give it to you?"

"I'm sorry, I need it now," Acosta said. "But give me the number and I'll call him on mine for you."

Hearing her husband's voice, Sheila came to the door and screeched, "Raymond, what in the hell have you done? What's going on here? Why are the police searching our home? And where the hell have you been all day?"

Raymond didn't know which question to answer first, and with

Detective Acosta and the uniformed officer standing there, he decided it was best not to answer any of them.

He stepped away from the door as DeLeon came on the line. "The cops are here searching my house," Raymond said. "They say they're going to search my office at work, too."

"That's routine," DeLeon said. "Just remember what I told you, don't say anything to anyone."

"So what am I supposed to do now?"

"Be cooperative, polite, and don't say anything. I told you, Raymond, this isn't going to just go away."

"Do you think they're going to arrest me now?"

"You have to be prepared for that. It's going to happen sooner or later."

"But I..."

"Yeah, Raymond, I know. You didn't do it. I'm not the one you have to convince. That's what juries are for. In the meantime, remember what I told you; be polite and cooperative, but don't say anything about the case at all. If they ask you where you were at any time, or about anything in the house, or whatever, don't say anything. If they take you in for questioning or arrest you, call me. Otherwise, we'll talk tomorrow."

DeLeon ended the call and Sheila pushed past the policeman in the doorway. "Raymond, I want to know what's going on! Why are these people in my house?"

"I can't talk about it right now, Sheila."

"What do you mean you can't talk about it? What's happening?"

"Sheila I...."

"And where you been all day? I've called and called. And I know you weren't at work!"

Her voice was shrill and was rising with each word.

"I said I can't talk about it!"

"I want to know what's going on," Sheila said, grabbing his shirt. "I have a right to know what these people are doing in my house!"

Raymond tried to pull her hand away and it turned into a shoving match, until the uniformed officer pushed them apart.

"Mrs. Winters, please go back inside the house."

"You can't tell me what to do in my own home!"

"Just do what the man said," Raymond told her.

"Shut up, Raymond! I don't know what you've done, but I'm going to find out."

Black Friday 77

The officer stepped between them and said, "This is your last warning, ma'am. You can either go back in the house or you can go to jail. Which is it going to be?"

For a moment Raymond thought she would challenge the officer, but instead she set her mouth in a hard line and said, "I've got your badge number!"

"That's fine, ma'am. Now go in the house, or else."

Sheila was not accustomed to anyone standing up to her, let alone ordering her to do anything. But she seemed to sense that the policeman would not tolerate any further resistance. With one last hateful glare at her husband, she turned and stomped back into the house. The officer shook his head and followed her back inside.

Not knowing what else to do, but not comfortable standing in the yard with all the neighbors gawking at him, Raymond went back across the street, to where Wayne stood in his driveway.

"Are you okay, buddy?"

"Do I look okay?" Raymond asked.

"Sorry. Dumb question."

"It's okay," Raymond said. "All this is just..."

"I understand. Come on, let's go inside."

Raymond watched through the window as the police came and went through the door of his house. They carried away the desktop computer he kept in his den, as well as two laptops, and several boxes of things he couldn't identify from that distance. Twice the young reporter from the news van knocked on Wayne's door, and both times Wayne told them to go away, that he had no comment and Mr. Winters was unavailable to speak to them. It was well past dark when the police finally finished and drove away, the news van following them.

"Are you going to go over and try to talk to her?"

Raymond felt that he should. Sheila deserved some sort of explanation, but what could he tell her? And would it matter anyway? He knew it was a matter of hours or days at best before the whole case blew wide open. Was suffering any more of his wife's abuse worth it to delay the explosion that was coming anyway?

"I guess I have to, don't I?"

"Probably."

Reluctantly, Raymond walked across the street, feeling like every eye in the neighborhood was watching him. The front door was locked, and when he used his key to unlock it, the security chain prevented the door from opening.

"Sheila, let me in."

She came to the door and said, "You've got your nerve! Do you really think you can just come waltzing in here after all of this?"

"Listen, I know this looks terrible. But..."

"Looks terrible? Looks terrible? Do you know how humiliated I am to have my home searched like I'm some kind of common criminal? Do you know how traumatized my children are right now? Do you even care what kind of hell you are putting us through? And we still don't even know what's going on! Nobody will tell us anything. That reporter was knocking on the door asking questions about you murdering somebody! God, Raymond, what the hell have you done?"

"It's all a big misunderstanding, Sheila. I promise, it's all going to work out."

"No, Raymond. A misunderstanding is when you go through a drive-through and they get your order wrong. This isn't a misunderstanding, this is a nightmare!"

"I'm sorry, Sheila. I really am."

"Get the hell out of here, Raymond, before I call the police."

"Come on, Sheila."

"I said go!"

"Can I at least get some clothes and my toothbrush?"

"I don't feel safe with you in the house. How can I when they're talking about you killing somebody?"

"I didn't kill anybody, Sheila. Don't you know anything at all about me after all these years?"

"Apparently not, Raymond. Now leave before I call the police."

"But I need some clothes." Raymond could hear the whine in his voice and hated himself for it.

"Forget it, I'm not letting you in here to kill me and my children, too!"

Raymond knew that arguing with her was futile, and the last thing he wanted was to have the police come back again. He turned and trudged back across the street, hearing the door slam behind him.

Back at Wayne's house, his friend shook his head. "No luck?"

"She wouldn't even let me get some clothes."

"Tell you what, let me go over and talk to her. I don't think she hates me as much as she does you right now. At least, not yet."

Raymond didn't want to involve Wayne any deeper than he already was in his problems, but didn't know what else to do. Wayne left and was back in a few minutes with two paper bags full of clothing and toiletries. "Nice luggage you got there, sport."

"Thanks, Wayne. I'm surprised she'd let you get anything."

"Maybe she still hopes to fix me up with that sister of hers. Who knows? With you out of the way, maybe she wants to keep me for herself." Seeing the pained look on his friend's face, Wayne said, "Sorry. Too soon?"

In spite of himself, Raymond chuckled. "I wouldn't wish that on my worst enemy."

Wayne laughed, then his expression grew somber and he said, "Really, man, I was out of line. This is some serious shit you're in."

"It's okay. Right now, I think I need all the laughs I can get."

His friend looked at him with concern and asked, "Have you eaten anything at all today?"

"No. I usually grab a breakfast burrito or something on the way in to work because Sheila doesn't like me making noise in the morning, and, well, you saw how that worked out today."

"How about I throw a couple of steaks on the grill?"

"I don't think I can eat, Wayne. And if I did I don't know if I could keep it down."

"Your body needs fuel. Let me get them started and then I'll help you carry all this stuff down to the bedroom."

In spite of himself, Raymond found the aroma of the cooking steaks overpowering, and wolfed down the ribeye and the baked potato Wayne had prepared for him.

"Did that help?"

"Yes it did, surprisingly. Thanks."

"Here, another of these will help, too," Wayne said, handing him a Heineken.

He offered to wash the dishes, but Wayne shooed him into the living room and made short work of loading the dishwasher. When he joined him and sat in his recliner, he asked, "So what did the lawyer have to say?"

Raymond knew that DeLeon had told him not to talk to anybody about the case, but he felt that Wayne was the exception and told him about their conversation. When he was finished, Wayne's face looked troubled.

"Damn, Raymond, what can I do to help?"

"You've done so much already," Raymond said. "I don't know what's going to happen, Wayne. And I'm scared. Do you think they'll really send me to prison?"

His friend shook his head and said, "Not if I have anything to do with it. Look, Raymond, I meant what I said before. Whatever you need, I'm here for you. Money, a place to stay, a shoulder to cry on, you don't even have to ask."

"I appreciate that more than you'll ever know," Raymond told him. "I've never had a friend like you, Wayne. Hell, I don't know if I've ever really had a friend before."

Wayne left the room, and when he returned he handed him a thick white envelope.

"What's this?"

"Just a little something to tide you over."

Raymond opened the envelope. It was full of $100 bills.

"God, Wayne, how much is in here?"

"$5,000. And there's more if you need it. I like to keep a little cash on hand, just in case of emergencies."

"I can't take this," Raymond said. "I appreciate it, I really do, but this is too much, Wayne. The way things are going, I don't know if I'd ever be able to pay you back."

"Don't worry about that. Just use it for whatever you need."

"No," Raymond said, handing the envelope back to him. "You know how much I appreciate it and how much it means to me, but I just can't."

"It's not going to change my life," Wayne told him. "I'm a bachelor, man. I make a shitload of money, and what am I going to spend it on?"

"Well you could get yourself a woman," Raymond suggested.

"No, that's why I *have* the money," Wayne said laughing. "I'll tell you what, I'm going to put it over here on the bookcase, and it's going to stay right there. If you need it for anything, Raymond, anything at all, help yourself."

"Why are you doing this?"

"Doing what?"

"All of this?" Raymond said, waving his arm around him. "Letting me stay here, the money, all of it? You don't have to do this. Why complicate your life with my problems?"

"It's called friendship, man. That's what friends do for each other. Now, before we get all mushy and start saying *I love you bro*, how about

I get us both another beer?"

Raymond couldn't trust himself to answer so he just nodded.

By the time he had finished the beer, the combination of the alcohol and the stressful day had taken their toll, and Raymond's eyelids were getting heavy. He yawned, and Wayne said, "You're beat, buddy. Why don't you take a long shower and hit the sack?"

Raymond started to shake his head and then realized that his friend was right. He was exhausted and it was all he could do to make his way down the hallway to the guest bedroom, strip, and get into the shower. He turned the water on as hot as he could stand it and stood there a long time before he finally soaped himself, rinsed, and turned the water off. Stepping out of the shower, he toweled himself dry and climbed into the queen size bed in the guest bedroom. He did not know what the next day held in store for him, but he didn't have the energy to think about it just then. Within minutes he was sound asleep.

Chapter 15

The hardest thing Raymond had ever had to do was to get out of bed and get dressed the next morning as if it was any a normal day. He almost turned around and went back to bed when he walked into Wayne's kitchen and saw the TV. The screen showed the reporter from the day before standing in front of his house. The reporter was saying, "In the latest on the Holly Coulter murder investigation, yesterday afternoon Titusville police executed a search warrant on a home and vehicles in the 300 block of Stardust Street. At the same time, detectives were also searching the office of the Palmetto Pantry grocery store on Cheney Highway. Police would not say if they had a suspect in the case, but Channel 17 has learned that the home belongs to Raymond Winters, who is also the manager of Palmetto Pantry. When we tried to speak to Mr. Winters, we were told he was unavailable. A spokesman for Palmetto Pantry said they had no comment at this time and would not acknowledge whether or not Mr. Winters is still employed by the company."

"Oh shit," Raymond said. "That's all I need."

"Do you think you should just stay here and lay low today?" Wayne asked. "You're more than welcome to."

Raymond wanted to take him up on the offer, but he had always followed the rules and done what was expected of him so he shook his head and said, "No, I'd better go in and face the music."

Wayne slid a key across the table to him and said, "I've got appointments in Winter Park on the north side of Orlando this morning, but you come and go anytime you need to, okay?"

Raymond nodded and accepted the key. "Wayne, I'm really worried about how this is going to affect you. I don't want my problems to become your problems."

"Don't worry about it."

"You have to live here after all this is over with, no matter how it works out. I don't want you ostracized by the neighborhood for helping me, or for it to cost you your job or something."

"Don't sweat it, buddy. What are they gonna do? Stop inviting me to the neighborhood cookouts? Kick me off the bowling league? Will Sheila stop trying to fix me up with somebody?"

"Still...."

Wayne interrupted him and said, "Okay, you need to get something straight in your head, Raymond. First of all, you're my friend, and I don't give a rat's ass what anybody thinks about me. Number two, this is America, and the last time I checked, people here were still innocent until proven guilty. And we both know you're not guilty. And as for my job, I've been their top producer in the entire Southeast region for the last five years in a row. No matter what you may have heard about pharmaceutical companies, the truth is that they don't give a damn whether or not their pills make you feel better or cure anything. It's all about the bucks, buddy. They need me more than I need them. I've got headhunters from half a dozen of our competitors knocking on my door all the time."

"I appreciate that. But..."

"Hey, what's the worst they can do? Fire both of us? If they do we'll hook that boat of yours to the back of your truck and head for the Keys. We'll live on fresh fish and beer, chase pretty tourist women, and if that doesn't work out, we'll become pirates!"

Raymond smiled and said, "I guess there are worse ways to spend the rest of our lives."

"Well there you go then." Wayne looked at the clock on the wall and said, "I've gotta go. Listen Raymond, I mean it, you treat this place just like your own home. Come and go whenever you need to, use that money sitting on the bookcase if you need it, it's all good, man."

He left, and Raymond followed soon after, wondering what kind of reception he would get at work.

***

Things were definitely tense at the Palmetto Pantry. He could feel it the moment he walked through the door. Dorothy Bernard and Suzanne Erickson were working the registers, and both stopped what they were doing and watched him as he walked past. Raymond nodded at both of them but they would not meet his eyes. Patrick Meyers stuttered out a hello when Raymond said good morning to him, but looked like he

Black Friday

wanted to run away. Dawn Forbes, a young mother who worked part time, was panic stricken when he said hello to her as she was arranging boxes of cereal on an aisle end cap.

Mike Rosemont, the weekend manager, met him in the doorway of the office.

"Hi Mike, what are you doing here on a Tuesday?" Raymond asked, though he already knew the answer.

Clearly uncomfortable, Mike said, "I'm sorry, Raymond. I'm not allowed to let you in the office and I'll have to ask you to leave the store."

"So it's come to that?"

"I'm really sorry, Raymond. I need your keys."

"It's not your fault," Raymond said as he took the company key ring from his pocket and handed it to the other man. "I understand. You're just doing your job."

Mike looked relieved and said again, "I'm sorry, Raymond. You're a great guy and you always treated all of us really well."

"Is Norma here? I'd like to say goodbye to her."

"She's... she doesn't want to talk to you."

That stung Raymond. While Norma had always been strong-willed and sometimes pushed too hard, they had enjoyed a good working relationship and had gotten along well. Raymond was hurt to realize that her assertion the day before that they were friends had only been lip service.

"Mr. Kirtridge said he tried to call you, but nobody was answering your phone."

"The police took it," Raymond told him.

"He said for you to call him. And I hate to say this, Raymond, but he said if you came here and wouldn't leave, I was supposed to call the police."

"It's okay, I'm leaving. I won't put you in that position, Mike." He offered his hand, not sure if the other man would take it, but Mike did, and there were tears in his eyes when he said, "When I started here you took me under your wing and really helped me get going. I owe you, Raymond, and you don't know how much this hurts me."

"Yeah, me too, Mike. Me too."

Raymond knew every inch of the grocery store as well as he did his own home, and he felt a strong sense of loss as he walked out the door, knowing he would never return. And every step of the way he felt the eyes of his former crew and customers on him.

***

From the store he drove to a nearby Walmart, purchased a cheap throwaway phone, not sure how long he would be free to make telephone calls. Back in the truck, he called the company's main office. After being on hold for what seemed like a long period of time, Stan Kirtridge came on the line.

"Mr. Winters, I'm afraid it's my duty to inform you that your employment with Palmetto Pantry has been terminated."

"Now it's Mr. Winters? Yesterday it was Raymond."

"Yesterday you weren't involved in a scandal that could cost this company its reputation and its customers."

"I didn't do anything, Stan."

"It doesn't matter. This company was built on strong community values and the very hint of something this messy doesn't look good. It doesn't look good at all."

"Dammit Stan, you know me!"

"I thought I did, Raymond. Apparently not."

"Doesn't all of my years of good service to the company count for anything? Doesn't all of the long days, all the nights and weekends, everything I did to build that store up, count for anything at all, Stan?"

"We appreciate what you've done for Palmetto Pantry, Raymond, and we wish you the best in the future. Now, Marcella from accounting will be in touch about your final check and distribution of funds you have in your profit-sharing account. As with standard company policy, the profit-sharing funds will not be released until after an internal audit."

Raymond felt his face grow hot. "Are you implying I'm a thief, Stan? I've never taken one penny that wasn't owed to me, never eaten a single grape I didn't pay for."

Kirtridge's voice grew formal when he said, "Again, we appreciate your contributions to the company over the years. Your group health insurance will continue for 90 days, and we wish you well. Oh, one final thing, Mr. Winters, please do not come onto our property again. We would hate to have you arrested for trespassing."

There was nothing else to say, so Raymond pushed the button to end the call. He had known it was coming but it still made him angry. While the job had been nothing more than a job to him, escaping to it every day had also been a sanctuary from his unhappy home life. He had given it everything he had and felt he deserved more than a quick brush off. Maybe Wayne had been right. Maybe when this was all over, *if* it was ever over, he should just go somewhere and spend the rest of his life fishing. Or become a pirate.

***

He wondered if Sheila had calmed down enough that he could talk to her, but got his answer as soon as he turned into the cul-de-sac and saw the mess in his front yard. His clothing, books, fishing gear, and everything else he owned was strewn across the grass. He parked the truck in the driveway and stood looking at the house and realized that it had never really been home to him. He began piling everything into the back of the pickup.

At some point Sheila came outside and stared at him with her arms folded across her chest. Raymond ignored her, and when everything was in the bed of the truck, he drove it across the street and into Wayne's garage and closed the door behind him.

Hauling everything out of the truck and into the guest bedroom left him feeling worn out. He realized he hadn't eaten anything that day, and even though Wayne told him to treat the place like his own, he did not feel comfortable going into the refrigerator or kitchen cabinets looking for something. So he drove to a nearby fast food place and got a burger.

Rationally, Raymond knew that not everybody in the restaurant was staring at him, from the young woman with the bright pink hair and pierced lip who took his order to the older couple seated at the next table, but he still felt like they had all seen the newscast and were judging him. He ate the sandwich without tasting it and left quickly.

Black Friday

Chapter 16

All of his life Raymond had a schedule, some place to be every day of the week. Monday through Friday he was at the store. Saturdays he did chores around the house or occasionally slipped away on his boat for a few hours of solitary fishing. Sunday mornings he was out on the water and Sunday afternoon always found him at Whispering Palms Nursing Home visiting his mother. Now, with nowhere to go and nothing to do, he was restless.

He drove across the bridge and causeway, stopped at the entrance booth at the Merritt Island National Wildlife Refuge to show the ranger on duty his annual Refuge Pass, and drove onto the vast preserve where he had spent so many hours fishing and enjoying the shorebirds, alligators, and other wildlife that inhabited it over the years. If Raymond felt at home anyplace, it was here.

Except for the John F. Kennedy Space Center at its southern end, the refuge was 140,000 acres of paradise to Raymond. He had spent uncountable hours driving the back roads and fishing the small ponds, Mosquito Lagoon, and Haulover Canal, where it was not uncommon to see manatee in the winter months when they came in from the ocean to the warmer waters of the canal. He felt a guilty sense of freedom, like a schoolboy playing hooky.

He turned left onto Black Point Wildlife Drive and followed the gravel road as it looped through the wetlands, stopping to admire a heron fishing for dinner in one of the shallow ponds, and again a mile or so down the road when he spotted an eight foot long alligator sunning itself on a dry hammock. Raymond had always been fascinated by the primeval creatures who had remained unchanged for eons and had adapted well to man's encroachment on their habitat. In spite of the occasional news story about a gator snatching someone's poodle for dinner, and even the rare incidents when some careless human got too close and was attacked, he never feared the big predators. He respected them and gave them their space, and had never felt threatened by the many he had seen when he was fishing on the refuge.

If the alligator even noticed him it didn't show it. Raymond wondered what it would be like to be the giant reptile, without a care in the world except what it was going to find for dinner that night. He realized that in that moment of time, he envied the creature.

He drove on further, passing a rusted old white station wagon and waving to the elderly couple fishing in a pond. He didn't know them, but they were regulars and occasionally would stop and exchange pleasantries while asking how the fish were biting. He remembered once, a year or two before, the woman had mentioned that it was their 50th anniversary and they were spending it doing what they loved most, just being together. Seeing them now, Raymond realized that he envied them, too. What must it be like to have somebody you could live happily with to that age and still enjoy doing things together?

His marriage to Sheila had never been happy, and for the most part even acrimonious, so why had he stayed? Yes, there was a sense of duty after the children were born, but what about before that? What caused him to stay when there was nothing to keep him from leaving? Some sense of guilt for what Royce had done? He had grown up knowing how badly the ongoing infidelity had hurt his mother until she reached the breaking point. But was he any better? Why had he so quickly been willing to barter his years of faithfulness for a few stolen hours with Holly? Were the sins of the father, indeed, passed down to the son?

And why Holly? There had been other opportunities, women employees who saw playing footsie with the boss as the quick route to promotion, bored housewives looking for a diversion from their humdrum life, even another manager who had once let it be known she was available during an out-of-town training retreat. Why not any of them? Holly had been no more attractive, and less refined than most of them. So why her? And why *that* morning of all mornings? And why had Holly chosen *him*?

Which led him to question once again, who had killed the woman? Had her husband followed her to the motel? And if so, why had he allowed Raymond to leave before going into the room to murder his wife? Was he a coward, afraid to confront another man but willing to attack a woman? Raymond knew that many abusers were cowards. But while Holly had made it clear that her husband was a loser and that their marriage was not happy, she had never given any indication of him being abusive.

Black Friday

Then what about the mysterious married man that Holly claimed to have been meeting at a motel that morning? Who was he? Had he been the jealous one who had discovered her cheating ways?

And last, but certainly not least, what was going to happen now? Raymond had already resigned himself to the fact that DeLeon had been telling him the truth the day before when he said that life as he knew it was over. He had accepted the fact that he was going to be arrested, but was there any possibility that he would actually be convicted? No, things like that didn't happen to everyday people like him. But then again, how often did everyday people like himself find themselves in such a situation?

While even the thought of arrest alone terrified him, Raymond knew that he could not live in prison. He was honest enough to admit to himself that he was too soft, too mild-mannered, to last long in an environment where the predators, though they walked on two legs, were even more deadly than the alligator he had just seen.

He drove further east to Playalinda Beach and parked the truck in one of the middle parking lots. He walked up the wooden ramp over the dunes and down onto the beach, enjoying the feel of the salt air on his skin, as he always did. There were over a dozen different beach access points, and while the ones to the south were popular with families, and the northernmost allowed nude sunbathing, which consisted mostly of fat old man, those in the center were popular with surf fisherman, surfers, and those who enjoyed being on some of Florida's last unspoiled beaches. With no condos and high-rise resorts towering over them, the beaches looked much like they must have 10,000 years ago.

There was one lone surf fisherman two hundred yards up the beach, but except for him and a few seagulls, Raymond had the place to himself. He sat down on the sand and watched the surf rolling in for the next hour, alone with his thoughts. He went over it all again and again, until his head began to spin and still, none of it made any sense to him.

Finally, he sighed and stood up, brushed the sand from his clothes, and made his way back up the ramp toward the parking lot. He paused and turned at the top, looking out at the Atlantic and wondering if it was last time he would ever see it.

***

"If that's the way they're going to treat you after all the years you put in, screw 'em," Wayne said. "You can do better."

Raymond knew his friend was trying to cheer him up, but it wasn't helping. Yes, he had had offers from other grocery chains over the years, but just as he had remained faithful to his domineering wife, he had also been faithful to Palmetto Pantry, where he had started as a stock boy and had gone up through the ranks. Now he wondered if, at his age and with the specter of the scandal hanging over him, if any of those offers would still be open to him.

"I don't know, Wayne. At this point, I can't even look past tomorrow or the next day. Last year an outfit out of North Carolina was trying to hire me away and I told them I was with Palmetto Pantry as long as they'd have me. I don't even know if they'd still be interested, after all this. And even if they did, what about Sheila and the kids?"

"Just take it one day at a time," Wayne advised. "As for Sheila and the kids, man, I can't tell you what to do. Be honest with yourself, Raymond, you've been miserable for about as long as I've known you. Maybe this is a chance for a new start for you."

"If I even get through all of this. Who knows what's going to happen at this point?"

"Hey, stop that shit right now," Wayne said. "You *will* get through this, and as bad as it looks now, maybe all of this will be a blessing in disguise. And who says you have to go back to running a grocery store?"

"It's all I know," Raymond said.

"That doesn't mean you can't do something else. Hell Raymond, I bet I could get you on with my company. We're expanding all the time and always looking for good people."

"I don't know, Wayne. I've never been much of a salesman."

"Sure you are! We're all salesman all the time, Raymond. Every day we're selling ourselves in some way. Way back when, you sold yourself to Palmetto Pantry to get hired. Then you sold yourself as you moved up from stock boy to cashier to department manager to assistant manager to store manager. And you sold your staff on you as their manager. That's how you've won so many awards and bonuses."

"Yeah, but that's different. I just can't see myself knocking on doors.

"You wouldn't be knocking on doors, you'd walk right in. And trust me buddy, some of the receptionists sitting on the other side of those doors make it worth the trip!"

"I don't know," Raymond said, still not convinced.

"Well, give it some thought, okay? I'm serious, Raymond, you're a great guy and I think you could do well at it. The pay is great, the benefits are fantastic, and as long as you're doing the job and making sales, you don't have anybody looking over your shoulder all the time. Look at me, I set my own schedule. If I want to take an afternoon or a day off, I just do it. I don't ask anybody's permission. All they care about is that I meet my sales quota every month. And since I always do a lot more than my quota, they treat me like royalty."

Raymond couldn't dispute that his friend seemed to do very well financially, and more than once he had envied him for all the free time he had with his flexible schedule. But still, he did not think he had the people skills to do what Wayne did. At any neighborhood gathering, Wayne was the center of attention, laughing and joking with everybody, and people seemed to gravitate to him. Raymond, on the other hand, was never comfortable in groups and always found himself standing unnoticed on the edge of the crowd.

"Listen, all I'm saying is that you have options, okay Raymond? I know things are looking really gloomy for you right now, but once this is all done and over with, it's not like you have to climb back into that same rut you've been in all along. There's a great big world out there, my friend, just waiting for you to explore it."

Raymond went to sleep that night in Wayne's guest bedroom, wondering if his friend was right. *Were* there other opportunities out there? While he had always been good at his job, it was because of his dedication to always giving his best, not some overwhelming love for the grocery business. More often than not, it *was* a rut. Raymond had heard someone say one time that the only difference between a rut and a grave was the length and the depth. Why shouldn't he consider other possibilities once this was all over? He had been depressed all day long over the loss of his job and not knowing what the future held in store for him. Maybe it was time for a new outlook on life. But what about Sheila and the kids? He couldn't just turn his back on them. He decided he would cross that bridge when he came to it. But he knew there was still a lot of bad road to travel before he got to that point.

Black Friday

Chapter 17

They came for him the next morning. Three marked police cars and the white Caprice descended on him as he backed the pickup out of Wayne's driveway. Officers jumped out of their cars and aimed their weapons at him.

"Keep your hands where I can see them," ordered a uniformed officer, who pointed a shotgun at Raymond from across the hood of his police car. The muzzle of the gun looked as large as a barrel to him and he quickly raised his hands as high as he could inside of the truck.

"Use your left hand to open the door from the outside and step out of the vehicle," the policeman said. "If you make any sudden moves, you will be shot."

Raymond started to reach down to shift the truck into Park and the policeman shouted, "Hands up! Show me your hands!"

Raymond quickly raised his hand again and said, "The truck's in gear. If I try to get out it's going to move or hit somebody."

"Okay, reach over with your left hand and put it in Park. Slowly!"

Raymond did as he was ordered, then opened the truck's door and stepped out into the street, keeping his hands as high as he could over his head.

"Turn around and face away from me, and keep your hands up."

As he turned, he saw Wayne watching from his doorway.

"Take two steps to the side," the policeman ordered. "Now drop to your knees and keep your hands in the air. If you make any sudden movements you will be shot. Do you understand me?"

"Yeah, yeah," Raymond said, terrified that he would do something wrong and they would shoot him. Once he was on his knees the officer ordered him to lie face down and to spread his arms out to his sides. He heard several policemen approach him and his arms were pulled roughly behind his back and he felt the cold steel of handcuffs locking into place around his wrists.

They pulled him to his feet and detective Hammond said, "Raymond

Winters, you are under arrest for the murder of Holly Lynn Coulter. You have the right to remain silent. If you choose to speak, anything you say can and will be used against you in a court of law. You have the right to have an attorney present during questioning. If you cannot afford an attorney, one will be appointed for you. You can exercise these rights at any time. Do you understand these rights as I've explained them to you, Mr. Winters?"

"Yes."

They led him to the back of a police car and put him inside.

Hammond leaned in the car's open door. "Do you have any questions at this point, Mr. Winters?"

"No."

"Is there anything you want to tell us at this time?"

He wanted to tell them that they had made a terrible mistake, that he had not killed anyone, that they had the wrong man. But he remembered DeLeon's advice and simply said, "I want my attorney."

"That's your right, sir. These officers are going to take you to jail now. I'll talk to you later."

He closed the door, and Raymond watched as the detectives and the other policemen walked to the door of his house. He didn't know if it was to search for any evidence they may have missed on their last visit, or to inform Sheila of his arrest.

As the police car pulled away he looked out the window and saw neighbors up and down the block watching the latest drama unfolding on their normally quiet cul-de-sac.

***

Raymond felt disconnected as he was taken through the booking process. A policeman watched as a bored looking young woman took his photograph, had him turn to his left and then right sides and photographed him again, and fingerprinted him. He was led into another room, where a male officer instructed him to take his clothing off, lean forward, and pull the cheeks of his buttocks apart. After that humiliation was done, he was handed an orange jumpsuit and rubber flip-flops to put on.

Then the handcuffs were put back on and he was led down another hallway to a small interview room where an officer with a clipboard asked him a series of questions about his health, any medications he took, if he smoked, drank alcohol, or used any narcotics. He was also asked for the name and contact information of his next of kin. He started to give them Sheila's name, then stopped and said, "Nobody."

"Nobody?"

"No, there's nobody."

"You have a wife? A sister or brother? Kids?"

"There's nobody that cares," Raymond told him.

"Look, there's got to be somebody, okay? Just give me a name. I don't need any grief from you."

Finally, he gave them Wayne's name and telephone number.

He had thought that once they were through booking him, the detectives or Janet Morrison would be there to talk to him, or that he would be allowed to call his attorney. But instead, he was taken through another series of hallways, where a guard pushed a button and a heavy steel door opened with a buzz. He was led into yet another hall, this one with barred cells on either side. There was another buzz. The door to the second cell on the left slid open and the guard pointed inside.

When the door slid closed behind him, Raymond felt a sense of panic. He wanted to throw himself against the bars, to tear them apart, to get out of there no matter what it took. But he knew the effort would be useless so he just stood there staring at the steel door of the cellblock as it closed behind the guard.

"Ain't no use standing there all day," a voice said from behind him. Raymond turned to see an immense black man sitting on one of the fold-down steel bunks. "Might as well cop a squat, bro, 'less you got someplace else to be."

There were three other prisoners in the cell, an old black man with leathery skin who sat staring at the floor, and two younger men who looked at him with hostile eyes but did not say anything.

"Dey call me Big Lucas. What's your name, man?"

"Raymond."

"And what brings your lily white ass in here on this fine morning?" Big Lucas asked.

Raymond shook his head and said, "Just a big mistake."

The big man laughed and said, "Well shit, man, I already knew that. It's always a mistake. There ain't a guilty man in this whole damn place! Me, I didn't have that rock and pipe those cops found on me. No man, I think I made a mistake and put on somebody else's pants that morning. And these two bloods here? They didn't jack anybody's car.

They thought it was a taxicab. Ain't that right, boys?"

The two younger men didn't answer, just gave him a stare that was meant to intimidate, but Big Lucas paid them no mind. "Now, Jester here? That old man, his mistake was just bein' born. So like I say, it's always a mistake."

Raymond didn't reply, and the other man laughed. "Hey, it's okay man, you don't gotta say nothing. Ain't nothing you're gonna say that anybody's gonna believe anyway. You can stand there all day or you can sit down or whatever. Makes no difference to me."

Finally Raymond moved to one of the bunks and started to sit down. "Hey man don't be sittin' your old white ass on my bunk," one of the younger men said to him.

"Now Hootie, is that any way to talk to our new cellie?"

"I ain't the fucking Welcome Wagon, man. Bitch wants to put his ass on my bunk he better be facedown."

Raymond moved aside and Hootie strolled over and stretched out on the bunk. He raised his eyes to the one above it and said, "Hey dog, this here white boy's eyeballin' your bunk, man."

His friend walked up to Raymond and stopped when their chests were almost touching. "That true, bitch? You trespassing?"

His breath was fetid and Raymond tried not to wince, worried that it would show his fear. "Sorry, I didn't know it was yours."

"Just to make it easy for you, bitch, it's all mine, okay? Every inch of this crib is mine, man. From the floor to the roof to the walls. You got that? Even the fucking air belongs to me."

Raymond had never been in a fight in his life, never played contact sports, and had always avoided confrontation anytime he could. He didn't know how to respond. He had read enough books and watched enough television to know that respect counted for everything in jail and that the slightest insult, whether perceived or real, was cause for violence. Now he expected to be attacked at any moment.

"Leave that man alone and shut your ignorant black ass up, young blood."

"You talkin' to me, Jester?"

"Ain't no other nigger I see running his mouth in here."

"Maybe you oughta mind your own business, old man."

"Maybe I oughta rip off your head and shit down your throat," Jester said. "Now I ain't goin' to tell you again, leave that man alone and try to act like you ain't some ignorant porch monkey."

Black Friday

The other man, who Raymond would later learn was called Droopy on the streets, shook his head and said, "You're lucky, man. I'm gonna let you live. For now." He stepped aside and Raymond walked to the other side of the cell, where Jester pointed at an empty bunk and said, "Make yourself at home."

Raymond sat on the bunk and the old man offered him his hand.

"They call me Jester. You just ignore them two fools over there. They're too young to have any sense yet and the way they're going they won't live long enough to get any."

Raymond shook his hand and said, "Nice to meet you, Jester."

"Make yourself comfortable, you're gonna be here a while."

Raymond certainly hoped not. He had not been in the cell more than half an hour and already knew that there was no way he could live very long inside those bars.

The cellblock was a noisy place, with prisoners hollering at each other and calling for the guards nonstop, the harsh buzz that opened and closed the doors, the slamming of steel on steel, and what seemed to be 100 prisoners talking all at once.

After a couple of hours he needed to empty his bladder, but he didn't think there was any way he would be able to use the stainless steel toilet built into the wall of the cell. He tried to ignore the growing discomfort, but by the third hour it was too much and he had to give in. A modest man by nature, Raymond felt that all eyes were on him, but his cellmates did not seem to notice.

Eventually the buzzer sounded again and two trustees came down the aisle pushing a large cart filled with brown paper bags. They handed them through the bars, one to a prisoner, accompanied by a small carton of warm milk.

"Damn, cold cheese and potato chips again," Big Lucas said, taking a sandwich out of his bag.

"What you expect, filet mignon?" Jester asked. "This is jail, man, not the Ritz."

"No, but would it kill them to slap on a piece of baloney now and then?"

Raymond had no appetite and did not even open his bag. "Hey man, ain't you hungry?"

"No," Raymond said, handing him the bag. "Help yourself."

"Now that ain't no way to be," Jester said. "You be wishin' you had that food inside you before too long."

"I'm not hungry."

"Maybe not now, but you will be before they bring us any dinner. 'Sides, in here you can't just be given' stuff to people. Makes them think you're weak or you want somethin' in return."

"I just....."

"You got to understand how it is in here," Jester told him. "In here nobody does somethin' for nothin' for nobody. If somebody offers you a cigarette or a piece of gum or anything, you better know they gonna come around wantin' somethin' in return."

"I'm hoping I won't be in here come dinnertime," Raymond said.

Jester laughed and said, "Now you bein' as big a fool as those two over there, pointing his chin at Hootie and Droopy.

Raymond couldn't believe he might be in there overnight. He was absolutely certain that if he was, he would not live to see daylight.

As if reading his mind, Jester chuckled and said, "Don't you be worrying now. Forget all that nonsense you heard and read. Ain't nobody in here gonna be rapin' you in the middle of the night. I done put three niggers in the ground that I'll admit to, and maybe a couple more I won't. The young gentlemen over there, they was just flexin' their muscles a bit and posturin' before. They heard me when I told 'em to leave you alone and they know what's goin' to happen if they don't. And Big Luca there, he got so much gut hangin' over it that he ain't seen whatever used to be between his legs in years."

"So that just leaves you to worry about," Raymond said.

Jester looked at him and started laughing, and kept it up until he had to wipe away tears. "Oh, man, you got to be shittin' me!" He slapped his thin vinyl mattress and said, "Don't you worry about that, you ain't exactly my type."

Jester started laughing again and it was infectious. Raymond found himself chuckling in spite of his situation.

Chapter 18

In mid-afternoon the main door buzzed open and a guard came in and called, "Winters. Hands through the bars."

Raymond wasn't sure what to do, and Jester said, "Put your hands through the slot there in the door."

Raymond did as he was instructed and the guard handcuffed him, then said "Step back."

When he did, there was another buzz and the cell door slid open. "Step out."

The cell door closed behind him and the guard led him to the main cellblock door, waited while it was buzzed open, and then led him down another long corridor and into an interview room. William DeLeon was waiting there for him.

"Can you take the handcuffs off, please?"

"Sorry sir, standard procedure for homicide suspects is..."

"I know what standard procedure is. I also know you have a certain degree of latitude during interviews with defense attorneys."

The guard shook his head. "Sorry. Can't do it."

"Fine," DeLeon said irritably, "I'd like to speak to my client please, in private."

The guard went out and Raymond heard the door lock behind him.

"How are you doing?"

"How am I doing? How do you think I'm doing? I thought I was supposed to call you when I got arrested and you'd be here. I've been in a cell for hours."

DeLeon raised his hand and said, "Calm down, Raymond."

"Don't tell me to calm down! I thought..."

"You thought you'd get a phone call right away and call me and I'd come running. But this isn't television, Raymond. Your friend Wayne called me less than an hour ago to tell me you had been arrested and to ask how he could help. I came here immediately and raised hell that you had not been allowed your phone call. Their excuse was that somebody dropped the ball."

Raymond was still angry, but he realized that DeLeon had come as fast as possible once he knew about the arrest. "So what happens next? When do I get out of here?"

"Unfortunately, your arraignment isn't scheduled until tomorrow at 11 a.m."

"Tomorrow?"

"I'm sorry. They stalled long enough that your name couldn't make it onto the docket for today."

"Why are they doing all of this to me?"

"It's all part of their strategy," DeLeon said. "They want to wear you down, make you desperate to get out of here, and hope you'll say anything to do it."

"I *am* desperate to get out of here!"

"Don't get too desperate," DeLeon warned him. "Look, I know this sucks, I know this is a totally new experience for you, but for these guys it's just business as usual. It's nothing personal, you're just one more perp in a long line of perps in a long line of cases."

"What happens between now and tomorrow, then?"

"They want to interview you again."

"What more can I tell them? I've talked to them twice now."

"Don't worry, I'll be right there with you this time around. Answer their questions truthfully and follow my directions. If I tell you not to answer a question, shut up and don't say a word. Got it?"

Raymond nodded.

"Okay, once the interview is over they're going to take you back to your cell and we won't talk again until tomorrow just before the arraignment. Is there anything I can do for you between now and then?"

"I don't know what it would be," Raymond said, resigning himself to the fact that he was going to be in jail at least overnight.

"Then let's do this," DeLeon said and called for the guard.

***

Janet Morrison and Detectives Harrison and Acosta were waiting for them in the same interrogation room where they had questioned Raymond before. Acosta pushed the button on the table to start the digital recorder, said the time and date, and identified the five people present. When he was done, the assistant district attorney asked him if his Miranda rights had been read to him. Raymond nodded and she said, "Please answer yes or no, Mr. Winters."

"Yes, they were read to me."

"And do you understand those rights as they were explained to you?"

"Yes, I do."

"You've been charged with first degree murder, Mr. Winters. Do you understand the seriousness of the charge against you?"

"Yes."

"Are you sure? Do you realize that you could receive the death penalty?"

"My client understands the penalties if he's convicted, but he didn't do it, so why don't we get this over with so you guys can get busy finding the real killer?"

"Save your legal arguments for the courtroom, Mr. DeLeon," Morrison advised.

She opened a folder on her desk and handed both Raymond and DeLeon typed transcripts of the statements Raymond had given to the police during the earlier interviews. "Please read this, Mr. Winters, and let me know if these are the statements you gave us previously."

Raymond read them and said, "Yes, they're correct."

"And do you stand by those statements today, Mr. Winters?"

"Yes, I do."

"And is there anything you would like to add to them?"

"No."

"Really? Because we have evidence that says you lied to us from the very first word, Mr. Winters."

"That's enough," DeLeon said. "My client has told you that the statements previously given are the truth."

"Your client has been lying all along," Morrison said. "Detective Harrison, why don't you share with Mr. DeLeon what you learned in a conversation with Melissa Ingram?"

"I've never heard of her," Raymond said.

"That's interesting," the detective said, "because she's certainly heard of you!"

"And who is this Melissa Ingram?" DeLeon asked.

"She's Holly Coulter's sister. And I have her statement here that the victim was having an affair with a married man. It'd been going on for several months, and she told her sister that she was going to be meeting that man on Friday morning at the TravelersRest motel."

"We know all this already," DeLeon said.

"Did you also know that the victim told her sister that her lover lived on Stardust Street, counselor? Don't you find it interesting that your client is a married man who lives on Stardust Street and who just so happened to be in that same motel room with the victim on the morning she was killed?"

"Mr. Winters has already acknowledged he was there with her. He's also stated over and over that she was alive and well when he left the room."

"And you expect us to believe that?"

"Ms. Morrison, with all due respect, I really don't care what you or these detectives believe. Now, do you have anything else, or are we going to sit here and beat the same dead horse all afternoon?"

"Oh, there's more," the assistant district attorney assured him. "We have your client's fingerprints on her van."

"You're grasping at straws. He's already said he went to the van to look at the tablet computers!"

"Computers that don't seem to exist. Computers that nobody has found. So where are these computers, Mr. Winters?"

"You don't have to answer that, Raymond. They're on a fishing expedition."

"Speaking of computers, Mr. Winters, why don't we talk about the e-mails that you have been exchanging with Ms. Coulter over the last six months?"

"E-mails? What e-mails? How can I have e-mailed her when I only met her that morning?"

"These e-mails," Harrison said, sliding a thick stack of papers in front of Raymond.

"What are these?"

"Those, Mr. DeLeon, are transcripts of e-mails from Mr. Winters' computer that prove he and the victim had an ongoing sexual relationship for months before she was killed."

"That's impossible," Raymond said. "I told you, I didn't know her before Friday!"

"There it is in black and white," Harrison said.

DeLeon looked at the first three pages and said, "I need a moment alone with my client."

"Certainly," Morrison said, pushing her chair back. She and the

Black Friday

detectives left the room.

As soon as they were alone, DeLeon turned to his client, his face dark with anger. "Goddamnit Raymond, I told you I needed one hundred percent honesty from you!"

"I have been honest!"

"Then how do you explain these?" he demanded, stabbing the e-mail transcripts with his finger.

"I don't know! I swear, I never met her before Friday. And I never e-mailed her!"

"Come on, Raymond, get real. You can't play these kinds of games and expect me to help you."

"I'm not playing any games! Why would I lie to you?"

"I don't know, Raymond. Why would you?"

"How many times do I have to tell you? I didn't write those e-mails."

"Well they didn't write themselves, Raymond. If you didn't write them, who did?"

The room was spinning, and Raymond felt like he was going to throw up.

"I don't know. Let me look at them."

For the most part the e-mails were short and they became more frequent over time:

Are we really going to do this? – Ray
I'm on my way now. See you there – Holly

Hey you, it was fun this afternoon. I'm glad we decided to meet. I had fun – Holly
Me too. You are amazing! – Ray
You weren't so bad yourself! – Holly

When can I see you again? – Ray
Today's bad for me. How 'bout tomorrow? – Holly
Same place? – Ray
Yeah. Noon? – Holly
Okay, see you there – Ray

What's happening with us? I can't get you out of my mind. Can't wait to be with you again – Holly
Me too. I can sneak out for an hour or so tonight. – Ray
Where at and what time? – Holly

Sand Point Park, say 10? – Ray
I'll be there – Holly

It's been five days, I need to be with you! – Ray
Sorry, had some family issues to take care of. Sister was sick and watching her kids. How about tonight? – Holly
9 o'clock? – Ray
I'll be there. I promise I'll make it up to you for being so busy – Holly

------

Did S give you any grief for getting home so late? – Holly
No, told her something came up at the store, – Ray
Good. I wish we could be together all the time – Holly
Me too. I promise, it'll happen. I just need some more time – Ray

------

I really need a job. My manager is a bitch – Holly
What did she do now? – Ray
Chewed me out because the floor didn't get mopped. But I was busy from the minute I clocked in and couldn't get to it. – Holly
Sorry – Ray
You said maybe you could get me on at your store. What's happening with that? – Holly
Is that really a good idea? What if people get suspicious? – Ray
How they gonna know unless they catch us doin' it on your desk? Oh, that sounds fun!
– Holly
You're bad! – Ray
And you love it! – Holly
Yes I do! – Ray

Hey, thanks for the money, it will really help. Love you – Holly
No problem, love you too. See you this afternoon? – Ray
I'll be there. I want to do that thing for you again – Holly
Really? – Ray
Yeah really – Holly
Can't wait - Ray

When can we be together forever? – Holly
These things take time. Please be patient. I'm working on it. – Ray

Black Friday

You keep saying that but it's been three months – Holly
I know. I'm working on it. I promise - Ray
My phone's gonna get shut off tomorrow if I can't pay the bill – Holly
How much? – Ray
$135 – Holly
Meet me at the regular place this afternoon. I'll take care of it – Ray
Thanks. Love you bunches – Holly

The e-mails went on for page after page, a documentary of two people carrying on an illicit affair, meeting at motels, public parks after dark, wherever they could sneak away to be together without arousing suspicion. The last was written late on Thanksgiving night, confirming their meeting at Denny's the next morning.

"Well?"

"Well what?"

"How do we explain these, Raymond?"

"I don't know. I've never seen these before. I never wrote them, and I never met that woman before Friday."

"This is bad, Raymond. Having an affair is one thing. But having an affair with a woman who turns up dead, and then denying you even knew her is just crazy."

"How can I make you understand that I did not write these e-mails, and that I wasn't having an affair with her and I didn't even know her?" Raymond was angry now, wondering how DeLeon could ever convince a judge or jury that he was innocent, when he obviously didn't believe it himself.

The attorney took a deep breath, closed his eyes and thought for a moment, and when he opened them again he said, "Raymond, look me in the eyes and tell me that you're not lying to me. Because if you are, I'm getting up and I'm walking out that door and you're on your own. Got it?"

"As God is my witness, I'm telling you the truth," Raymond said, looking him in the eyes, unwavering. "I didn't do any of this. The only thing I did was get stupid and go to bed with her, once. I never saw her before, I never had any contact with her before, and I didn't hurt her. Please believe me."

The attorney kept his eyes locked on Raymond's for a long moment, then nodded and said, "Okay, I believe you. I don't know why I do, but I do."

He stood up and opened the door and said to the guard stationed outside, "Would you please tell Ms. Morrison that we're ready to proceed?"

When the assistant district attorney and detectives returned, DeLeon said, "My client denies any knowledge of these e-mails and stands by his earlier statements that he met Ms. Coulter for the first time on Friday morning. He admits that he did have sex with her at the TravelersRest Motel, but that was it. She was alive when he left that room and he did not assault her in any way."

"You're really going to stick with that story?"

"Yes, we are. Now, do we have anything new to discuss or is this it?"

"Mr. Winters, do you have anything else you'd like to tell us?" Morrison asked.

"No ma'am. On the advice of my attorney I've said all that I'm going to."

She looked at him and shook her head, then sighed and said, "It's your funeral. We're done here."

Chapter 19

The same guard led Raymond through the same hallways to the cellblock. Once he was back in his cell and he had put his hands through the slot in the bars for the handcuffs to be removed, he walked wordlessly to his bunk and sat down.

"You look like they put you through the ringer," Jester said.

Raymond shook his head, but all he said was, "This nightmare just keeps getting worse and worse."

Sensing that he wasn't up to any further conversation, Jester moved away and sat back on his own bunk. Raymond suddenly felt exhausted, and it was all he could do to stretch out on the thin plastic covered mattress. In spite of all the noise around him and the strange environment that was so different than anything he had ever experienced before, he closed his eyes and was asleep in minutes.

***

Dinner was some sort of thick beef stew, accompanied by green beans and a thick slice of coarse bread. Raymond had no appetite, but Jester urged him to eat.

"You gonna need your strength, boy. Last thing you wanna do is pass out because you ain't ate anythin'. If they haul your ass down to the medical ward, they might lose your paperwork and your arraignment could get put off for another day."

Raymond ate the stew, which had a scorched taste, and washed it down with a foam cup of tepid tea. There was a television mounted high on the wall outside the cells that was tuned to a cartoon channel, with the volume turned off and closed captioning on. The evening seemed to drag on forever until the disembodied voice from the loudspeaker informed them that lights out would be in ten minutes.

In spite of Jester's assurances that he would be safe, Raymond feared what might happen to him during the long night hours. But his concerns were unfounded, and except for the noise of his cellmates snoring or getting up to use the toilet, and the sounds from the other nearby cells, nothing disturbed him.

At 9 a.m. a guard called a dozen prisoners' names and they put their hands through the bars to be handcuffed, then were lined up in the aisle and shackled together in groups of three. They were led into a holding area adjacent to the courtroom where arraignments were held and where they could consult with their attorneys, who sat on the other side of a glass divider, by telephone.

"How are you doing, Raymond?" DeLeon asked.

"What can I say? I'm here. What happens now?"

"You'll be arraigned in about an hour, the judge will explain the charges against you and she'll ask for your plea. You say not guilty, and then I'll ask for bail. The DA will argue against that, and the judge will decide."

"Will they let me out on bail?"

"If they do, it's going to be high. But I think we've got a pretty good shot, since your friend Wayne Lamb has stepped up to the plate and offered to cover it for you."

Raymond was surprised because Wayne had not mentioned anything about that, but relieved that once again his friend was there for him.

"Now you need to understand something, Raymond. Even if you do get bail, it is revocable at any time if the court decides that you are a flight risk or danger to the public. So you need to really watch everything you do so as not to give them any cause to revoke you, got it?"

Raymond nodded, and DeLeon said, "Okay, just bide your time, and hopefully you'll be back out on the street in a little while."

"What if the judge says no? Then what?"

"We're not even going to think about that right now," DeLeon said. "Just try to relax and I'll see you in the courtroom in a little bit."

The next hour seem to take forever, but finally Raymond's name was called and he was led into the courtroom. The judge, a gray haired woman wearing half glasses, read the charges against him and asked if he was ready to make a plea at that time. When Raymond said not guilty, DeLeon asked that he be released on his personal recognizance.

"Objection, Your Honor," Morrison said. "The defendant is charged with a capital crime and the State has reason to believe that he poses a significant risk to the community. We ask that he be remanded for trial without bail."

"That's nonsense, Your Honor," DeLeon argued. "Mr. Winters has cooperated with police throughout this investigation. He voluntarily went to the Titusville Police Station for questioning on Saturday and again on Monday, he agreed to a DNA test, and while he admits he had a sexual encounter with the victim on the day she was murdered, he has insisted all along that he is innocent. I have submitted several letters from his neighbors and coworkers attesting to his good character. He is a homeowner, he has a family, he has a long work history in this community, and there's no reason to think that he would be a danger to anyone, or a flight risk."

The judge looked at the letters DeLeon had referenced, the police report, and booking slip, then asked, "Ms. Morrison, did the defendant resist arrest or physically threaten anyone during the course of this investigation?"

"No ma'am, he hasn't."

"Is what Mr. DeLeon said correct? Did the defendant voluntarily come in for questioning and agree to a DNA test?"

"Yes, Your Honor, he did. However there is a history of domestic violence. I think that shows Mr. Winters could be a danger if he were released."

The judge looked through her paperwork, and then held up a police report. "Is this what you're talking about? It says both Mr. Winters and his wife were cited for an incident years ago, but that nothing came of it."

"Still, Your Honor, we believe it demonstrates that he is capable of violence."

"I'm sorry, I'm not buying that, Ms. Morrison. What else do you have?"

"The victim in this case, Holly Coulter, was brutally murdered, Your Honor. Mr. Winters was the last person seen with her while she was alive, he acknowledges he was in the motel room with her before she was killed, and there is no reason to believe that he isn't the one responsible for her death."

"I understand that," the judge said. "But we're not going to try the case here today. This is an arraignment, and while you've presented enough evidence to take this to trial, you still haven't convinced me that Mr. Winters should not be released on bail."

"Your Honor, I strongly object to any bail for this defendant."

"Your objection is noted, Ms. Morrison." She looked at Raymond and said, "Mr. Winters, you're looking at a very serious charge. Normally, I would be very hesitant to release you on bail, but your attorney has presented letters from three of your neighbors and four of your coworkers attesting to your responsibility and good citizenship. If I were to release you on significant bail, do I have your word that you will abide by the terms of your release?"

"Yes, Your Honor. You have my word."

She was silent for a moment, and then said, "Sir, if I set bail for one million dollars, you have to understand that I'm placing a lot of trust in you. Don't let me down."

"I won't, Your Honor."

"Mr. DeLeon, according to you, a Mr. Wayne Lamb is prepared to ensure that Mr. Winters will comply with the terms of release on bail and will post the necessary security for that bail. Is that correct?"

"Yes, Your Honor. Mr. Lamb is here in the courtroom."

Raymond had not seen Wayne in the gallery, but he stood up when the judge asked him to come forward.

"Mr. Lamb, before we proceed you do need to understand that by guaranteeing the defendant's bail you are taking on a serious financial risk. If he were to fail to appear for trial you are responsible for the total amount pledged. Do you understand that?"

"Yes, Your Honor, I do. I've known Mr. Winters for several years and I believe he is innocent. I don't believe he poses any risk to anyone and that he will show up whenever he's supposed to."

"And how will you secure his bail, Mr. Lamb?"

"Your Honor, Mr. Lamb has offered the title to his home, which has no mortgage, as well as cash, CDs, and securities to cover the bail. That's how much he believes in the defendant. I think that has to say something for both men's character."

"Your Honor, I have, here, a restraining order that has not yet been served on Mr. Winters, asking that he not be allowed to come within one thousand feet of his wife, his children, or their home on Stardust Drive, and that he not be allowed to contact them verbally, by telephone, by e-mail, or through a third party. Mrs. Winters has informed me that she will be filing for divorce from the defendant in the next few days and she fears for her safety and the safety of her children if he is released on bail."

"May I see the restraining order, Ms. Morrison?"

"Certainly, Your Honor."

Black Friday

She read it, then asked, "Mr. Winters, are you prepared to follow the terms of this restraining order?"

Raymond had known it was only a matter of time before Sheila filed for divorce, and while it was something that his moral code would not allow him to do, he also felt relief that she had taken the action. "Yes, Your Honor."

"Where will you live if I release you on bail?"

"If I may, Your Honor, I have already told Mr. Winters that he is welcome to stay at my home for as long as he needs to," Wayne said.

"Objection, Your Honor, that's directly across the street from Mrs. Winters and their children."

"It's a cul-de-sac, Your Honor," DeLeon said. "It comes within fifty feet of being the distance requested in the restraining order. The man's got to live somewhere. And again, Mr. Winters has not shown any indications of being violent or a danger to anyone."

The judge shuffled paperwork on her desk for a moment, and then said, "Mr. DeLeon, while your client is facing a very serious charge, I believe that as our system says, one is innocent until proven guilty. So I'm going to grant bail at one million dollars. But," and with that she turned to Raymond and held up a cautioning finger, "let me make this very clear, Mr. Winters. If you step over the line, if you fail to appear for any hearings in this case, if you violate the terms of your release, if you violate the restraining order, if you give me *any* reason to regret my decision, I'll have you back sitting in a cell and you won't get out of it until your trial. Do you understand me, sir?"

"Yes I do. Thank you, Your Honor."

"You have to understand, sir, that I'm putting my professional reputation on the line for you. Your friend here, Mr. Lamb, is putting a lot of his money, and his very home on the line for you. I'm not sure I would do that for anybody I know, to be honest with you. Like I said, don't let us down!'

"I won't," Raymond promised.

He thought he would be released right then, but it took time for all the paperwork to be processed, for Wayne to surrender the title to his home, his certificates of deposit, and to pledge his assets to cover the bail. The last step before Raymond was brought out of the cell and allowed to get dressed in his street clothes was for a deputy to hand him the restraining order from his wife. As he left the cell, he had shaken Jester's hand and thanked him for his friendship. And Raymond really meant that. He didn't know what crimes the old man was incarcerated for, but it didn't matter. In his darkest hour, Jester had been there for him, and Raymond realized that sometimes even the worst among us have good inside of them.

Chapter 20

Raymond felt oddly disjointed when he walked out of the jail with DeLeon and Wayne. Had he really only been inside for a little over 24 hours? It seemed so much longer.

"Okay, you know the rules. Stay away from your wife and kids, don't try to contact them, don't leave the county limits without permission from the court, surrender your passport to the court clerk by the end of the day, and stay out of trouble. Got it?"

"Yeah, thank you Mr. DeLeon. I really appreciate you believing in me."

The attorney put his hands on Raymond's shoulders and said, "Listen, I don't know what happened in that motel room and I don't know how those e-mails got on your computer, but we're going to get through this. Come see me tomorrow morning at 10 o'clock. By then I should have the preliminary background check back from my investigator on Holly Coulter. Maybe it will give us something to go on."

"Thank you. You're great," Raymond said.

"You need to give your buddy here a lot of the credit. He's the one that went around the neighborhood getting those letters of recommendation for you and then went to the store and got them from your former coworkers. And he's the one who put his money on the line for you. Okay, I've got to run, I've got an appointment in Melbourne this afternoon that I'm barely going to make as it is."

When they were in the Camry, Raymond said, "Man, I just want to hug you, Wayne. Nobody's ever been there for me like you have."

"Probably not a good idea," Wayne said, "half the people in the neighborhood think I'm gay as it is. No need to add fuel to the fire."

"Seriously, Wayne, I can never repay you. I just..."

Raymond's voice broke and he couldn't say anything more. Wayne reached across to squeeze his shoulder and said, "It's okay. You'd do the same for me." Then, changing the subject, he asked, "Are you hungry?"

Raymond had been too nervous to eat breakfast when they brought it to his cell, and had given it to Big Lucas and Jester. It was noon and he was indeed hungry, but he didn't feel comfortable going to a restaurant and enduring the stares from the waitresses and the other customers.

"Nonsense," Wayne said. "Half the people wouldn't know who you were if you were wearing a big sign around your neck with your name on it. And the other half are so busy scarfing down lunch that they don't even know anybody else is in the place. Besides, I'm so damn handsome they won't even notice you."

They went to El Leoncito, an excellent place on Washington Street that served some of the best Mexican and Cuban food on the Space Coast. Sitting in a booth at the rear of the restaurant, Raymond finally let himself relax. He had not realized how tense he had been ever since the police cars had surrounded him the morning before and the officers all jumped out with guns pointed at him.

"Man, this is a lot better than the stuff they fed us in there," Raymond said, savoring his lunch combination plate after their waitress served it.

"So does this mean I'm gonna have to listen to you talk about life in the joint for the next month?"

"No," Raymond said with a wry smile. "I'd just as soon forget about that place as fast as I can."

"Seriously, how bad was it?"

"It wasn't pleasant," Raymond said. "There were five of us in the cell and I was the only white guy. A couple of them were real thug types who wanted to impress me with how tough they were. They scared me. But there was another one named Big Lucas, and I'm telling you Wayne, this guy was big! But he was friendly to me. And then there was an older guy named Jester, he looked like he was a hundred years old. He was nice. In fact, when one of the younger guys was starting to push me around, he told him to back off, and I'll be damned if he didn't do it right then. He said he had killed a couple of people, and the way they deferred to him kind of made me think it was true."

"So you didn't get any marriage proposals or anything like that?"

"No, but I won't lie to you Wayne. I was terrified."

"Well, you're out now, and we need to make sure you stay out."

"Yeah, but how do we do that?"

"I guess we wait and see what this private investigator of DeLeon's comes up with first. None of this makes any sense, Raymond. How can that woman know what street you live on? And how did those damned e-mails get on your computer?"

Black Friday 117

"I don't know. I keep wracking my brain trying to figure it out. If I were a paranoid person I would think it's all some part of some big conspiracy."

"Well, if you're not a paranoid person yet, maybe you should become one."

Wayne ate a spoonful of black beans, and then said, "Let me ask you something, Raymond. Do you think Sheila could have done this?"

"Huh? Why would she do that?"

"I don't know," Wayne admitted. "Because she hates you? Because she wants you out of her life?"

"I never thought of her actually hating me," Raymond said. "I mean, Sheila's never been a pleasant person. You know how she is. She's always pissed off about something and arguing with somebody. Well, except you, and her mom and sister, I guess. But hate me? Why?"

Who knows? Because familiarity breeds contempt? Because you haven't given her the life she thought she deserved?"

"I gave her everything I possibly could," Raymond said, somewhat defensively. "But no matter what I did, it was never enough."

"Oh, I get that," Wayne said. "But she's one of those women that always wants more. I don't think any man could measure up to her expectations. You just happen to be the unlucky slob she chose to make miserable till death do you part. Or divorce, in this case, I guess."

Raymond looked skeptical, and Wayne said, "Think about it. Who else had access to the computers in your house? The kids? No offense, but your spawn don't seem smart enough to pull off something like this."

"But kill somebody?"

"How many times has Sheila gotten mad and said she was going to kill you? Because I remember two or three, including at the Fourth of July block party when she went off on you."

The incident he referred to had been an ugly one. Sheila never liked interacting with the neighbors, many of whom had been involved in arguments with her over the years. She considered most of them no more than drones and worker bees who went through life blindly performing whatever tasks were assigned to them with no thought or imagination. Raymond often thought that she saw herself as the Queen Bee, much better than those around her, and she made no attempt to hide it.

On that day Raymond had supplied the hamburgers and buns for the cookout, and when Sheila realized the buns had sesame seeds on them, she had thrown one of her tantrums.

"My God, Raymond, how long have we been married? You know I hate sesame seeds! How hard is it to do a simple thing like bring home plain buns?"

"I'm sorry," Raymond had said. "I got both. I guess somebody just opened these first. I'll get you another bun."

"That's not the point," Sheila said. "If you would have just got what I told you to in the first place we wouldn't be having this problem now, would we Raymond? But no, that would show some consideration for me on your part."

Her voice had risen, and neighbors were looking their way. "Calm down, Sheila, it's not the end of the world. I said I would get you another bun."

"Oh, that is *so* like you, Raymond! First you do something to annoy me and then you want to make it all better. How about you just get it right the first time? Is that possible? Are you too stupid to do that, Raymond? Just get it right the first time!"

"Calm down Sheila, people are looking at you."

"Do you think I care what these losers think of me? If you were man enough to make a real living for your family we wouldn't have to live here with all these rednecks and white trash!"

She had thrown the hamburger in Raymond's face and stood up, knocking over Wayne's can of beer in the process. Raymond had tried to take her hand, but Sheila had shook him off and screamed, "Don't touch me or I'll kill you. Just stay away from me you worthless son-of-a-bitch!"

She had stomped across the yard and into the house, slamming the front door so hard that the glass in one pane had shattered. Around him Raymond heard the murmurs of the neighbors talking, but he had been unable to meet their eyes as he wiped the ketchup from Sheila's hamburger off of his face.

"I don't know, Wayne. She's got a crazy temper, but why go to all that trouble? Why didn't she just poison me, or put ground glass in my food, or whatever? Why go to all this trouble?"

"Don't ask me to explain the workings of a deranged mind," Wayne said.

"Do you really think she's behind this?"

"If not her, who else? Who hates you enough to do this?"

Raymond couldn't answer that question. He had lived the kind of life where he remained almost invisible outside of his small circle. He didn't get involved in politics, he got along well with his neighbors in spite of his wife's reputation among them, and he always assumed he was well regarded by his crew at work. He couldn't think of anyone who would want to harm him or do something to upset his life like all of this had done.

"Do you have anybody at work who's trying to climb the ladder that sees you as an obstacle? Or maybe somebody you fired that's out to get you?"

"Not that I can think of. I've always gone out of my way to recommend my people for promotions. And I can't remember the last time I've had to fire somebody."

"What about this weekend guy that's taking your place? Could it be him?"

"Mike? No way! We had a great relationship. And besides, he's not the kind of person who would hurt anybody."

"That's what I say about you," Wayne said. "But somebody killed that woman."

"Maybe we're looking at this from the wrong direction."

"What do you mean?"

"What if it's not about me at all? What if it's about Holly?"

"I'm not sure I follow you."

"Think about it, Wayne. What if somebody wanted her dead and I was a handy way to keep the police from looking at them?"

"Like who?"

"I don't know. Her husband, maybe? She told her sister she was having an affair, so maybe word got back to him and he's the one who set this all up?"

"Then how did he get in your house to get your computers? Is he some cat burglar who can slip in and out whenever he wants to without getting caught? And what about this man the woman was meeting? Did he put on some kind of disguise and go to bed with her over and over and she didn't know it was her husband?"

"No, that doesn't make sense. But then again, neither does your theory about Sheila. If Holly was meeting some man, how did Sheila set that up. Did she hire some kind of gigolo to impersonate me? It's all too far-fetched, Wayne."

"You've got a point," Wayne said. "I guess until we know what that investigator of DeLeon's comes up with, all we can do is wait.

Chapter 21

"Holly Coulter didn't have a husband," DeLeon said the next morning."

"What?"

"She was divorced, and her husband's name wasn't Ricky, it was Tony. Anthony, actually. He works out at the Space Center, some kind of maintenance guy."

"Could he be the one who killed her?"

"I don't see how," said Phil Bixler, the private investigator who was looking into the victim's background. "His parents live up in Lake City and he was there with them from the day before Thanksgiving until Saturday evening when he got the word about his ex-wife and came back to town. He's got a whole family for alibis, and besides, he seems genuinely broken up about her death. Apparently they still had a good relationship even though they've been divorced for over five years."

"So what does that mean?"

"I don't know what it means, Raymond. But I can tell you this, Janet Morrison is going to seize on it and say it's just one more lie that you've told to attack your credibility even more."

Raymond started to say that he had not been lying, but before he could, DeLeon raised his hand and said, "I know what you're going to say. But you're preaching to the choir here. This is going to be one more thing they use against you when this gets to court."

"What else do we know about Holly?"

Bixler picked up a copy of his report and said," She was born Holly Erickson. Her father worked for the railroad and was gone a lot. Her mother was an alcoholic who seemed to get lonely when hubby was away and spent a lot of time looking for company, if you get my drift. Apparently the marriage broke up when Holly was about six or seven years old, and dad dropped out of the picture. Holly quit school in the 10th grade, got pregnant when she was 17 and gave the baby up for adoption. Her work history is spotty. She was a dancer at a couple of gentlemen's clubs up in Jacksonville, worked at a convenience store in Daytona Beach for a while, and three or four other menial jobs along the way."

"Gentlemen's clubs? You're saying she was a stripper?"

"Yes, among other things."

"Other things?"

Bixler looked at his papers again, and said, "She had two arrests for prostitution. She was using one of those online ad sites and meeting men from them at motels. She got busted in Orlando two years ago when the john was an undercover cop. She paid a fine and that was it. Last year the same thing happened in Daytona Beach. That time she got another fine and six months probation."

Raymond felt disappointed and betrayed, though he couldn't understand why. He already knew that Holly had lied to him about being married and other things, so why did the deceit about her background bother him? He couldn't explain it to himself, but it did. It was like he had expected more from her, but how could that be when he didn't even know her?

"Anything else?"

"Not really," Bixler said. "She moved around a lot, mostly between Jacksonville, Daytona Beach, Titusville, and the Orlando area. Lived in trailer parks, cheap apartments, crashing with friends, you get the picture. Basically, she was one of those women who live on the fringe of society. I guess if you had to describe her lifestyle in some way, it would be white trash."

"What about the husband?"

Bixler turned pages in his report, then said, "Anthony Coulter, 35 years old, everybody calls him Tony. He seems like an everyday blue-collar guy. Like I said, he works in the maintenance department at the Space Center. High school education, a couple of minor traffic citations over the years, but except for that, his record is clean. Nothing stands out about him; he goes to work every day, comes home, pays his bills, and seems to get along with everybody. He and Holly were married for a couple of years, and eventually she moved out and filed for divorce. But like I said, they stayed in contact and seemed to get along fine. In fact, the last time she was busted, he was the one who put up bail for her."

"Anybody else? Another husband, a boyfriend, somebody?"

"A woman like Holly, she's usually got a man or two in her life. But nothing serious that I could find. At the time of her death she was living

Black Friday

in a small apartment over on Barna Avenue. She wasn't employed, but she paid her rent on time every month."

"If she didn't have a job, how was she paying her bills?" Raymond asked.

"I don't know. She told a couple of people that she had a married boyfriend who was helping her out."

"A sugar daddy?"

"Sounds like it," Bixler agreed. "But we don't know who that person is."

"We've got to find out who this guy is," Raymond said. "He's got to be the one that killed her."

"But why would he do that?"

"I don't know. Because he was tired of her? Because he found out she was cheating on him? Maybe she threatened to tell his wife about the affair?"

"Those are all good questions, Raymond," DeLeon said. "But the only way we're going to get any answers is to keep digging. And I don't mean to be rude, but this isn't cheap. How much can you afford? I mean, you're unemployed at this point. Don't get me wrong, I'm not saying I'm not going to be here for you, but Phil here needs to be paid, and I've got expenses too."

Raymond didn't know what to say. He had what was left of his secret stash, but DeLeon was right, there was nothing else coming in.

Before he could say anything, Wayne spoke up, "You just keep digging. Do whatever it takes and I'll make sure the bills get paid."

Raymond started to object, to say that his friend couldn't continue funding his defense, but Wayne held up a hand. "Don't even say it, Raymond. It's handled. Okay?"

Raymond couldn't have said anything even if he had tried. All he could do was blink away tears and nod his head gratefully.

"Alright then, we'll keep poking. In the meantime, I can't say this often enough, Raymond. Keep a low profile. Don't let your wife goad you into an argument, don't go near the house, and for God's sake, don't even get a ticket for jaywalking. And don't talk to anybody, especially the police or the media. Got it?"

"Yeah, I got it. You don't have to keep repeating it. I got it, okay?"

"Easy there, buddy," Wayne cautioned him. "The man's on our side."

"I know," Raymond said, "I'm sorry. I just feel like everybody's waiting for me to screw up and do something stupid. I've already done that, and look where it got me. Sorry, Mr. DeLeon."

"It's okay," the attorney told him. "I *am* on your side, Raymond. And we're going to beat this. I know it's hard, and it's going to get harder, but just keep doing what you're doing. I just keep cautioning you because it's just like this thing about Holly telling you she was married when she wasn't. When this gets to court, Ms. Morrison is going to use every tiny little thing she can to discredit you in front of a jury. Like I said, don't even get a jaywalking ticket, because when it gets to court, it will be that you were cited for breaking the law again while out on bail waiting for trial."

Raymond nodded.

"Speaking of which," DeLeon continued, "we do have one little factor on our side at this point."

"What is it?" Raymond asked, eager for any glimmer of hope.

"Rumor has it that there is bad blood between Morrison and Judge Stewart. I'm not sure what about, but I do know that Janet Morrison was very open in her support for Carl Meredith when he ran against Judge Stewart in last year's election. I think that's one reason the judge agreed to bail in the first place. Now, that doesn't mean we have a cakewalk. Judge Stewart is very good and very fair, and if she decides you're guilty, she'll work to see you put in prison, no matter what her personal feelings are about Ms. Morrison. And if Morison feels that the judge might take their personal differences into account, she could petition the court to have the judge replaced with somebody else. But from a political standpoint, that could come back and bite her on the butt down the road. So I don't know if she'll take it that far."

"So what does that mean for me?" Raymond asked.

"Not much, really, except that I think the judge will take a long hard look at any motions the prosecution might make to have you rearrested for some little technicality. So like I said, don't give anybody any reason to do anything like that. Got it?"

"Yeah, I've got it," Raymond said again.

***

"Man, this just gets more confusing all the time," Raymond said. They were back in Wayne's Camry headed north on US Highway 1 toward Titusville. "Why did Holly lie about having a husband?"

Wayne shook his head as he changed lanes to pass a big motorhome that was pulling into Manatee Hammock Campground. "I don't know. Why did any of it happen? If we knew the answer to that, life would be a whole lot simpler."

Raymond knew his friend didn't need to hear it, but he still said, "Listen, Wayne, about the money. I can't tell you how much it means to me. And if it takes me the rest of my life, I'll make this up to you, I promise."

"Nada," Wayne told him, "it's only money and they print that every day. Besides, what else am I going spend it on? Wining and dining your soon to be ex sister-in-law? Cozying up to one of the soccer moms in the neighborhood? We've been over that route already. No thanks."

Raymond laughed. "Sometimes I think you really are gay."

Wayne laughed with him and said, "I promise you, I'm not. But even if I was, you're not my type."

Raymond laughed again, and said, "That hurts."

"Seriously," Wayne said, as he stopped for a traffic light, "I've got money, Raymond. More than I can ever spend. I don't need or want much in life. I've got a nice house, a nice car, a great stereo system, and a giant screen TV. What more does a guy really need?"

"I don't know. Somebody to share it all with?"

"Now I'm wondering if *you're* the gay one," Wayne said. "Anyway, Raymond, don't sweat the money, okay? Do you need any more or do you still have some left from that $5,000 I gave you?"

"I haven't touched it," Raymond said. "It's still sitting there on the bookshelf."

"Well, it's there if you need it. Now, how about we grab a bite to eat before I drop you off at home? I've got a couple of appointments up in New Smyrna Beach this afternoon."

Raymond wanted to say that he would have preferred to just go home and not have to deal with anybody else, but he didn't want to say no to Wayne's generosity and hurt his feelings. Besides, the thought of sitting in the empty house all day with nothing to do did not appeal to him.

They chose a barbecue place on Cheney Highway, and after the waitress brought their food, Wayne said, "Tomorrow I have to be in Ocala early, and then in the afternoon I've got appointments at four different medical offices in Gainesville. The company is introducing a new antihistamine inhaler and I've got to push it hard. So I don't know how late it will be when I get in. And I may just spend the night somewhere. Will you be okay by yourself?"

"I'll be fine," Raymond assured him. "I promise not to do anything stupid."

"I'd invite you to ride along but you'd be pretty bored while I'm busy giving my sales presentations. And besides, the judge said you couldn't leave the county without permission."

"I'll be fine," Raymond said again. "What's the worst that could happen?"

As it turned out, he would find out all too soon.

Chapter 22

After Wayne left for New Smyrna Beach, Raymond occupied himself with household chores. As bachelors went, Wayne was pretty tidy. But the carpet needed vacuumed and when he was done with that Raymond stripped the beds and did laundry. While the washing machine was churning away, he dusted things. Those were the same chores he had always done at home, as well as dishes and whatever else needed done that Sheila and the kids neglected.

Thinking about his wife and children, who were so close but yet so far away, Raymond tried to examine his feelings about the fact that he was no longer a welcome part of the family. He was surprised that while he regretted his actions that had put him in that position, he really felt no sense of loss. Yes, he loved his children. But if he had to be honest with himself, he would have to admit that he didn't really like them as people.

From the time they were very little, Sheila had always been a barrier between them and their father. If they did something wrong and Raymond tried to discipline them, she overruled him and told them it was okay, just don't make the same mistake again. When Raymond tried to express his displeasure with their low grades, Sheila went on the defensive, claiming that the teachers were all against her babies and that Raymond was, too. Even something as simple as expecting them to help around the house became an argument every time. "My God, Raymond, they're children. What do you expect of them? Leave them alone, it's not going to kill you to mow the grass or take out the garbage!" As a result, his children did not respect him, did not obey him, and did nothing to hide their scorn for him.

As for Sheila, any affection Raymond had for her had died long ago. There were too many fights, too many insults, and too much rejection to keep whatever love he might have had for her alive. So why had he stayed? He knew the answer to that; because Royce hadn't. His own father had abandoned *his* family, and despite what his mother had preached to him for as long as he could remember, he wasn't like his father! Raymond had been willing to suffer whatever it took to hold his marriage together. But what had it mattered? He and his father may have taken different routes, but hadn't they ended up at the same place?

No! He was not like his father even if he had made the same mistakes his father had. For a moment Raymond was tempted to walk across the street and reclaim his family, restraining order be damned. Was he willing to let a piece of paper keep him from becoming Royce? He opened the door and took a step out onto the walkway that led to the sidewalk, but then he remembered the warnings from Judge Stewart, and DeLeon, and even Wayne. All he would accomplish would be to get himself arrested again, and give the district attorney more ammunition to use against him when his case went to trial.

While he was standing on the walkway two women came by on the sidewalk.

"Hello Joyce, Andrea."

He had known both women for years. Joyce Paulson was a plump, happy-go-lucky mother of four who worked part time for an insurance company and lived two doors down from Raymond's house. Her husband, Frank, was a sports addict, and anytime a game was on television one could hear him loudly berating the umpires or a player who had fumbled the ball. Andrea Metoff lived on the far side of the Paulson house and was a divorcee who had escaped a bad marriage and made it very plain to any man who approached that she wasn't interested. Raymond had always gotten along well with both women, but now they seemed startled to see him, and after nodding quickly but not meeting his eyes, they had hurried on down the sidewalk.

Raymond watched them go, hurt and embarrassed by their reaction. He knew it was not going to be the last time someone treated him like a pariah on the cul-de-sac he had always called home. He shook his head and went back into the house.

With nothing else to do, he tried to watch a movie on one of the cable channels but couldn't follow the storyline and finally switched to a music channel and took a nap on Wayne's plush velour sofa. When he woke up it was dark and he was hungry. He found a TV dinner in the freezer and microwaved it, making the beds while it cooked.

Wayne got home just as he was finishing his meal, and when Raymond offered to make him something, he said he had had dinner with one of his clients. "It's all part of the smoozing that comes with the job," Wayne said. "But what the hell, that's what expense accounts are for, right?"

They made small talk the rest of the evening, neither of them touching on Raymond's case because there was really nothing else to be said that they hadn't been over many times already. About 10 PM, Wayne said he was going to bed because he had to be up and on the road early the next morning, and he reminded Raymond that he may not be back that night.

After his long nap, Raymond wasn't really tired, but he didn't know what to do with himself. Nothing on television interested him, he tried to read a couple of magazines but couldn't follow the stories in them, and he finally went to bed just after midnight. He tossed and turned and was still wide awake at 3 AM. Staring at the ceiling, the only light the red LEDs on the alarm clock on the nightstand, he wondered about Holly and why fate had brought the two of them together on that terrible morning.

Was somebody setting him up, as Wayne had suggested? If so, who? Wayne had suggested Sheila, but Raymond believed that despite her many faults, his estranged wife was not a murderer. If nothing else, Sheila was too lazy to go to that much effort to get him out of her life. Then what about his son or daughter? That didn't make any sense either. They hardly acknowledged his existence, so why would they go to so much trouble? Could he have been right when he said that maybe Holly had been the target all along, and he just happened to have been the unlucky schmuck who came along at the most inopportune time. But that didn't explain the e-mails.

Eventually Raymond drifted off to sleep, and in his dreams he was out on his boat. It was a warm, sunny day and the sea was calm. Holly was there with him, sitting in the bow and smiling back at him as the wind blew through her hair. He cut the engine and dropped anchor in a secluded cove. She grinned mischievously at him as she stripped off her clothing and dived over the side. She was laughing when she surfaced and paddled back to the side of the boat, inviting him to join her in the water. In the dream, Raymond was reluctant, but she finally coaxed him to undress and he slipped over the side. She wrapped her arms around him and they kissed, and he could taste the salt water on her lips. With her arms around his shoulders, Holly wrapped her legs around his waist and he entered her.

Black Friday
***

Raymond woke up aroused, the dream still very real in his mind. It was daylight. He glanced at the clock beside the bed and was surprised to see that it was almost 11. He had never slept that late in his life. He got out of bed and crossed to the bathroom to relieve himself, then flushed the toilet and got in the shower, where he stood under the hot water, feeling guilty.

What kind of sick bastard was he to have a sex dream about a dead woman? And then he found himself crying and could not understand why. In the dream Holly had been real, not just alive, but real; someone he could spend his life with, happily cruising over the crystal clear waters of the Keys and dropping anchor to swim naked and make love on a whim. Of course it was a fantasy. But why couldn't it have been real? Why couldn't *she* have been real? Why had she deceived him? And though they had only spent a few hours together, why did he miss her so much?

He toweled off and dressed, then wondered what to do with himself for the rest of the day. Raymond had never been one who could just sit idly, possibly because Sheila had never allowed it. If she saw him relaxing on the couch, she always found some chore that needed to be done and nagged him for being lazy.

He wasn't hungry, but he put two frozen waffles in the toaster and ate them standing up over the sink, washing them down with orange juice. The doorbell rang as he was washing out the glass and when he peered out the window he saw the news van parked in front of the house. Raymond did not answer the door, and after knocking several times and calling his name, the reporter gave up and left.

Was this going to be what the rest of his life would be like, Raymond wondered, scorned by his neighbors, hounded by the press, and hiding behind closed doors? What kind of life would that be? But then he thought about the alternative; locked in a cell forever, or strapped to a gurney with a needle in his arm, pumping in a lethal dose of misdirected justice. Raymond was not sure which would be worse.

Daytime television was terrible mind-numbing swill. He tried to get interested in a talk show in which a tattooed woman with green hair and multiple piercings on her lips and nose was relating all of the abuse she had suffered at the hands of her live-in boyfriend, a grungy character in a stained T-shirt who tried to justify his cheating and drug abuse by citing his rough childhood. All while the show's host feigned interest and tried to look concerned. Raymond switched to some silly game show where contestants were pushing big plastic balls up a steep incline with their foreheads while the audience shouted with the excitement one would think they would have reserved for the World Series or a NASCAR race. Wayne had 162 channels and Raymond tried them all before giving up and settling on an oldies music channel, the same one he had listened to the day before.

By mid-afternoon Raymond was bored to distraction and felt like the walls were closing in on him. The thought went through his mind that if he could not handle being cooped up inside of Wayne's comfortable house, with his television and stereo system, and a full bookshelf, how would he handle years of incarceration? That was when Raymond came to the decision that he would not. If it came to that, if everything went to hell and they really did find him guilty, rather than spend his life in a cell he would end it on his own terms. He wasn't sure how he would go about that, but he knew that a quick death would be preferable to lingering in prison for years before the state or old age finally put an end to it.

For a while he contemplated how he would do it. Grab a policeman's gun and shoot himself when the judge sentenced him to prison? Or maybe let another officer do the shooting for him? He didn't know if that would even be possible if he were shackled like he had been when they brought him into court. Maybe he could hang himself in his cell? Or slit his wrists? Raymond did not consider himself a brave man. Could he really do any of that? Maybe the answer would be to just take his boat far out into the Atlantic until it ran out of fuel and then just jump overboard. That would be the better alternative, by far. He loved being on the water. Would there be a better way to end it all? But rationally, he realized that if it reached the point where he was sentenced, he was not going to be allowed to be on his boat ever again. Should he take preemptive action and do it while he could?

"*Stop it. You haven't been convicted of anything yet, and you're not going to be. You didn't kill anybody. This is all going to work out.*" He told himself that, but did he really believe it? Raymond wasn't sure.

Chapter 23

By 4 o'clock, Raymond was pacing and his thoughts were growing darker in spite of himself. He needed to get out, he needed to be doing something. He got in his truck and drove to the Veterans Memorial Fishing Pier, next to the A. Max Brewer Bridge. Actually there were three piers in the complex, and he chose the longest one for no other reason than it was the longest.

There were a couple of people fishing who nodded at him and went about their business. Raymond used a soft jig for a while, without success, and then put on a Gulp artificial minnow and cast his line out and did a slow retrieval. On his second cast he got a strike and the rod tip bent over. He set the hook and reeled in a large skate. The flat fish resembled a ray, though it's tail was longer and not barbed like a ray. Raymond pulled the skate over the rail and dropped it on the dock, then held it down with his foot while he worked the hook loose with a pair of needle nose pliers. When it was free he used his toe to nudge it back into the water and re-baited his hook.

Over the next three hours he caught and released two more skates, several small catfish, and one respectable snapper. It was dark and he was getting cold, and he realized that he was the only person left on the pier. He also realized he was hungry. Raymond reeled in his line, took the leader and hook off, and left the pier.

While the pier was a busy place during the daytime, and even at night in the summer, on this chilly December evening the only vehicles in the parking lot were his pickup and a rusty old mustard yellow half-ton Chevy 4x4. The engine was running and there were two men in the cab. Raymond was almost to his truck when he heard doors slam and rapid footsteps behind him. He looked over his shoulder just in time to see one of the men from the Chevy swinging a fist at him, and then the night exploded in a shower of orange and red fireworks. He was rocked back by the blow, and immediately a second one landed along the side of his head. He threw up his hands to try to shield his face, and felt a solid jolt to his stomach. Raymond stumbled backwards, trying to stay on his feet, but his legs failed him and he crashed onto the pavement.

"No good murdering son-of-a-bitch, we're gonna stomp your ass!"

"Stop! I didn't..."

Before Raymond could say anything else he was jerked to his feet and one of the men held his hands behind him while the other punched him in the face. He felt blood in his mouth, and then a second blow hit him on the cheek. There were more fireworks going off in his head and Raymond struggled to get free, but the man holding him was too strong.

"Hit the motherfucker again," said the man holding him. "Knock his teeth down his throat!"

The fist struck him in the face again, then the man stepped back and punched him in the stomach three times before moving back up to his face. Raymond could no longer struggle to get free and at some point the man holding him let him go and he collapsed. He thought they were done with him then, but he was wrong. The first kick caught him in the groin, sending agony throughout his body. But they weren't done yet. He was kicked again and again in the stomach, the back, the side. He managed to roll into a fetal position and tried to shield his head but the attack continued. It could have been only a moment or two or it could have been hours. He didn't know, but it seemed like an eternity.

"Let him go! Stop, you're going to kill him, Donald."

"We plan to kill him, just like he did Holly."

"Stop! Stop it right now!"

"Mind your own business. This don't concern you."

"I said stop, Goddammit! You two back off right now or I swear I'll bust both your heads open."

"Get out of here, Tony, or you're gonna get the same."

"Don't even try it, Kyle. Now back off, right now."

"You chickenshit asshole. No wonder Holly divorced you!"

"Yeah, you're a big man with that baseball bat in your hand, ain't ya?"

"This is your last warning. You guys get out of here right now or else."

"What do you care about this asshole, anyway?"

"Go!"

"This ain't over. We're gonna fix your ass, Tony. And his, too!"

"Maybe so, but it's not going to be tonight."

Raymond managed to get an eye open, and in the yellow light cast by the parking lot lights and the lights on the bridge, he saw his two attackers walking away, pausing to look over their shoulders and giving the finger. A moment later the tires squealed as the Chevy sped out of the parking lot. A man was standing over Raymond, an aluminum baseball bat in his hands. He closed his eye, waiting for the blow to land that would end it all. But it never came.

He heard the bat fall to the pavement and the man was leaning over him. "Can you hear me?"

Raymond tried to respond but could not make his mouth work.

"Open your eyes. Look at me."

He managed to get one eye open again.

"Those assholes might come back any time. I've got to get you out of here. Do you understand?"

Raymond couldn't speak, but managed a grunt that the man must have taken as an affirmative.

"I don't want to move you, but I'm afraid to leave you here while I go for help and I don't have a cell phone. Those two have always got a gun or two in their truck and this baseball bat won't do much against that. Are the keys to your truck in your pocket?"

Raymond grunted again, then felt hands patting his jeans, and a hand going into his pocket. A moment later he was pulled to his feet and half carried to his truck. He groaned when the other man pushed him into the passenger seat and lifted his legs inside. The door closed and he leaned against it. He heard the driver's door open and felt the weight of the other man getting behind the wheel. The truck started and they drove to the street.

Raymond worked his mouth again, and managed to ask, "Who... who are you?"

"I'm Tony Coulter. Holly's ex-husband."

***

Somewhere during the beating Raymond had stopped feeling the individual blows and kicks that struck him, and his body had become one massive ball of pain. While he wasn't unconscious as the truck moved through the darkness, he was only vaguely aware of what was happening. At some point he was realized they were crossing under Interstate 95, and a few minutes later they bounced down a long driveway and he heard dogs barking. Then the passenger door was open again and he felt the cold night air. It helped revive him a little bit, and he opened his eye to see a mobile home.

"Where are we?" he managed to mumble.

"This is my place. Don't worry, they won't come here. They know the dogs would eat them alive. Besides, facing someone head on isn't their style."

"Who were those guys?"

"Donald and Kyle. They're Holly's brothers. A couple of real losers."

"And you... you're her husband?"

"Ex-husband. But don't worry, I'm not going to hurt you. If I wanted you dead I'd have left you with those two. Now let's get you inside before we both freeze to death."

Raymond's head was clearing now and the pain was coming from every direction. He winced with every step as Tony helped him into the mobile home and eased him onto a chair in the small kitchen. The other man stepped away and came back with a warm washcloth, which he used to clean up Raymond's face.

"I don't mean to hurt you," Tony said when Raymond winced as he dabbed at the cuts on his face. He held his hand up with three fingers extended and asked, "Can you see my fingers? How many am I holding up?"

"Three."

"That's not bad for one eye. The other one's pretty well swollen shut but I think you're going to live."

"Thanks to you," Raymond said.

Tony laughed, and said, "You may not thank me in the morning. You're numb now, but once that wears off you're going to be in a world of hurt."

"I hurt already."

"Just you wait and see. I've had a good ass kicking a time or two myself. I know what you've got coming."

He handed Raymond a glass of warm water and held a large plastic bowl in front of his face and said, "Rinse your mouth out and spit."

Raymond did, and saw that the water was red with blood.

"Do it again. Okay, one more time."

"Open your mouth. I know it hurts, but I want to see if you've lost any teeth. Okay, that's good. I think you've got a few loose ones, so I wouldn't advise eating any steak or saltwater taffy in the next few days.

Black Friday

But they'll tighten up."

"Are you a doctor or something?"

Tony laughed and shook his head. "No, I'm just a janitor. But I was a Navy corpsman for four years and I've patched up a lot of guys who came back from shore leave looking just like you so they wouldn't have to go on sick call and get themselves on report."

"Why did you save me from those guys? Why are you taking care of me?"

"Because I didn't want them to kill you."

"Saving me for yourself?"

"Man, are you paranoid or what? Then again, I guess you got good reason. But like I said, if I wanted you dead, I'd have left you with Donald and Kyle."

"I don't understand any of this," Raymond said, but before Tony could reply, he felt the room spinning and everything went black.

Chapter 24

Something warm and wet moving across his face woke him up. Raymond managed to open his eye enough to see the blocky head of a large brown and white pit bull who was licking his face. He tried to pull backward, afraid the animal would attack him, but he was lying on a couch and there was nowhere to go. The dog licked him again and Raymond managed to move a hand up to block it. The dog started licking his hand.

"Ginger, stop it!"

The dog sat back on its haunches.

"Don't worry, she won't bite you, but she may lick you to death. That's Ginger, and that one over there is Murphy."

Raymond saw another pit, this one a gray brindle, sleeping in front of a small television that was perched on a wobbly bookcase. As he became more aware, his whole body throbbed with pain. He winced, and a groan escaped his lips as he sat up.

He heard somebody laugh and then say, "I warned you that you were going to feel a lot worse this morning than you did last night."

"What happened?"

"You blacked out on me. I managed to drag you over here to the couch."

"No, I mean...."

"You got your ass whipped. A couple rednecks jumped you out at the fishing pier. Do you remember any of it?"

It all came back to him at once. The two men in the Chevy 4x4 attacking him, his inability to fight them off, and then his savior showing up with a baseball bat to drive them away.

"Yeah, I remember now."

Tony Coulter squatted in front of him and examined his face and said, "Well, you're not going to win any beauty contests anytime soon, that's for sure."

"Those guys, you said they were Holly's brothers?"

"Yeah. Donald and Kyle Erickson. The two of them together don't have as much brains as a turtle, but they're both as mean as gators."

"Why did they jump me?"

"Because they think you killed their sister."

"But I didn't."

"I believe you, or else I'd have left you to them last night."

"Why were you there?"

"What? You don't believe in coincidence?"

"Man, I don't know what to believe anymore," Raymond said.

"My buddy Dean and I stopped at the Green Lantern to shoot some pool and have a beer and somebody came in and told them you were down there fishing. They said they were going to go teach you a lesson and I told them to just let the police do their job. But they weren't buying that. They kind of feel like you being out walking around while Holly's dead means the police aren't getting the job done. So when they left the bar I tried to get Dean to go with me and make sure they didn't kill you. But he didn't want any part of that, because he didn't want to take those two on, and probably because he thinks like a lot of folks around here, that you probably have it coming. So I grabbed that bat out of his car and followed them. What were you doing out there all by yourself, anyway?"

"I was fishing," Raymond said with a shrug that sent pain lancing through his back and rib cage.

"You were setting yourself up for just what you got. That was a damn fool thing to do if you ask me."

It seemed like people had been telling him everything he had been doing wrong all of his life, and Raymond couldn't hide his irritation when he said, "Nobody asked you. Since when can't a guy go fishing without getting jumped in this town?"

"Since he's suspected of killing someone, maybe?"

"I told you, I didn't kill anybody."

"And I told you, I believe you. Or else I would have minded my own business and let them pound you into mush. So don't get all snarky with me, okay? Just because I kept them from killing you doesn't mean I'm your buddy or anything like that. I mean, you *were* screwing my ex-wife."

Raymond felt guilty, not just for his encounter with Holly, but for his lack of appreciation for Tony coming to his rescue and for not being sensitive to the fact that the man had obviously lost somebody he cared

Black Friday

about. "I'm sorry, it's just been a rough week."

"Yeah, it hasn't been a great one for me, either."

"I'm sorry about Holly, about being there with her, and, well everything. I'm sorry, man."

"You weren't the first, and you wouldn't of been the last. Even when we were married she didn't have a problem spreading her legs for somebody else. And she didn't try to hide it."

"I'm sorry," Raymond said again. "That sucks."

Now it was Tony's turn to shrug, and he said, "What can I say? Holly had a lot of good points, but she was who she was. I kind of knew that when I married her, and she didn't try real hard to hide it while we were married."

"But you still had feelings for her, after all that? I know about the arrests and all that."

"Yeah, people kept telling me I was a fool, but I still loved her. I didn't want her back, I couldn't handle all that drama, coming home and finding the house empty and her being gone for a week or two, and then just showing back up like she just walked down to the store to get a pack of cigarettes. Seeing hickeys on her neck that I didn't put there. I wasn't gonna live like that anymore. But whenever she called and said she was in trouble, I dropped whatever I was doing and came running."

Raymond wondered how the man could be that devoted to someone who had done him wrong so many times. Would he had been there for Sheila? He knew the answer to that. He would, but not because of love. He'd do it because he wasn't his father.

"Holly was a bad woman in a lot of ways. But at the same time there was a lot of good in her if that makes any sense. Take animals, for example. She was always hauling home some stray dog or cat she found someplace. Hell, once she brought home a baby armadillo she found out on the highway. Thing couldn't have been more than a few weeks old. She nursed it for two or three weeks, until the game warden showed up because some neighbor turned her in. He told her he could cite her for keeping a wild animal, but instead he just took it to some rehabilitation center and that was the end of it. Well, maybe not the end of it, because I heard later that the game warden's truck was at my place two or three times when I was at work."

Tony talked about his wife's cheating ways as nonchalantly as he would have said she was a good cook or enjoyed pizza and a cold beer on Friday night. He had accepted that it was just part of who Holly was.

Ginger pressed her head against his leg and Raymond patted her. "I've always been afraid of these things. I've heard so many stories about them attacking people and tearing them apart."

"Pits have a bad reputation," Tony acknowledged. "And some of it's deserved. They have amazing strength in their jaws and when they latch onto something, they don't let go. But a big part of the problem is the assholes who fight them or want a big mean dog to brag about. So they breed the most aggressive tendencies into them and then abuse them. What do you expect? Now these two, they're just as sweet as can be, and they're two of the smartest dogs I've ever had. It's like they can read people. I think a lot of dogs can do that, really. They just seem to know who's good and who's bad. Take Donald and Kyle? First time they came over here, these guys about tore the doors off that old Chevy of theirs trying to get to them. But look how she is with you. That tells me something. Tells me a lot."

"So now what?"

"I want to know what happened to Holly."

"I don't know what happened to her," Raymond told him. "She was alive when I left her in that motel room."

"Holly had something going on," Tony said. "I saw her a couple of weeks before she died and she was telling me that she had a new boyfriend who was loaded and that he was going to leave his wife for her right after the holidays. I told her that was the oldest story in the book, but she didn't want to hear that. She said this boyfriend had a big deal lined up and all she had to do was play along for a little while and she'd be rich."

"Did she give you any idea what this deal was about?"

"Nope, but it was obvious it was some kind of scam. That's the only kind of deal Holly ever got involved in. I asked her and she wouldn't say. Then when I asked her if this boyfriend of hers was so rich already, why did they need whatever kind of deal it was they were working on? She just told me to mind my own business. But after she drank a couple of beers she did let something slip about it was a set up, some rich guy who was going to put them both on Easy Street."

"Apparently Holly took her sister to my street and said that was where her boyfriend lived. Why would she be there?"

"I don't know, maybe you were the target for whatever kind of scam they had going on?"

"But why me? I'm not rich. I'm just an everyday working guy. I

Black Friday

mean, I've got a little bit of savings, but not all that much. What were they going to get from me?"

"Maybe they were setting you up to blackmail you? Holly takes you to that room and then they threaten to tell your wife or something?"

"But again, why me? I don't have anything worth taking."

"I don't know," Tony said again. "You run that grocery store, right?"

"I did until all of this came out and I got fired. But I was just the manager. I didn't own the place."

"No, but you had access to a lot of money there, didn't you? Maybe they planned to make you rip off the store or something?"

"It's not like we had millions of dollars in there at any one time. I mean, even after a busy weekend, it wasn't that much money. Certainly not enough to go to all that trouble."

"When you were with Holly, did she say anything to you about her boyfriend or anything like that?"

"No. She said she was married to some guy name Ricky and that it wasn't a very good marriage, but that was it. Holly told somebody else that she had some rich guy who was paying the bills for her. Like a sugar daddy type of thing maybe. Could that be the boyfriend?"

"Holly had a lot of men over the years who footed the bill for her. But it never lasted very long. They get tired of her bullshit and running around on them and end it, or she'd get bored and take off on them."

Raymond stroked the dog's head and shifted on the couch and the pain hit him again. Tony saw him wince and said, "They really worked you over good, didn't they?"

"Yeah, they did." He thought about how to say what he felt, and finally said, "This sounds weird, telling you this, you being her ex-husband and all, but I think I fell for Holly. I mean, we were only together a few hours. But I felt something for her. Does that make any sense at all?"

"Makes perfect sense to me," Tony told him. "It was the same way with me. I remember the first time I laid eyes on her. I was at the car wash cleaning up my truck and she came in driving an old green Volkswagen Bug. She couldn't get the bill changer to work because she had this worn out old torn five dollar bill. So I gave her one of mine and she got her change and we got to talking. She was wearing short, cut off jeans and a halter top, and man, I fell for her right then and there. Next thing I knew we're in bed back at my place. I should've known a woman you pick up that easy wasn't wife material, but if you told me that back then, I wouldn't have believed you. And to be honest with you, even today, knowing everything I do, I'd have done the same thing."

They were quiet after that, both seeming to have run out of things to say. Finally, Tony said, "You've probably got stuff to do, and I do, too. Are you okay to drive home?"

"Yeah, I'll be okay," Raymond said, standing up and groaning. "I appreciate it, Tony, I really do. I don't think there's many men who would do what you did for me, under the same circumstances"

"Like I said, you weren't the first, and you wouldn't of been the last. But you're a link to what happened to Holly, one way or another. And you being dead wouldn't help figure out who killed her."

"You know how I keep asking why me? Why did Holly and this boyfriend of hers pick me? I guess the next question is, why do you believe me? It seemes like most everybody else in this town thinks I did it."

Tony stood up and said, "I didn't know one way or the other last night, when I saved your ass. I just wanted you alive so I could figure out what happened to Holly."

"But you know it now? Why?"

"Because my dog likes you. That's good enough for me."

Chapter 25

"Jesus Christ, what happened to you? And where have you been?" Wayne asked when Raymond came through the door. "Are you all right?"

"Yeah, I'm fine," Raymond assured him.

"You don't look fine!"

"Okay, maybe not fine, but I think I'm going to live."

"What happened, Raymond? Did you get into an accident? Or a fight?"

"I think a fight is defined when both sides are taking part in it," Raymond told him. "I was more of a punching and kicking bag for a couple of rednecks out at the pier."

"Who were they? And what did you do to piss them off so bad that they'd do this to you?"

"A couple of guys named Donald and Kyle Erickson. Holly's brothers."

"Oh shit. It's a wonder they didn't kill you."

"They were trying pretty hard. And if Tony Coulter hadn't shown up and saved my ass, I think they would have gotten the job done."

"Tony Coulter? Wasn't that her husband's name?"

"That's the guy."

"And he saved you from them?"

"Yeah, it's a long story," Raymond said. "Let me take a shower and get some clean clothes on and I'll tell you all about it."

Standing naked in front of the mirror in Wayne's guest bathroom, Raymond inspected his body to see how much damage had been done. There were dark blue bruises on his torso, his right eye was still swollen shut, and there was a lump the size of a golf ball on the right side of his head. His entire face was one giant ugly bruise, his lips were swollen and split, and there were cuts in several places. He was surprised to realize that he could breathe through his nose and wondered how it had survived not being broken during the beating.

He started to brush his teeth, but it hurt so much that he was fearful of loosening them even more than they already were. He settled for rinsing his mouth with Scope and the alcohol in it burned so much that he quickly spit it out into the sink. He stood for a long time under the hot water of the shower, trying to avoid letting it hit him directly in the face. He held a thick terrycloth washrag under the water and pressed it to his face, feeling the warmth soak in. Then he soaped the rest of his body gingerly and rinsed. When he finally got out he felt somewhat better. Dressed in jeans and a light blue T-shirt, he went back into the living room, where Wayne was waiting for him.

"When you came back last night and I wasn't here, did you think I had skipped out on you?"

"Actually, I didn't get back until this morning. By the time I wrapped up in Gainesville it was too late to drive home, so I stayed over. But no, I'm not worried about you running out on me, Raymond. I guess I would've been worried that you were okay if I was here and you didn't show up. Now, tell me, what the hell happened?"

Raymond told him the whole story, from getting cabin fever, being cooped up in the house all day, to going to Veterans Pier to go fishing, to getting attacked by Donald and Kyle, and Tony coming to his rescue and taking him back to his mobile home. When he was done, Wayne's jaw was set tight.

"We need to do something about this, Raymond."

"What can we do?"

"I don't know. File a police report, I guess."

"I'd rather leave the police out of this," Raymond told him. "I'm not exactly their favorite person right now, and I'm not really too fond of them myself, the way things been going for me lately."

"We can't just let them get away with this!"

"Let's just let it go, okay?"

"Let it go?"

"Yes, let it go. Put yourself in their place, Wayne. If you had a sister or somebody else you loved, and somebody hurt them and then was walking around free and easy, what would you do? I'm just a friend, and you're ready to go after them. What if it was your sister or your wife, or whatever?"

"But they could've killed you!"

"I know, and I think if they had the chance they would do it again."

"Then you have to *do* something, Raymond!"

Black Friday

"What else can we do? These guys are barroom brawlers, Wayne. The kind that started fighting as soon as they could walk and never stopped. You and me, we're not like that. So what are we supposed to do? Hunt them down and jump them? We're way out of our league. They'd kick our ass for sure, and I don't think I'm up to that again anytime soon."

"Damn it, Raymond... "

"All I can do is try to keep a low profile and hope they catch whoever did all of this. That's what's really driving me crazy. Why would whoever this boyfriend of Holly's is think that there was anything to be gained by blackmailing me or whatever they were planning to do? I mean, think about it, Wayne. If you were going to work a scam like that on somebody, why a grocery store manager? Why not the owner of the company, or a doctor, or some rich guy? Tony said something about maybe they planned to have me rip off the store, but even then we're not talking about very much money. It's not like they could come back and make me tap the till over and over again if I did it. It wouldn't take very long at all for that to get discovered."

He could tell that Wayne was still angry about the attack on him, but he knew that he understood that what Raymond was telling him made sense.

"And whatever their big plan was, why did it blow up on them? And why did Holly end up dead? What did that accomplish?"

"I know that private investigator said that her ex-husband had a lot of alibis for where he was during the time she was killed." Wayne said. "But that doesn't mean he didn't have something to do with it, does it?"

"What do you mean?"

"He told you Holly had been cheating on him all the time they were married, and she was still hitting him up for money. Could he have paid somebody else to do it?"

"It didn't look like he had a lot of money to pay a hit man. And besides, why would he do that?"

"It's obvious he still had feelings for her. Jealousy? Or maybe he just got tired of giving her money and getting nothing in return?"

"I really don't think so," Raymond said. "He still loved her."

"That's my point." Wayne argued "Maybe with her having this new guy in her life, this mysterious boyfriend of hers who supposedly had a lot of money, he realized she was never going to come back to him. There have been a lot of women killed by jealous husbands and boyfriends who decided that if they couldn't have them, nobody else could either."

"I guess anything's possible," Raymond agreed. "But I really don't think so. He just didn't seem like that type to me. It was almost like he knew she slept around, and he didn't like it, but it's like having somebody who smokes or pops bubblegum, or whatever. It irritated him but he had learned to live with it."

"Sleeping with every guy that comes along is a lot more than smoking or chewing gum."

"To you or me, maybe. But Tony, he just seemed to have resigned himself to the point of view that it was part of who she was. And besides, if he did it or had it done, or whatever, why save me from her brothers last night? If they had killed me that probably would've been the end of the investigation. With the main suspect dead, how hard would the police have kept looking?"

"I guess you've got a point there," Wayne admitted grudgingly. "I don't think I could've handled having a woman that jumped into bed with somebody else whenever she got the chance. But that's just me."

"Maybe that's one of the reasons you don't have a woman in your life."

Wayne chuckled and said, "One more on a long, long list of reasons, old buddy." He changed the subject and asked, "Are you hungry? Have you had anything to eat since yesterday?"

Raymond realized that he was hungry, once Wayne brought it up, but he hoped his friend did not suggest going out to eat. It'd been bad enough thinking that everybody was staring at him because they thought he had killed Holly. The way he looked now would only make it worse. But Wayne seem to understand that and said, "Let me fix something here. What sounds good?"

"Right now I'm so hungry that anything sounds good," Raymond told him. "But my mouth is so sore and I've got some loose teeth, so I'm not sure what I can eat."

"Not to worry, I'm a bachelor. I've got plenty of quick comfort food. Let's see what we can round up."

Raymond followed him into the kitchen, where Wayne opened cabinets and took out cans, asking, "How about beef stew? Or SpaghettiOs? If that's not to your liking, I've got chicken noodle soup, Ramen, and tuna. Name your poison."

They settled on canned tuna and Ramen noodles. It may not have been the perfect combination, but it got the job done and Raymond felt a lot better after he ate. Better, but suddenly very tired.

Wayne noticed his one eye drooping and said, "you look beat in more ways than one, buddy. Why don't you get some rest?"

"I haven't exactly been the best houseguest, have I?"

"Don't worry about it. I've got a lot of paperwork to catch up on from the last couple of days' appointments. Playing mother hen to you would just keep me from concentrating on it. Go ahead, hit the sack."

Too tired to argue with him, Raymond put his bowl and spoon in the sink and went to bed.

***

The ringing doorbell woke him three hours later. He walked down the hallway and into the living room, and Wayne turned to say, "It's for you."

The visitor was a middle-aged man who asked from the doorway, "Are you Raymond Alan Winters?"

"Yes."

He handed Raymond a large manila envelope and said, "Mr. Winters, I'm a process server. You have been served, sir." With that he turned and walked away.

Raymond opened the envelope as Wayne closed the door and turned back to him. The first page of the stack of legal papers inside was titled Petition for Marriage Dissolution. He had been expecting their arrival and sat down on the couch to read them.

"How bad is it?"

"She wants everything. No surprise there. The house, our savings, CDs, my boat and truck, sole custody of the kids, $4,000 a month child support, and $1,000 a week alimony."

Wayne whistled. "Wow, talk about going for the jugular! Did you even make that kind of money before you got fired?"

"Not even close," Raymond told him.

"I'd say when it rains it pours, but this isn't rain. You're in the middle of the shit storm, buddy."

"Well, what's that old saying? You can't get blood out of a turnip?"

Raymond had been hit by so many things in the last week that he didn't give the divorce papers much thought at that point. He had bigger things to worry about, and was reminded of another old saying about being up to one's ass in alligators.

"Well, I have to say, you're handling it pretty well," Wayne said.

"What else can I do? Even if I wanted to fight it, it's Friday. I can't get in to see DeLeon again until Monday. And I don't know what he could do for me, he's a criminal defense attorney. And who knows, I could be sitting in prison before long."

"Don't even go there," Wayne admonished him. "You are *not* going to prison! We are going to beat this thing, Raymond."

Raymond wanted to believe him, he wanted to be positive, but so much had happened that it was hard to have any positive thoughts at that moment.

Chapter 26

Raymond hurt too much and looked too bad to want to go anywhere, so he spent the weekend in the house, never stepping outside. Several times he looked through the window to his house across the street and saw his and their friends coming and going, and at one point he heard the sound of Sheila's Pathfinder and saw her driving away. None of them even glanced at Wayne's house, almost as if it, and he, did not exist.

Then he wondered how much he *had* ever existed in their minds. He had never been anything more than a paycheck, an occasional irritation, and a constant object of ridicule. As much as he wanted to roll back the clock to before that fateful Black Friday morning, he also knew that even if the police caught the real murderer that day, his life in the house across the street was over, and he would not have wanted to return to it.

Wayne left early Monday morning on a sales trip that would take him up to Saint Augustine and then further north to Jacksonville, and told Raymond he probably would not get back to town until Thursday evening.

"Treat the place like your own," Wayne said. "If you need anything, give me a call. I turn my phone off when I'm with a client, but I check for messages as soon as I break free, and again before I go into the next meeting. So if I miss your call, leave me a message and I'll get back to you soon as I can."

Raymond had an 11 AM appointment at DeLeon's office in Cocoa, and when he told him about the divorce papers and Sheila's demands, the attorney laughed.

"I don't mean to make light of your problems, Raymond, but this broad is crazy," he said, looking at the papers Raymond showed him. "I practice criminal law now, but my wife is a divorce attorney and I was in partnership with her for a while, before we both decided that would lead to our own divorce. But I know enough to know that your wife is not going to be able to stick it to you this bad. I mean, she's going to stick it to you, but she's totally unrealistic."

"That's good to know," Raymond said, "because even if I get out of this mess I'm in, there's no way I could meet all of her demands."

"Well don't sweat it. I'm going to give my wife a call, and when you get done here you go over and see her. Now, tell me everything about these two punks who jumped you, and Holly Coulter's husband."

Raymond told him the story and when he was done, DeLeon sat with his elbows on his desk and his hands steepled as he had during their first meeting as he thought about what Raymond had told him.

"Okay, my first instinct is to tell you to go file a police report."

"I really don't want to do that," Raymond told him. "I guess I'm afraid if I get anywhere near a cop right now they're going to lock me up again."

"I understand that," DeLeon said. "But these guys are not the kind who are going to forgive and forget. They're going to take another run at you, no question about that."

Raymond didn't reply, though he was sure that the attorney was right.

"And you feel like this Tony Coulter, the ex-husband, is a pretty good guy?"

"I may be influenced by the fact that he saved my life, but yeah, I think he's a good guy. I liked him."

"Saving your hide is a pretty good way to influence somebody," DeLeon agreed. "I need to get Phil Bixler in here and tell him about this scam or whatever it was that Holly and her boyfriend were involved in."

"Has he found out anything about who the boyfriend might be?" Raymond asked.

"It would seem that Holly liked to brag, and she told several people about him and how much money he had. And while she didn't say anything about this grandiose scheme of theirs, she did say that they were going to be getting married and that her life was going to change big time. Phil looked at the lease agreement on her apartment, and it didn't show anybody's name but hers. She had really grungy credit and no job, so they almost didn't let her in, but she put down $2000 cash as a security deposit, and money talks. A couple of the neighbors have said they saw her coming and going a lot, but there was never a guy with her. So she was meeting her boyfriend someplace else, and if she was playing footsie with anybody on the side, she wasn't doing it there."

"Now what?"

"Now, we keep doing what we're doing. I know it seems like a slow process Raymond, and it is, but this isn't the movies or television. We keep working on this and following up every lead we uncover, and something's going to turn up. In the meantime, keep your nose clean, try not to get it broken, and keep a low profile. Got it?"

Raymond nodded.

"Good," DeLeon said, opening his desk drawer to take out a business card, which he handed to Raymond. "This is Georgette's office, it's just down the block. Go see her right now. I'm going to call and tell her you're on your way. And when you're done there, go to the police department and file that report about what happened to you Friday night. Don't worry, they're not going to lock you up or anything. If they had something to warrant it they would have come looking for you already. You're the victim here, Raymond, and we need that on record. I'm thinking about filing a restraining order against those two. Not that a piece of paper is going to slow them down, but it can help get them locked up if they do get too close."

"Do you really think they're going to come looking for me again?"

DeLeon nodded. "Under other circumstances I'd advise you to get a gun. It's still not a bad idea."

"I've never fired a gun in my life," Raymond said. "With my luck, I'd probably shoot myself in the foot or something. And to be honest with you, I don't know if I could use it even if I had to."

"You'd be surprised what you can do when you don't have any choice. Anyway, go talk to Georgette, get that police report filed, and I'll be in touch."

***

Georgette Keeler was a tall, thick bodied woman who wore her hair cropped close to her head and had amazingly long fingernails painted purple to match her lipstick. The first thing she did was ask Raymond for a $1000 retainer, and once he had given her that and signed yet another power of attorney authorizing her to act in his behalf, she read the divorce papers that had been served on him.

When she was finished she told her secretary to make copies of them and then to give the originals back to Raymond.

"What's this lady been smoking?"

"There's no way I can pay that kind of money. Even before I got fired, I wasn't earning $8,000 a month. Nowhere close to that."

"You won't have to. Florida isn't a community property state, but it has what is known as Equitable Distribution when it comes to divorce. That means that the marital property, anything that the two of you acquired while you have been married, is fairly divided between both parties. So your wife is entitled to half of the value of the home, one vehicle if they're both paid for and of equal value, and half the value of your boat."

"I don't care about the house," Raymond said. "I've come to realize that it was never home to me anyway."

"Be that as it may, you're entitled to half the equity in the home. Now, as for child support and alimony, or spousal maintenance as it's called, Florida law has a formula to determine child support. You were making what, $60,000 a year?"

"That's about right, with bonuses," Raymond told her.

She consulted her computer, then said, "You're looking at somewhere around $1350 a month in child support."

"That's a big difference," Raymond said.

"Yes it is. That's based upon your past income. Right now you're unemployed so I doubt she can even get that. And when you do get a new job, if it pays less than you have been earning, that will be factored in. As for alimony, the law provides for five different types of alimony: temporary, bridge-the-gap, rehabilitative, durational, and permanent. And how that is determined depends on the circumstances. Has Sheila ever been employed?"

"When we first got married she had a couple of jobs, but they never lasted very long. She either got sick and couldn't work or got fired for arguing with her bosses and the other employees. She hasn't worked for at least eighteen years."

"Now, when you say she got sick, what are we talking about?"

"Sheila has migraines. Lots of migraines."

"Reading between the lines here, I get the impression that you don't think they're real?"

"They only seem to happen when she doesn't want to do something," Raymond told her. "And if her mom or sister calls and wants her to come over, she suddenly has a miraculous recovery.

"Has she ever been treated by a doctor for them?"

"No. A couple of times, early on, I insisted she go see somebody. But she always went once and never went back again. She said they were all quacks."

"How convenient. What's her educational level?"

"She was a few credits short of a degree when we got married, but she never went back to school after the wedding."

"But she *is* capable of working, right? Aside from these migraines of hers? Which have never been medically diagnosed?"

"Yes, I guess so. I mean, except for her personality."

The attorney smiled and said, "Okay, so we've ruled out rehabilitative alimony. She is capable of working, she's just enjoyed an easy ride at your expense for all these years."

Out of habit, Raymond started to defend her by saying that Sheila had been a stay-at-home mom, but then he thought about the many times he had come home and made dinner and taken care of the household chores because Sheila was at bingo with her mother and sister, or involved in some drama with one or the other of them.

"The court may award one or more types of alimony in some combination that is fair, under the circumstances. The responsible spouse may be required to make monthly or quarterly payments to their ex, or sometimes a single lump-sum payment. And if there was an unequal division of the property, say for example that you allowed your wife to keep the house and all of the equity in it, that would be deducted from any alimony obligation the court might assign you. However, things have changed. We women wanted equal rights, we darned sure deserved them, but with those rights came the same responsibilities as our male counterparts."

"What does that mean?"

"What it means, Raymond, is that if your wife is physically and mentally capable of working, there is no reason why she shouldn't support herself. In fact, if for some reason you became incapacitated or unable to work because of an injury or illness while you are still married, Sheila might be required to pay *you* alimony. As it is right now, I wouldn't be surprised when this gets to court if the most a judge would order is for you to pay alimony for a short term to give her time to find employment. Her attorney might even make an argument that she needs to take some kind of refresher courses or something to make her more employable, but these days the courts don't always look very favorably upon that. Especially since you're unemployed yourself at the moment. And even if that happens, based upon your past income, it's not going be anywhere near $1000 a week. Maybe a month, but not a week."

Raymond was surprised to hear that news and his sigh of relief was audible.

"Now, what I'm going to need from you is a complete listing of all the marital assets you two have accumulated together, as well as your debts. Because just like the assets, under the Equitable Distribution law the debts are also divided equally."

"Sheila is not going to like that at all," Raymond said.

"Well, she's the one asking for a divorce, so she's just going to have to put on her big girl panties and deal with it," Georgette replied.

Chapter 27

As he walked into the police station, Raymond had a panic attack. It came out of nowhere without warning, and suddenly he had trouble getting his breath, he felt hot and dizzy, and his legs felt like two stretched out rubber bands that couldn't hold him up. He stopped just inside the door and tried to catch his breath. He felt sweat breaking out on his forehead.

"Sir, are you all right? Sir?"

The voice seemed to come from far away. He realized his one good eye was closed. He opened it to see a young policeman looking at him with concern.

"Are you all right, sir?" the officer asked again.

Raymond managed to draw a deep breath and nodded his head. "Yes, sorry, I just got a little dizzy."

"Do you need to sit down, sir?"

"No. No, I'm okay. I need to report a crime."

The policeman took him to an interview room and Raymond felt a new wave of panic as they walked down the same hallway that he had with the detectives. But somehow he managed to control his breathing. When they were seated in the room the policeman, whose name tag identified him as B. Walton, asked Raymond to tell him about the crime he was reporting.

As Raymond told him about the attack, he saw the change in the way the young officer looked at him. The concern he had first shown in the police station's lobby changed to something hard. He had been taking notes on a yellow legal pad when they first began talking, but as he listened, he stopped writing. When Raymond was finished describing the incident at the fishing pier, the officer asked, "Were there any witnesses to this alleged attack?"

"Alleged?" Raymond pointed to his face and asked, "Does this look alleged to you?"

Instead of answering his question, the officer asked, "Did you do anything to provoke these guys that you say jumped you?"

"I told you, they think I killed their sister."

"Well then, I'm not surprised, Mr. Winters. There are probably a lot of people that would do the same thing in their position."

"So that makes it okay? I'm supposed to just walk around with a big target drawn on my back, waiting for them to come after me again?"

"I could talk to Detectives Harrison and Acosta and see about the possibility of placing you in protective custody."

"You're joking, right?"

"Do I look like I find this amusing?"

"I want to talk to your supervisor," Raymond said.

Officer Walton stared at him for a long, hard minute, and then said, "That's up to you. Wait right here."

Sitting alone in the interview room, Raymond had to fight his anger at the policeman's indifference and the panic that wanted to rise within him again. Why had he listened to DeLeon and come here in the first place? He wanted to get up and walk out of there, but he didn't know if they would let him. He had decided to at least try when the door opened and Officer Harris and an older man with three chevrons on his uniform shirt came in and sat down across from him.

"Mr. Winters, this is Sergeant Zukkerman. Why don't you tell him what you told me?"

Raymond could already tell that it was a waste of time, but he told the story again. And again, neither officer wrote anything down while he talked. When he finished, Zuckerman said, "I'm sorry this happened to you, Mr. Winters, but I'm not surprised. There are a lot of people in this town that know what happened to Ms. Coulter. I'm sure there are more than these two you're talking about who might want to take the law into their own hands."

"So what am I supposed to do? Hide inside the house? Go into protective custody like this clown suggested?"

"I don't appreciate you calling one of my officers a clown, sir."

"Well guess what? I don't appreciate being jerked around like this! I'm a taxpayer in this town, and unless something has changed since my college civics classes, people in this country are still innocent until proven guilty. Or did that change and I missed the memo?"

Sergeant Zuckerman stared at him, and Raymond stared back defiantly. Finally Zuckerman slid the legal pad across the table to him and said, "Write it down, all of it, and I'll kick it up to the detectives to see what they want to do about it."

Knowing that it was a waste of time and that he would get no help from the police, he still wrote down the details of his encounter with Donald and Kyle Erickson. When he was finished he signed it and put the pen down.

"Alright Mr. Winters, I'll pass this along."

"And that's it?"

"What is it you want us to do, Mr. Winters?"

"What I want is some kind of protection."

"Then I would suggest you get yourself a dog, sir."

"Thank you very much for your concern," Raymond said sarcastically. "Am I free to go?"

"Yes sir. For now. Officer Walton will be happy to show you out."

They stood up and the young officer opened the door for him. Before they left the room Sergeant Zuckerman said, "Officer Walton, be sure you don't trip over those big clown feet of yours."

Neither man said anything as Walton led him down the hallway and back out into the lobby. When Raymond got back to his truck he was shaking, but this time it was from anger, not from fear or panic. He had not wanted to go to the police in the first place because he feared they would not take the attack upon him seriously, and he had been right. And even though he had been reluctant to report the incident, it angered him that the police did not seem to feel he deserved protection from Holly's brothers.

He was trying to decide what to do next when his cell phone rang. He answered it, expecting the caller to be Wayne, but he was wrong.

"Raymond? It's Norma. We need to talk."

***

The lunch rush was over at Dixie Crossroads, and though she looked strangely at his battered face, the young hostess didn't say anything as she led him to a table. Raymond asked for a glass of sweet tea and told her that he was meeting someone and would wait to order until she arrived. She had barely returned with his drink order when Norma got there.

Raymond stood up, not sure of the proper protocol given the change in their status, and extended his hand.

Norma looked at him, unable to hide the shock on her face when she saw his condition. She covered her mouth with her hand, then asked, "My God, Raymond, what happened to you?"

"It's nothing," he told her. "Have a seat, Norma, please."

She stared at his face with something akin to horror, which did nothing to help Raymond's already shaken self-confidence. Finally she took a seat across the table from him and said, "Oh, Raymond. I am so sorry!"

"It's okay," he said, trying to reassure her.

The waitress brought them the restaurant's signature complimentary corn fritters dusted with powdered sugar, and a glass of tea for Norma. Raymond ordered a rock shrimp basket, and Norma opted for clam strips.

When she left with their order, Raymond asked Norma, "So how are things at the store?"

"It's been kind of crazy," Norma told him. "There's been a lot of talking, a lot of whispering, the auditors have been there going over everything, and customers are asking what's going on with you."

"I have to admit I was kind of surprised when you called," Raymond said. "When I was there the other day, Mike said you didn't want to talk to me."

Norma's face colored and she lowered her eyes. "I'm sorry, Raymond. You deserved better than that from me."

Neither of them said anything for what seemed a long time, until finally Norma cleared her throat and looked up. "I'm not proud of acting that way and there's no excuse for it. I was hurt, shocked. I guess I felt betrayed."

"Betrayed?"

"I thought I knew you, and then all of this came out and I was asking myself how I could've been so naïve. I was angry at you, Raymond, for being this... this monster they were talking about on television and not being the man I thought I knew. I mean, you work with somebody every day as close as we did, you think you know them. And then..."

"I didn't kill that woman, Norma. I swear to God, I didn't do it."

"But you were in that room with her."

Raymond nodded his head. "Yes, I was. I'm not proud of it, and I can't explain why I did it. I was always faithful to my wife. Always. And then... there's no excuse for it. I screwed up. I screwed up big time."

"And that's the thing," Norma said, "I knew you weren't that kind of guy. The kind that cheats. It's something I've always respected about you, Raymond. You're a good guy. I've worked with other managers who weren't like you. I knew the way you always interacted with me. With all of the women at the store. So that's why I was so shocked. But the point is, you're my friend, and whether you made a mistake and did something stupid doesn't change who you are or what you are. And I apologize for forgetting that."

"It's okay. Don't worry about it."

"And, this is hard to say, but I was jealous, Raymond."

"Jealous? Jealous of what?"

"Jealous of the fact that in all the years we worked together, you never showed any interest in me at all, and then you're in some motel room with some woman? I know that doesn't make any sense, but it was like... why would you be with some stranger when I was available?"

He didn't know what to say, but felt that he should say something. Before he could, she continued, "And I was available, Raymond."

"Norma, I never... I never thought of you that way. Not because of you. I just never thought of any woman that way. This woman, Holly, I didn't go looking for it, I didn't expect it, and like I've said over and over, I can't explain it."

"And that's the thing I had to figure out in my own head," Norma said. "You never would notice me, or any other women at work, because that's not you. I know what your marriage is like, Raymond. I've sat across the office from you and heard Sheila ranting and raving over the telephone. I've taken her messages when she called and you were busy. But never in all the years we were together did I hear you say a bad word about her. Not once did I see you looking at one of the women employees or customers as they walked away, like a lot of guys do."

The waitress brought their order and refilled their drinks. Dixie Crossroads had a well deserved reputation for excellent food and service, and was Raymond's favorite restaurant. He had dined there more times than he could count over the years and he was relieved to discover that his mouth had healed enough that he could eat comfortably.

When they were alone again, Norma said, "Here's the thing, Raymond. There's a lot of talk going on and there are a couple of women who are claiming that you made passes at them or tried to pressure them."

He started to say something, but Norma held up her hand. "You don't need to say it, I know it's a lot of bull. But I just thought you should know. Because at least one of them has talked to the news people."

"Who?"

"Nancy."

"Nancy? Nancy Chambers?"

Norma nodded.

Raymond wasn't completely surprised that if anybody on his team would have betrayed him, it would be Nancy. She had only been at the store a little over a year, but in that time he had had to talk to her twice about her tardiness, and the third time he had given her a written warning. She had stalked out of the office without a word, slamming the door behind her. After that she had lodged a complaint against him for being rude to her. It was the only time he had ever had an employee grievance filed with the company. The human resources department had sent a mediator to talk to the two of them together, and after listening to both sides, reading the notations Raymond had made in the woman's file about the previous verbal warnings, and reading the written warning he had given her, all strictly following company guidelines, the mediator had ruled that her complaint was groundless.

"You said a couple of women? Who else?"

"Nancy is the one who talked to the TV station, but after that, I overheard Paula saying that she caught you looking down her blouse twice when she was stocking shelves. I took her into the office right then and we had it out. I asked her why she had never reported it and she said she was afraid of losing her job. I told her I didn't believe a word she said and asked for specific details. She began hemming and hawing, and finally said well, maybe she had been wrong."

Raymond didn't know what to say. He was both hurt and angry at the accusations, and wondered how they would affect his case.

"But you need to understand something, Raymond. Those are two women out of 37 employees. When your neighbor came in asking for character references, he got them from several people. And there are a lot of people at the store who miss you, who respect you, and who believe in you. And I'm one of them. I need you to know that."

In spite of himself, Raymond felt tears welling up in his eyes. "That means more to me than you'll ever know, Norma. It really does." He looked away, uncomfortable showing his emotions.

"Raymond, I believe the system works. I believe this is all going to work out and life will get back to normal."

"Normal? I don't know what normal is any more. No matter what happens, my career with Palmetto Pantry is over, my marriage is over, and I don't know where I'm going to go from here, or what I'm going to do, Norma."

"Well, know that you've got a friend, okay?"

They finished their meal, making small talk, trying not to touch on the subject that was on both of their minds. Raymond couldn't help but wonder how many more opportunities he would ever have to share a casual meal with a friend. When they finished eating and walked out to the parking lot Norma hugged him, and Raymond surprised himself by returning it.

He had never been a demonstrative man. Growing up, physical expressions of affection had always been rare in his family, and he could not remember the last time he had hugged Sheila. For years, any attempt to do so had earned him a push away, and usually, not gently. It had seemed like the kids had quickly adopted their mother's aversion to his embrace at an early age. Now, he found himself clinging to Norma in a way that would have embarrassed him before. It was an expression of affection between two good friends, something that was alien to him, and he didn't want it to end. When it did, Norma gently laid her hand alongside his bruised cheek and said, "Take care of yourself, Raymond. If you ever need to talk, I'm just a phone call away."

Black Friday

Chapter 28

The news crew's van was parked in front of Wayne's house, and Raymond was tempted to keep on driving, but there was nowhere to escape in the cul-de-sac except to go to the end and turn around and leave, and he figured they would follow him anyway. So he parked in the driveway and ignored the eager young reporter who jumped out of the van, followed by his cameraman.

"Mr. Winters, do you have any comment about the revelation by one of your former employees at Prairie Pantry that you sexually harassed her?"

As Raymond was unlocking the door, the reporter persisted with his questions. "Mr. Winters, don't you have anything to say in your defense? Is it true that you sexually harassed one of your employees? Can you tell us anything about your relationship with Holly Coulter?"

Raymond hoped his shaking hands were not evident to the camera as he unlocked the door and got inside, quickly closing it behind him. He leaned against the door and took a deep breath, and then another. The reporter knocked on the door but Raymond ignored him. Through the door he heard the reporter asking, "Mr. Winters? Mr. Winters, why won't you talk to us? Why won't you tell our viewers your side of the story. What do you have to hide, Mr. Winters?"

His knees suddenly felt weak and Raymond was afraid he was going to collapse right there in the entryway. He managed to make his way across the living room and down the hall to his bedroom, where he threw himself face down on the bed and could not hold back his tears. And in the background, he could still hear the reporter knocking on the door and asking his questions.

***

"Breaking news in the Holly Coulter murder case," the anchorman on the 6 o'clock news said. "Channel 17 has learned that Raymond

Winters, charged with killing Ms. Coulter at the TravelersRest Motel here in Titusville on Black Friday, was also accused of sexually harassing an employee of the Palmetto Pantry grocery store on Cheney Highway, where Winters was the manager before being arrested in connection with the homicide. Here is Leonard Delgado with more."

The scene switched to a sobbing Nancy Chambers and the voice of the reporter saying, "That's right, Frank. This is Nancy Chambers, an employee of Palmetto Pantry, who told me that while he was the store's manager, Raymond Winters sexually harassed her and threatened her with being fired if she did not give in to his demands."

The camera zoomed in on the crying woman, who said, "All I wanted was a job, a chance to feed my family. And this man... this man who I trusted and respected, he...," she paused to wipe her eyes and sobbed again, then said, "he tried to force me to... he told me if I wanted my job I had to do things with him."

"Can you tell us what kind of things, Ms. Chambers?" the reporter asked.

She shook her head and said, "I can't say them on TV. They were filthy, disgusting things, things that I just could not do, *would* not do!" She buried her face in her hands and the camera stayed on her as she tried to get control of herself.

"Did you report this to the company, Ms. Chambers?"

She nodded behind her hands, then raised her face and said, "They sent in an investigator, but it ended just the way Mr. Winters said it would. I got a reprimand, and nothing was done to him at all."

"Nothing? Are you telling me the company allowed this to go on?"

"No, nothing. I guess he got scared though, because after that he never approached me again. But I always got the worst hours and the worst shifts after that."

The camera switched to the reporter, who said, "When contacted about Ms. Chambers's allegations, a Palmetto Pantry spokesman would only say that Ms. Chambers had filed a complaint against Mr. Winters, but confidentiality rules do not allow them to go into any details about the incident."

Then the screen switched again, this time to footage of Raymond pulling into Wayne's driveway and the reporter asking him about the woman's allegations, and then Raymond going into the house without answering. That was followed by the reporter knocking on the door and asking why Raymond would not talk to him. "And there you have it,

Frank. As he has ever since this story began, Mr. Winters refused to comment when we tried to get his side of the story."

The anchorman came back on the screen and said, "Mr. Winters remains on bail, awaiting trial in the Coulter murder case. When we contacted the District Attorney's Office about these latest allegations against him, Assistant District Attorney Janet Morrison said that they would be a civil matter and would have no bearing on the Coulter case. When I asked her why a man accused of so much is still walking around free, all Ms. Morrison would say was that she does not always agree with the way the system works, but it is the system we have."

The newsman shook his head as if to imply that it did not make sense to him, and then they went on to the next story, something about a new company coming to the Space Coast and how many jobs it might bring to the area with it.

Raymond stared at the television for a long time, his mind numb. He knew Nancy Chambers resented him, but he never thought she would take it that far, and actually lie to get revenge.

Things got worse by the 10 o'clock news, when they replayed the earlier footage, accompanied by another woman who had come forward to claim that when she accidentally bounced a check at the grocery store, Raymond had threatened her with arrest if she did not have sex with him. He knew the name immediately. Alecia Garvin had not bounced just one check, but seven, at the store. And while he had not propositioned or threatened her in any way, he *had* reported the checks to the police, and she had been arrested. As he recalled, she had also written bad checks to at least half a dozen other stores in town.

But that wasn't the worst of it. The anchorman said that two of his daughter Kimberly's friends were now saying that while Raymond had never touched them or made suggestive comments to them, he was always "creepy and staring at them" whenever they visited, and they felt he was undressing them with his eyes.

"And yet this man is still walking around, a danger to every woman in this community," said the station's co-anchor when her colleague had finished his report.

"Well, keep in mind, Laura, as the District Attorney's office tells us, this is the system we have, whether we like it or not."

While they were not identified because of their age, Raymond was pretty sure the girls were Heather Jordan and Kyra Landry, Kimberly's constant companions. The three were always together, and when they weren't, they were either talking or texting each other on their cell phones.

Raymond wished that Wayne was there to provide a sounding board but he didn't want to call and bother him when he was on the road. Twice he picked up the phone and started to dial Norma's number, but then he put it back down. He had spent too much of his life keeping his feelings bottled up inside to feel comfortable opening up now, even though she had told him she was just a phone call away anytime he needed to talk. And while he believed her, old habits die hard.

Raymond wasn't a drinking man. He would occasionally have a few beers with Wayne, or a can now and then at the neighborhood get-togethers, but that was it. He did not enjoy the taste of alcohol and he had only been intoxicated twice in his life, both times in college. In each instance, he had woken up sick and hung over and vowed never to do that again. But he still turned off the television, opened a beer and drank it, and then opened a second one. He had not eaten since lunch and had no appetite, though he knew he should. Instead, he drank a third beer and then went to bed, where he stared at the ceiling for hours.

Try as he might, he could not turn off his mind. Over and over he relived the conversation with the two policeman that day, thought about his meeting with Norma, ran the news programs through his mind, and then his thoughts went to Holly. He wished he had never seen her. So why, after all of this, did he still wish that she was with him right then, somewhere out on the water in his boat? Eventually he did drift off to sleep, but his dreams were a kaleidoscope of images - scenes from the store, from his time spent in jail, fishing on Mosquito Lagoon, and more than once Holly cupping her breasts and smiling down at him as she rode him.

Chapter 29

By Tuesday the worst of the swelling had gone down in his face and the bruises were beginning to fade to a yellow color. But Raymond knew that it was not his appearance alone that caused the nervous reaction in the same young nurse aide when he signed in at Whispering Palms Nursing Home.

"Umm... can you wait here just a minute, please?"

She walked to a phone as far away from him as she could on the curved reception desk, pushed in three numbers on the keypad and he heard her murmuring to somebody. She hung up and did not meet his eyes, and a moment later a smartly dressed black woman approached him.

"Mr. Winters?"

"Yes?"

"I'm Amanda Shoals, the assistant director here at Whispering Palms. Can we talk for a minute?"

Raymond nodded and followed her across the lobby and down a short hall to her office.

"Please, have a seat, Mr. Winters."

Raymond did, and then asked, "Is there a problem Ms. Shoals?"

"Not a problem, per se, as much as a... potential problem, I guess you could say."

"Potential problem?"

She nodded. "Your sister has requested that you not be allowed to see your mother."

"Why would Julia do that?"

"She told us that in light of recent events, she feels that you might be a danger to your mother."

"That's ridiculous," Raymond said.

"I understand how you must feel, Mr. Winters. But given your situation..."

"No, you don't understand how I feel," Raymond told her. "How could you understand? I keep hearing that a person is innocent until proven guilty in this country. I have never been a danger to my mother or anybody else."

"I'm sorry, Mr. Winters. I sympathize."

"She can't do this. What gives her the right to decide if I get to see our mother or not?"

"Well, Mr. Winters, she does pay a significant amount of the cost of your mother's care here."

"And I also contribute," Raymond said. "Maybe not as much as Julia does, but I pay $500 every month towards our mother's care. That's all I can afford." It was actually more than he could afford and had been one more bone of contention between Raymond and Sheila.

"That's commendable," the woman said. "However..."

"However, you can't buy or prevent access to another human being," Raymond interrupted. "Now, unless you have a court order or something legally keeping me from seeing my mother, this conversation is over."

"Sir, we don't need an incident here."

"Then I would suggest that we end this conversation right here and I go visit my mother like I came here for. I don't mean to be rude, Ms. Shoals, but I've had just about enough people pushing me around and telling me what I can and can't do and what a terrible person I am lately. So you can either call the police and report a man is just here to see his mother, or you can go back to whatever it was you were doing and I'll go on about my business."

The woman blinked her eyes, and stared at him for a moment. "Can I say something off the record, Mr. Winters?"

"I didn't know any of this was on a record," Raymond told her.

"Your mother can be rather a difficult woman, as you know. And so can your sister. I really don't want to be involved in a family feud and if you ever quote me on this I'll deny it. But I have no idea why you would want to put up with the abuse I personally have heard your mother lay on you during your visits."

"Taking abuse from the women in my life seems to be something I've become very good at," Raymond said. "Look, Ms. Shoals, I'm not here to make your life more difficult. And I damn sure don't need to make mine any more difficult, either. I just want to see my mother while I can. I know she can be a bitch, and I know that Julia can, too. But she's still my mother."

Amanda Shoals regarded him thoughtfully for a moment, then nodded and said, "As you wish. Have a nice visit."

***

His mother was playing with a handheld video poker machine that the kids had given her last Christmas when Raymond knocked and poked his head into her room.

"Hello Mother."

"You're two days late. You always visit on Sunday afternoon."

"I know, it's been pretty crazy lately."

"That's what I hear. I guess killing women and being on the run from the police does take a toll on one's time, doesn't it, Raymond?"

Her words stung him. "Mother, I didn't kill anybody and I'm not on the run. I'm out on bail pending trial and when I do go to trial I'll be found not guilty, because I didn't do anything."

"And what about those other women Raymond? What about those from the store that say you tried to get into their pants? And I don't even want to think about the way you looked at Kimberly's friends, because it makes me sick. The same age as your own daughter!"

"I would have hoped that my own mother would have had a little more faith in me than that," he told her.

"What? Are you going to tell me that none of it ever happened? That all these women are coming out of the woodwork just to pick on you and you're totally innocent?"

"Yes, Mother. Because I am innocent!"

"So you weren't in that motel room with that woman?"

"Yes, I was there with her. But I didn't kill her, and I didn't do any of the other things they're claiming I did."

"Really? And you expect me to believe that because?"

"Because I'm your son. Because you know me. Because you raised me better than that."

"Lord knows I tried, Raymond. But obviously I failed, didn't I?"

"No mother, you didn't fail because I didn't do any of this."

"Except for going to that room with that whore?"

"She wasn't a whore, mother. She was a..."

"I know exactly what she was, Raymond. She was no better than all those tramps that your father got involved with over the years. And you're no better than he was. The first chance you had to jump into bed with somebody else you took it. Assuming it was the first time."

"Yes, it was the first time, Mother. And I can't tell you how much I regret it. Or how much I hate myself for doing it. But I can't roll back the clock and undo it. I didn't kill that woman, and I didn't try to make those other women sleep with me, and for God's sake, I never looked at Kimberly's friends like they are saying. Give me a little bit of credit, will you?"

"I don't want to hear it," his mother said shrilly. "The same lies I heard from your father over and over until I was just sick of it. And now my own son... You're no better than him, Raymond! You make me sick just looking at you."

"Mother, how many times do I have to tell you, I didn't kill anybody. I didn't do any of the things they're accusing me of. Yes, I screwed up and went to that room with that woman. I could tell you it's because Sheila has treated me so bad for so long, or because she has ignored my needs for so long, or make a hundred other excuses. But it all comes down to one thing, I had a choice and I made the wrong one. I'm not making excuses for it. It happened, and I wish it never did. But that doesn't make me a murderer, that doesn't make me some kind of pervert chasing little girls around, or trying to force women to go to bed with me. I may not be the son you always wanted, but I'm not the person you seem to think I am, either."

"How many, Raymond?"

"I told you, it was the only time I ever cheated on Sheila."

"I don't believe you. But my question is, how many more will there be? You're following in your father's footsteps every inch of the way. How many people will have to die for your sick pleasure, Raymond? Will you stop at this one, or are you going to try to beat his score?"

By then she was shouting at him. The door opened abruptly and Amanda Shoals asked, "What's going on in here?"

"We're just talking," Raymond said.

"Get him out of here," his mother said. "Get him out of here and don't ever let him come back!"

"What are you talking about, Mother?"

"Mr. Winters, you're going to have to leave."

"Mother? What do you mean about my father's score?"

"Mr. Winters, please. Don't make me call the police."

"I said get him out of here," his mother screamed.

By then two other staff members were in the doorway, their faces alarmed..

"Mr. Winters, you have to leave right now or I'm calling the police."

"I just want to know..."

"Joyce, please call 911."

"Okay, okay, I'm leaving," Raymond said. "I'm going."

He turned back to his mother and saw pure hatred in her eyes. The look hurt more than any words she had ever spoken to him.

***

He was three blocks from Wayne's house when his cell phone rang.

"Are you out of your mind, Raymond?"

"Hello, Julia."

"Don't hello Julia me! What is wrong with you?"

"Nothing's wrong with me that wouldn't be better if people would stop lying about me, and stop accusing me of things I didn't do, and stop treating me like I'm some kind of wild animal."

"Try telling that to our mother, Raymond! I just got a call from Whispering Palms. Do you know that she is hysterical right now? Do you know what you've put her through. I wouldn't be surprised if they have to sedate her."

"That's ridiculous, Julia. She wasn't hysterical. She was just our mother, throwing one of her tantrums."

"Mrs. Shoals at the nursing home said she was shouting so loudly that they could hear her out in the lobby."

"That's what people do when they throw tantrums," Raymond said. "They shout."

Now it was Julia's turn to shout, "Now you listen to me Raymond, and you listen good. You are not to go back to Whispering Palms, you are not to call, you are not to contact our mother in any way. Do you understand me?"

"Since when do you make the rules?" Raymond asked.

"Since I pay most of the bills for her. Since the whole world knows that you're a murdering pervert. That's when!"

"I've always done what I could to help out with Mother's expenses," Raymond said.

"Oh, please! Do you have any idea what it costs to keep her there? Do you really think your pathetic little contribution amounts to anything at all?"

"God, Julia, do you really think your money makes you that much better than me?"

"It's not about money, Raymond. Lord knows you could've made something of yourself. You were smart enough to do something with your life. But you took the easy way out like you have all your life. Maybe you don't have any self-respect, but I do!"

He started to reply but he was shaking so badly that he had to pull the pickup to the side of the road. It didn't matter, Julia still had plenty more to say.

"I've already called Brian, and he is going to have his secretary do the paperwork to request a restraining order barring you from coming anywhere near Whispering Palms or our mother. And don't think I won't have you arrested if you violate it, do you understand me?"

"Yeah Julia, I understand. It doesn't matter that I'm innocent, it doesn't matter that I'm your brother. I'm the bad guy. I get it, I've always been the bad guy."

"Mother always said you would turn out just like Royce. I guess she was right about that."

That reminded him of what his mother had said at the nursing home. "Julia, Mother said something about me trying to match Royce's score and asked me how many people would have to die? What was she talking about?"

"What?"

"She asked if I was going to try to match his score. Do you know what she meant?"

"Who knows? You had her so upset that there's no telling what she was talking about."

"You were what, twelve or thirteen when they split up? Do you know what happened?"

"What do you think happened, Raymond? Mother got tired of him sleeping with every slut that came along. She was tired of being cheated on and humiliated."

"But what was she talking about? What did she mean about people dying?"

"I don't want to talk about Royce. He's dead to me. We're talking about you, and how upset you made our mother. So stay away! Do you understand me, Raymond? Stay away or else!"

Before he could reply, she broke the connection and ended the call.

Chapter 30

If Raymond thought he had had enough drama for the day, he was mistaken. He had barely parked the truck in Wayne's driveway and was just reaching for the door handle when a beefy man with short cropped hair and a red face shouted at him.

"Hey, asshole, I want to talk to you!"

He strode across the front yard, fists balled. Visions of the beating he had taken at the boat ramp raced through Raymond's mind, and he wanted to turn and run, but there was nowhere to go.

"I ought to kill you, you goddamn pervert! Where do you get off looking at my daughter like that?"

Raymond was surprised that his voice was as steady as it was considering how shaky he felt. "I don't know what you're talking about."

"Yes you do, you son-of-a-bitch! Heather told me how you kept looking at her all the time."

"Heather. You must be Mr. Jordan."

"You got that right, and I'll tell you something right now, you sick bastard. If you ever come near my daughter, if you even look in her direction again, I'm gonna kill you. I'll take my shotgun and blow your ass away. Do you understand me?"

"I never..."

The man poked him hard in the chest with a thick finger and said, "Don't you try to deny it! Everybody knows what a twisted pervert you are. Now you remember what I said. You come anywhere near my daughter again and you're dead. The cops can lock me up and throw away the key, I don't care. You don't look at her. You don't talk to her. You stay away from her. Do I make myself clear, asshole?"

Five or six neighbors had gathered on the sidewalk to see the confrontation, and Raymond was sure others were watching from their windows. He wondered what would happen if the verbal assault turned physical. Would any of them come to his aid? Or would they think he deserved whatever he was getting and mind their own business, even cheer the enraged father on?

"I don't know what kind of father you are, but I love my kids and they're all that matter to me. So don't you forget, I'll kill you and not think about it for one second. Just give me an excuse."

Jordan was close enough that Raymond could feel the spittle when he talked spray on his face. He was backed up tight against Wayne's door, and not knowing what he could say, and realizing that anything he did say would only exacerbate the situation, he remained silent.

He expected the man to hit him at any second, but his message delivered, Jordan seemed to have run out of things to say. Finally, he jabbed Raymond with his finger a final time and stepped back. He gave Raymond one last threatening look before turning and walking away.

Raymond closed his eyes, relieved that the encounter had not become more physical than it had. When he opened them, most of the neighbors had gone away except for John and Rachel Lowman, who lived two doors down from Wayne. Raymond had always gotten along well with them, and John had been one of the people who had provided a character reference at his arraignment hearing. Now the man shook his head and said, "Go away, Raymond. You're not doing yourself any good staying here. Find an apartment or someplace else to stay. We don't need this here on our street. All the cops, and the reporters, and now this. Just... just go away, Raymond."

***

Once inside and away from the eyes of his neighbors, Raymond sank down into the closest chair and let the tremors that he had held in check overtake him. He thought he would cry again, but the tears didn't come.

Though he had never really noticed his teenaged daughter's friends, and had certainly not leered at them the way they had reported, he could understand the man's rage. He thought he would have reacted the same way in his place. Or would he? Did he really know how he would react in any given situation? Raymond didn't honestly know.

Lately he did not know who he was or what he would do from one moment to the next. In his darkest moments, lying in bed staring at the ceiling when sleep wouldn't come, he had even asked himself it was possible that he *had* gone into a fit of rage and murdered Holly when she told him their encounter had only been a one-time thing and they would not be meeting again. He had heard of people who had committed crimes of passion and claimed not to remember it later. He had always been skeptical of such claims, but maybe they were right after all.

But what about the e-mails between himself and Holly? How could he have blocked all of *that* out? Did he have some kind of split personality? A Jekyll and Hyde thing going on where the good Raymond was unaware of the misdeeds of the bad Raymond? He shook his head. He wasn't crazy, he was just an average man caught up in some crazy nightmare. The only thing was, he knew he wasn't going to wake up and realize it was all just a bad dream.

***

He spent the rest of that day and the next inside, afraid to go out and risk another confrontation, and not knowing where he would go anyhow. As he had done for what seemed the hundredth time, he went over everything in his head again and again, from the first time Holly had spoken to him standing in line outside of the store that cold, wet morning, to their conversation later in the parking lot, going to the restaurant for coffee, Holly putting her hand on his arm and him realizing that the conversation had gone in a new direction, to their tryst in the motel room.

None of it made sense, let alone any of the events that had followed. Why *had* an attractive, younger woman like Holly Coulter singled him out? Why had she lied about who she was? Why had she brought her sister to Stardust Street and said her boyfriend lived there? What about the e-mails between himself and Holly, or the big deal she had told her ex-husband she was working on? What had he gotten himself into? And again, why him? What did he have to offer anybody that would make it worth all of this?

And lastly, what had his mother been talking about when she asked if he was going to beat his father's score? After the divorce and the move across the state, Raymond had not seen his father for many years, and there had been no communication between them. Then, on his twelfth birthday, he had come home from school and found a birthday card in the mailbox. It had a drawing of a boy with a baseball bat over his shoulder, and said Happy Birthday on the outside. On the inside there had been two lines of printed birthday greetings, and under that the words "Happy Birthday, Dad" scrawled in blue pen along with a five dollar bill.

When Raymond had excitedly ran inside the house and shown his mother, she had torn it from his hand and ripped the card and the money into pieces and threw them in the trash, telling him that his father was a terrible man and she never wanted to hear his name or anything else about him ever again.

Twice more over the years, on his fourteenth and sixteenth birthdays, he had received the same generic card, the same written message, and another five dollar bill. But having learned from the first experience, Raymond had hid them away in one of his schoolbooks and never said a word to his mother or sister about them.

He had only seen his father twice that he could remember. Once Royce had shown up at his doorstep soon after he and Sheila were married, saying he had come to meet his daughter-in-law. He was accompanied by a pretty woman with bleached blonde hair who wasn't much older than Raymond was, and only stayed half an hour before saying he had a long drive home.

A few years later Royce had made an appearance at the grocery store where Raymond was the assistant manager, accompanied by a different younger woman. They had invited him to lunch, an uncomfortable affair that showed they had nothing in common and little to say to each other. When they had gone their separate ways there had been no hug, no handshake, no suggestion that they get together again sometime. Just a simple "see you around" and Royce and the woman had climbed into a red Miata sports car and were gone.

There had been a couple of Christmas cards after that, the most recent last year. Again, they were impersonal cards with no greeting, just his father's name signed on the inside.

Raymond knew nothing about his father except for things his mother had told him over the years, all of them bad. He seemed to recall that Royce was a salesman of some kind, and that at some point he had been a partner in an automobile dealership that ended badly. He recalled his maternal grandfather, long dead now, once saying that Royce could "sell ice cubes to Eskimos" but that he would steal the pennies off a dead man's eyes.

So what had his mother been talking about? What kind of score? How many dead people would he leave in his wake? He wanted to drive back to Whispering Palms and ask her what she meant by all of that, but he knew that would only turn out badly. And to be honest, he had

Black Friday

no interest in seeing her again, no matter what kind of information she might have.

Or had her words been simply the ranting of the hateful woman who could never forgive nor forget? The official diagnosis was that his mother had early onset Alzheimer's, and there were times she seemed totally out of it when he visited. Could whatever she was referring to be some fantasy she had conjured up in her mind? Then again, Raymond was never totally convinced that there was any type of mental impairment. More than once he had suspected that his mother simply used that as a way to disassociate herself from him or whomever she did not feel like dealing with at the moment.

He realized he was pacing the living room like a caged animal, but was that surprising? In many ways he felt like a caged animal under constant scrutiny from the curious, who saw him as something disgusting and dangerous. It was late in the day and the living room was dark when he finally went into the kitchen and microwaved some type of frozen dinner, eating it and cleaning up after himself with no idea what it had even been.

An hour later, his mind still in turmoil, he went through his wallet and found the slip of paper tucked away behind his Social Security card and dialed the number on it. He immediately had second thoughts and was about to hang up when the call was answered.

"Hi. It's Raymond. I need to see you."

Chapter 31

Norma lived in a small bungalow on Pinecrest Street, tucked away in a lot sheltered by a pair of ancient live oak trees that dripped Spanish moss. She greeted him at the door with another hug, and again, just as he had at their last meeting, Raymond did not want to let go.

"I really appreciate this," he told her.

"No problem, but do you really think this is a good idea?"

"Probably not, but it's something I have to do. If you're not comfortable with it, I understand. I don't want to put you on the spot."

Norma shook her head, "No. Don't worry about that. I just don't want you to get into any more trouble than you already are."

"I don't think anybody followed me," Raymond said.

"Okay. If you're sure?"

"I'm sure."

"Do you want me to go with you? I can call in sick."

"You've never called in sick in your life, Norma."

"No, but I would for you."

"Thank you, but it's not necessary. This is something I have to do by myself, I think."

"Well, here you go," she said handing him the keys to her car, a five year old Buick Lucerne.

"Thank you," Raymond said. "This means a lot to me."

***

He didn't believe the police had him under surveillance, and if they did, he didn't know if switching cars would really make any difference. But on the drive to Norma's house he had made several left and right turns in succession, watching for any vehicles that might be following him, and had not seen any. He didn't know where he had picked that trick up, probably from some television show or movie, and he didn't really know if it was effective anyway. For all he knew, they had some type of electronic tracking device in his truck, but he couldn't worry about all of the what ifs.

Nevertheless he made another series of turns when he left Norma's house, always watching the rearview mirror for anybody who might be following him. Then he drove through the crowded WalMart parking lot, crossed Cheney Highway and did the same thing at Lowes, always watching to see if the same car or any other vehicle was in sight behind him. Satisfied that he was not being followed, he got onto Interstate 95 and drove south a few miles before exiting.

He took the Beeline Expressway west, skirted the southern edge of the Orlando metropolitan area, then followed the turnpike north to Wildwood. From there it was only a few miles to The Villages, the upscale retirement community that was his destination. Using the GPS in Norma's car, he was able to find the address he wanted. He had second-guessed himself through the entire 120 mile drive, and more than once he had been tempted to turn around and forget the whole thing. And now that he was there, he asked himself what he hoped to accomplish. He felt his stomach cramping and he had to fight down a wave of nausea before he got out of the car and went to the door. He pushed the button and heard a bell ringing somewhere inside and a moment later the door opened.

"Hello, Raymond, it's been a while."

"Hello, Royce."

***

They sat in the backyard at a patio table covered by an umbrella. His father's latest woman was a big breasted redhead named Yvette, and while she was at least 20 years younger than him, she was still older than his usual companions. She brought them orange juice, made small talk for a moment or two, and then went back inside.

They watched her walk away, and Royce said, "She's dumb as a rock, but I don't keep her around for conversation. Look at that ass. And when she puts it in gear all you've got to do is hold on. If those rodeo cowboys think they've had some wild rides, they have no idea."

Raymond didn't know what to say, so he didn't say anything, just looked at his father as he lit a cigarette. In his early 70s, Royce Winters was still in very good physical shape. He was tanned, his hair was still dark with just a hint of gray at the temples, and Raymond wasn't sure whether or not it was dyed. He wore a pencil thin mustache, and a thick gold chain around his neck. As he exhaled the smoke he regarded his son with open frankness.

"I was surprised to get your call last night."

"Thank you for seeing me on such short notice."

"Anytime, son."

Raymond was surprised that his father had used the term, and did not know how to respond.

"I hear on the news you've got some problems."

"It's a mess," Raymond said. "I know it looks bad, but I didn't kill that woman."

"Women," Royce said derisively. "They're the best thing ever put on this earth, and the worst thing, too. How can anything that can give you that much pleasure cause that much grief, too? I've had a bunch of them in my life, and the secret is to not get attached. They're like a cheap pair of tennis shoes. Use them as long as they're comfortable to slip into, and then throw them away and get some new ones when they start to smell." He laughed at his own joke, then took another long drag on his cigarette

Raymond was uncomfortable with his father's crudeness but Royce did not seem to notice, or if he did, he ignored it..

"So what is it you need, Raymond? Money? Advice? What?"

"No, I just need to ask you about something."

"Okay, what is it?"

"My mother said something... something about you."

Royce laughed, but there was no humor in it. "I'm sure she's said a lot of things about me. I'm not exactly her favorite person. How is Alice doing these days?"

"She's in a nursing home. She has good days and bad days."

"That's too bad," Royce said, but Raymond could tell it was more a platitude than a true expression of concern for the woman that had been his wife and had borne his children.

"Yeah. Anyway, she said something the other day that I can't figure out."

"What was that?"

"She asked me something about was I going to try to match your score, and how many people had to die for me to do that. Do you have any idea what that was about?"

"I think you're probably starting a little late in life if you want to try to match my score," Royce boasted. "I've had so many broads that I stopped counting somewhere past a hundred."

Raymond had never fit in when he was in high school. He never played sports, or poker, or golf, or hung out with a bunch of guys so he wasn't accustomed to or comfortable with locker room humor. Especially coming from his father, though they had never had a normal father-son relationship, or any kind of relationship for that matter.

"Whatever. But what was she talking about people dying? That didn't make any sense."

"How the hell should I know?" Royce asked, a trace of irritation in his voice as he took a final drag on his cigarette and stubbed it out in an ashtray. "You said she's in a nursing home. Maybe she's senile. Who knows?"

In spite of himself, Raymond felt like he should defend his mother, though he didn't know why. "Like I said, she has good days and bad days. But when she said this she sounded like she knew what she was talking about."

"Maybe she did, but I sure as hell don't."

"Why did you guys get divorced?"

"Oh hell, I don't know. It's been so long I forgot. Why does anybody get divorced?"

"I was pretty young when it happened," Raymond said. "But I remember there was some big something that happened. And after that, anytime I asked about it I was hushed up. But once in a while I'd hear Mother talking to her parents or somebody and hear your name come up, but as soon as they noticed me, they shut right up."

"Whatever. It's all ancient history," Royce said, waving his hand dismissively. "Why dredge up the past?"

"I don't give a damn about the past," Raymond said, "I'm worried about my future!"

"What's this all about, Raymond? I've never heard from you, not so much as a Father's Day card or a birthday card ever, and suddenly you're here asking me all kinds of shit about things that happened a lifetime ago. What do you want from me?"

"How come you never came around when I was growing up? I got like three birthday cards from you in my whole life. Then you show up out of the blue a couple of times, and I get a Christmas card every few years."

"Look, kid, it wasn't exactly a good breakup, okay? Those things happen and sometimes it's best just to keep your distance. It's better for everybody."

"Everybody? Or better for you?"

"What the hell does that mean?"

"Lots of people get divorced," Raymond said. "That doesn't mean they forget their kids or act like they were never born."

"Who the hell do you think you are?" Royce demanded. "The telephone and the mail are two-way streets. At least I tried a couple of times. The only time I've ever heard from you is last night, now that you're in trouble. So if you just came here to ask me a bunch of silly-assed questions, and try to make me the bad guy about what happened between your mother and me, you can just turn your ass right around and go back to Titusville."

"All I'm trying to do is..."

"I don't give a rat's ass what you're trying to do! Whatever it is, I want no part of it and it's none of my business. If you stuck your dick in some broad who wound up dead, don't expect me to come up with some magic solution to your problem."

Royce was shouting by then, and the back door opened and Yvette asked, "What's going on out here?"

"Nothing's going on out here," Royce told her. "Get your ass back inside and mind your own god damn business."

He turned back to Raymond and said, "Go on, get out of here. I've got nothing more to say to you."

"That's it? You've got nothing else to say at all?"

"Are you leaving or do I need to drag your ass out to the street?"

Raymond had never been prone to violence but he wanted to slam his fist into the face of this man who was nominally his father, if only because he had created a child with a woman. He didn't know what sins his parents may have committed that led to their separation, and in his experience, neither of them had been a typical mother or father. Though he didn't know his father, he had always believed that his mother's constant comments belittling him were wildly exaggerated. Now he wasn't so sure. But when he stood up and walked away from the table, he knew that no matter what the outcome of his own legal problems might be, he would never see or speak to Royce Winters again.

Black Friday

Chapter 32

He didn't want to deal with the traffic around Orlando again, so on the return trip he took US Highway 27 south to Leesburg, where he picked up US 441 east, passing through the lake country to Mount Dora, where he got onto State Route 46. Somewhere between Sanford and Geneva he glanced in the rearview mirror to see a Highway Patrol car following him.

Panic hit him hard. It was all he could do to keep the Buick between the lanes and not stomp on the accelerator in an attempt to escape. Maybe it was just coincidence. After all, it was a state highway. How could they have known he had violated the judge's order by leaving the county? Had they followed him? That didn't make any sense. If so, why hadn't they stopped him on the way to The Villages? Had Royce called and reported his visit?

The police car stayed behind him for five miles and Raymond tried not to keep looking in the rearview mirror or to do anything else that might tip the patrolmen off that there might be a problem. He knew that if he did anything to get pulled over he would give himself away by his sweaty palms and the rapid heartbeat that he could feel pounding in his chest so much that he was sure it must show under the fabric of his shirt.

Why had he even gone to see Royce? Nothing had been accomplished and he had put himself in jeopardy. What had he expected to get out of the visit? Whatever it was, the trip was one more failure in a long list of failures in his life.

As they approached Geneva the police car pulled off the road into a convenience store, and the relief that Raymond felt was huge. He was tempted to speed up and put some distance between them in case the patrolmen pulled back onto the highway, but he forced himself to keep his speed steady, right at the limit, in the hope of not drawing any further attention to himself.

He made it back to Titusville without incident, breathing a deep sigh of relief when he crossed back into Brevard County. He called Norma's cell phone and she told him she would take a late lunch and meet him at a sandwich shop two blocks from the Palmetto Pantry. She pulled in with his truck five minutes after he arrived.

"How did it go?" Norma asked with concern.

"Not as well as I hoped. But then again, I don't know what I was hoping for or expecting," Raymond admitted.

"Well, there's news at the store," Norma told him after they had ordered their sandwiches and were seated.

"What's that?"

"Nancy Chambers is gone."

"Really?"

Norma nodded her head as she bit into her pastrami sandwich. She chewed, swallowed, and dabbed at a bit of mustard on the corner of her lip, then said, "I don't know what she expected to accomplish by going on the news with all that crap she said, but this morning Mr. Kirtridge came in and told her to punch out and leave and not to come back."

"The company is devoted to their family values image," Raymond said. "For her to say that they ignored her so-called complaint about me was stepping way over the line."

"She would not have lasted very long anyway. After she went on TV and did that, the rest of the crew was so danged mad at her that it was only a matter of time before something happened. You may not know it Raymond, but there are a lot of people at that store who really care about you. They know how many times you shared your bonuses with them, how many times you went to bat for them with the head office over something, how many times you fought to keep their benefits when the company was cutting back. They miss you. We all miss you."

Raymond felt a lump in his throat and was surprised at how much he missed them. Though he had never felt like he had a close personal relationship with any of his crew, he now realized that in many ways they were all part of an extended family. He missed the people, he missed the routines, he missed everything about his old life. Then he corrected himself; he did not miss his wife and the kids. Why was that? Why did his former coworkers mean more to him than his own family? Was it one more indication that, no matter how hard he tried to deny it to himself, he was more like Royce than he was willing to acknowledge?

"Raymond?"

Norma's voice brought him back to the present. She looked at him quizzically. "Where did you go?"

Black Friday

"I'm sorry, I was just thinking about the people at the store. What were you saying?"

"I was saying that Paula Cunningham came to me yesterday, after all this stuff with Nancy started, and apologized for what she had said. She said she knew you were better than that, and that she kind of got caught up in Nancy's nonsense and started believing things that weren't real. I think she really regrets it."

"That's good to know," Raymond said, though he didn't really feel any vindication.

"What are you going to do now, Raymond?"

"I don't know. I want to know what my mother was talking about, the whole thing about beating my father's score, and dead people."

"Dead people? I'm sorry, you lost me there," Norma said with confusion.

Raymond realized he had not revealed anything to her about the reason for his visit to his father. He had just told her he needed to make a trip to The Villages to see Royce and did not want to take his truck since he was prohibited from leaving the county. He was surprised that Norma had not questioned him more, but she had just told him that she would do whatever he needed and was happy to help. He felt that she deserved more than that and told her what his mother had said about trying to match Royce's score, and what his father had said when he asked him about it.

"Do you think he was right? Could it just be something your mother made up? Something she just said to hurt you or whatever?"

"I have no idea. But I think there was something there. As soon as I brought it up he seemed to get agitated and it went downhill from there."

"Is there anybody else you can ask about it? Maybe your sister or your grandparents or some other relative who might know something about it?"

"My sister would just as soon see me sitting in a cell right now," Raymond said. "I did ask her, but if she knows anything she wouldn't say. My grandparents are dead and I don't really have any other relatives."

Norma thought for a minute, then asked, "What are you doing this afternoon?"

"I don't have any plans," Raymond said.

"I've got an idea. I get off work at four. Meet me at my place."

***

Raymond drove back to Stardust Street and spent the next three hours cleaning Wayne's house, not because it needed it but because he had nothing else to do and it kept him busy. The physical activity did not prevent him from thinking, and as he worked he went over his conversation with his father again, wondering what he had said that caused the sudden change in Royce's attitude. One minute the man had been boasting crudely about his conquests, and the next he was dismissing Raymond and closing the door on any chance for a future relationship between them.

He was surprised that he felt some sense of loss about that. How can you lose something you never had? There never *had* been a relationship, and upon reflection, Raymond had to admit that Royce had been right in that any overtures, what few there were, had been made by his father. Raymond had not been comfortable in their rare meetings, and though Royce had given him his phone number and address on his last visit, Raymond had never made any effort to contact him. So why had he kept the information?

Had it been because, as far as he knew, Royce had never attempted to contact Julia? His mother and sister had always had a close bond that he was excluded from, and had always longed for. Had that simple piece of paper symbolized something more in his mind?

He didn't have any answers. It seemed like more and more he realized that he understood himself less and less. The one thing he did know now was that the shadowy image of a father no longer existed in his life. He pulled the paper with his father's name and address from his wallet, found a box of wooden matches in a kitchen drawer and struck one. He held the paper over the sink as it burned. dropping it only when the flames got too close to his fingers. He pulled the strainer from the drain and washed the ashes away. As the last shreds of black disappeared, the thought went through his brain that so much of his old life had been washed down the drain recently.

Chapter 33

Norma had changed out of the blue slacks and blue and white striped blouse that was the required uniform for work and was wearing jeans and a loose fitting top. She greeted him with a hug and asked if he wanted something to drink.

"No thanks," Raymond told her. "I don't do much drinking."

"How about a soda?" she asked.

"Sounds good," he said, more to be polite than because he was thirsty.

"I usually have a drink to unwind from the day," Norma told him. "Do you mind?"

"No, not at all."

"Make yourself comfortable, I'll be right back."

He stood in her living room, which was simply furnished with a television, couch, upholstered rocking chair, and a large bookcase holding an eclectic collection of mysteries, books on art, and cookbooks. He was admiring a painting on the wall, a tropical scene with palm trees and a long stretch of white sand beach, when Norma returned, handing him a glass with ice and Pepsi.

"Sit down, make yourself comfortable."

"This is a nice painting," Raymond told her.

"Oh, that? It's one of my favorites. I think I did that in... '99, maybe 2000?"

"You did it?" He looked closer and saw her name in the bottom right corner of the painting. "I'm impressed!"

"What? You thought I came home every day and spent my spare time thinking about the price of asparagus and the best way to display Tide laundry detergent?"

"No, I guess I never gave it much thought."

Norma pouted and said, "Gee, you sure know how to make a girl feel special, you sweet talking devil you."

"I'm sorry, I didn't mean..."

She laughed and said, "Boy, you're so easy. Relax, I'm just picking on you."

He laughed with her and she sat at one end of the couch.

"Are you just going to stand there all evening? Sit down, I don't bite."

Raymond took a seat at the other end.

"So what did you expect? That I was the neighborhood cat lady, spending my time reading trash romance novels?"

Raymond laughed, "I saw some mysteries and thrillers, but no trashy romances on your bookshelf."

Norma shook her head, "No, I keep those under the bed next to the whips and chains."

Raymond stared at her for a moment, and she burst out laughing again. "Will you relax? I'm not Mistress Norma the Space Coast Dominatrix. I promise, your virtue is safe with me."

He found himself laughing with her, enjoying the sense of humor that she had never displayed at the store. Norma sipped her drink, something clear with ice in it, then sat it on the coffee table and said, "You said something about not knowing much about your family background. Not having anybody who you could ask about your father and whatever your mother was talking about."

Raymond nodded, "I don't really know anything at all about my old man except what my mother always said."

"Which is?"

"That he was a no good, cheating SOB. Irresponsible, untrustworthy, you name it, and if it was bad, he probably did it."

"And what did he have to say about things?"

Raymond shrugged. "The longest conversation I ever had with him about what happened between him and my mother was today, and it probably lasted fifteen minutes. I never knew him when I was growing up. There was never any contact except for a couple of birthday cards that I had to hide from my mother. He visited me a couple of times, no advance notice, he just showed up and he was gone just as quick."

"Did you ever hear from his side of the family? Birthday cards? Anything?"

"If there was, my mother must have destroyed them and never told me or my sister anything about them. I don't even know who my grandparents are on his side of the family are. I couldn't tell you their names."

"Well, let's see what we can find out," Norma said, standing up and taking her glass in hand, "Follow me."

She took him through a doorway and into a small room that he assumed had been a bedroom at one time but was now outfitted with a desk, more bookcases, and an easel. A computer sat next to the desk, with a large monitor on the desktop. Norma sat down at a wheeled office chair and turned it on, then nodded to an extra chair while it booted up. "Pull that over here and have a seat."

Raymond had used the computers at work for filing reports and other job-related duties, as well as company e-mail. His computer at home didn't see much use unless he had paperwork to do when he left the store, or to visit a few boating and fishing websites that he followed. Norma, on the other hand, seemed to know her way around the Internet very well, and in just a click or two of her mouse, she had logged onto Ancestry.com.

"Okay your full name is....?"

" Raymond Alan Winters."

"And what is your date of birth?"

"December 14, 1974."

"Where were you born?"

"Cincinnati, Ohio."

She asked him a couple of other questions, mother and father's names, his mother's maiden name, and their birthdates. He didn't know his father's, but Norma said that didn't matter. She entered the information into the computer as he answered and then hit the Search button. A moment later a screen opened up showing Raymond's name. She did another search for Royce Winters, waited a moment, and said, "There you go. Royce Alan Winters, born April 9, 1943, in Cincinnati."

"That's him?"

"Same name, also born in Cincinnati, and the age would be about right. Royce isn't exactly a common name like Sam or Bill, so I think this must be the guy. Let me try this." She worked the mouse again, typed in his mother's name and birth date, did a marriage records search, and said, "Bingo!"

Raymond read the screen. Royce Alan Winters and Alice Marie Keppler had been married in Cincinnati on February 14, 1964. "That Valentine's Day marriage didn't work out too well, did it?"

Norma laughed and said, "Go figure." She took another drink from her glass and said "Now let's see what else we can dig up."

Over the next 45 minutes, Norma was able to give him the names of his paternal grandparents, Jeffrey and Suzanne Winters, who had both lived and died in southern Ohio, confirmed the little he knew about his maternal grandparents, Paul and Louise Keppler, who had lived in Ohio and later Florida, and that his mother and father had divorced in 1983, and that the divorce had been granted in Titusville.

Raymond stared at the computer screen in fascination. This was more than he had ever known about his family. "It's amazing that you can find that much information so quickly," he said.

"Ancestry is incredible. Genealogy is one of my hobbies and it's absolutely the best resource out there," Norma told him. "I've traced my family all the way back to Scotland."

"Swirensky doesn't sound Scottish," Raymond said.

"My maiden name was McDermott."

Raymond had never realized she had been married. Norma had never mentioned a husband, and seeing the look in his eye, she laughed again. "Don't worry, he's not going to come busting in the door ready to beat you to a pulp. He's been gone a long time."

"Gone as in...?"

"Gone as in he was too lazy to work and I didn't feel like supporting him, so I kicked him to the curb years ago."

"But you kept his name."

"He was worthless, but his mother and father were two of the sweetest people you'd ever know. I was closer to them than I was to my own parents, and I loved those two right up to the day they died. I don't know, Raymond. Maybe I didn't want to hurt their feelings. I just never got around to changing my name back. It just didn't seem all that important."

"I'm sorry, I didn't mean to pry."

She shook her head. "It's okay, that was a long time ago. I haven't seen him in probably fifteen years, maybe more. He didn't even come back for his father's funeral."

Raymond looked at the computer monitor again, and shook his head. "You make this all look so easy. It's all I can do to log on to a couple of websites to check the fishing reports and the marine weather forecast. Half the time when I try to get online I screw something up and have to have Wayne come over and reboot the computer to figure out what I've done wrong."

"It's just a machine, Raymond. It does what you tell it to do."

Black Friday

"The problem is, sometimes I think I tell it to do one thing and it misunderstands me and does something entirely different," he said ruefully.

Norma took another drink, draining the glass, and said, "At least now you know something about your father. That's the starting point. You would be surprised how much you can find just doing a few simple online searches. You want me to print this information out for you?"

"If you wouldn't mind."

"No problem," she told him. She hit the print button on the computer and said, "While that's printing out I'm going to refresh my drink. Are you sure you won't have one with me?"

"Okay, just one," Raymond said. He didn't really want the drink but felt he should to be social.

The printer had finished by the time Norma returned and he took a sip of the drink, surprised at how strong the vodka was, as he read over the family history he had never known.

"Let's see what else we can dig up on your father," she said, sitting back down and clicking the mouse again. In less than an hour their research showed his father and mother living together in Pensacola from 1977 until 1982, and then two other residences listed for his father over the years, first in Tallahassee and then Gainesville. Norma also turned up three other marriages, none of which had lasted more than a year or two.

"Looks like your old man gets around," she said.

They had finished their drinks and were well into another round by then. "Well, at least my mother was right about that," Raymond said.

"What about you, Raymond? How come you didn't take after him?"

"What do you mean?"

"It's like your father was a horn dog chasing anything with a skirt. And here you are, a total Boy Scout."

He shrugged, "I don't know, I guess maybe because all the while I was growing up I kept hearing what a bastard he was, and that I was just like him. So I tried very hard not to be. And the one time I did step over the line, look what happened."

Their chairs were close together and Norma turned to him and said, "I have to ask, Raymond. Why that woman?"

"What do you mean?"

"Like I said at Dixie Crossroads the other day, you never came on to any of the women at work, and we both know there are managers who do, and women who are more than agreeable. So how come you never did anything before?"

"I don't know," he told her. "I've asked myself that more than once. I slipped, that's all I can say. I'm not proud of it and I wish I never had. My marriage was far from perfect, but up until then I'd never cheated."

"You said was, as in past tense. Is the marriage over?"

"All except for the paperwork. What can I say, Norma? It was over a long time ago. I knew that but I still hung on."

"And now?"

"And now what?"

"And now," she said leaning forward until her face was close to his. "And now you don't have any reason not to, Raymond."

The kiss started out gently but quickly became passionate. Their tongues met and Norma moaned into his mouth. He felt her hands in his hair and on the back of his head. When it ended, neither said a word. She stood up, took him by the hand, and led him to her bedroom.

Chapter 34

The room was dark and they lay side by side. Neither said anything for a long time, and then Norma got up and went into the bathroom. A moment later he heard the toilet flush and she returned. She lay down beside him and squeezed his hand.

"This was a mistake, wasn't it?"

Not for the first time that day Raymond found himself not knowing how to respond. Finally he said, "I thought you enjoyed it."

She had left the light on in the bathroom and he saw her smile. "Oh, don't get me wrong, I enjoyed it. It's been a long time."

"But?"

"But I think we both know it was a one-time thing."

Raymond remembered that the last woman who had said that to him had ended up dead, but thought better of saying it.

"Listen, Norma, it's just that...."

She sat up, comfortable in her nudity, and said, "It's okay, Raymond. I understand, I really do. It's something I've wanted for a long time, and it was good. Better than I had imagined. But right now I think you and I make a lot better friends than we do lovers."

She must have seen the relief in his face, because she laughed. "Don't worry, I don't expect any commitments from you. I know you've got too much going on in your life right now to even consider any kind of a relationship. I was curious, I needed the physical release, and I think you did too."

He couldn't deny that, and nodded.

She was still holding his hand and she kissed the back of it. "I don't want this to be weird between us, Raymond. Okay? It happened, it was good, and on a purely physical level I'd say call me anytime. But I care too much about you as a person to let sex come between us. Who knows? A year from now..."

"A year from now I might be in jail," he said.

"Don't even think that, Raymond. You *will* put all this behind you!

You've got to keep positive. And you're not alone in this. I'm here for you every step of the way. So is your friend Wayne. And like I said, you've got a lot of people at the store pulling for you."

"I wish I had all of you guys on my jury."

"Don't worry. I believe in karma, Raymond, and you've been a good guy to so many people for so long that I don't think karma is going to let you down."

"Maybe so," he replied, "but right now Karma is kicking my ass."

***

Wayne was watching a sitcom on television and turned it off when Raymond walked in, a little after 9 P.M.

"Hey guy, what's going on?"

"How was your trip?"

"Typical," Wayne told him. "Schmoozing doctors and office managers, buying them lunches and dinners, and telling them how great they are and how much they need whatever pills we're pushing this week."

"You make it sound like a grind," Raymond said.

"It is a grind sometimes. But what the hell, it pays the bills, right? What have you been up to while I was gone?"

"Well, let's see; Monday I talked to a divorce lawyer, and then I went to see the cops about getting jumped at the boat dock. That was a lot of fun. Then the next day I went to see my mother to get my weekly dose of humiliation. Oh yeah, and when I got home a man threatened to kill me. And today I had a visit with my father."

"Your father? Really? How did that go?"

"About as well as the rest of my life has been going lately. Let's just say he didn't welcome me with open arms."

"Okay, I'm gonna need a beer to hear all of this," Wayne said, getting up and going into the kitchen. "Do you want one?"

"No thanks," Raymond said, still feeling the effects of the drinks he had with Norma.

"Oh, have one," Wayne said, returning with two bottles in his hands. "My old man used to always say never trust a guy who won't drink with you."

Raymond took the bottle from him and took a sip to be polite, then set it on the coffee table. After taking a long pull from his, Wayne said,

"It sounds like you've been busy. Start at the beginning and tell me all about it."

He listened without interrupting while Raymond recounted the details of the last three days, and when he was finished, Wayne said, "Well, I'm glad Sheila is not going to be able to completely screw you in the divorce. And as for the cops, that just sucks. It's like they've made up their minds that you're guilty, so you don't deserve any kind of protection. Our tax dollars at work."

"Yeah, they didn't make any secret of the fact that they felt like I deserved whatever I got."

"As for these women coming out of the woodwork claiming you did this and did that, that's typical. Either somebody with an ax to grind like these two, or someone looking for attention like Kimberly's friends. I'm just glad that girl's father didn't take it any further."

"Me too," Raymond said. "And I have to admit I was scared, Wayne."

"Have you thought about getting a gun?"

"A gun? Mr. DeLeon said something about that, too. Like I told him, I'd probably shoot myself in the foot with it."

"With all this going on, you might want to give it some consideration. Between that dead woman's brothers and the guy yesterday, you need something to protect yourself."

"I don't know if I could ever shoot anybody," Raymond said. "Besides, I don't know if I can legally own one right now."

"I don't see why not. You haven't been convicted of anything."

"I don't think so," Raymond said, shaking his head, still unconvinced that having a firearm would be a good move for a man in his position.

"Well, you've got to do something. You can't be a punching bag for everybody that comes along."

"Maybe not, but I've just never had any interest in guns. I've never even held one. I mean, if a guy had training and was comfortable with one, that's one thing. I don't have anything against somebody else having one, it's just not me."

Wayne nodded in agreement, then said, "Still, you need some way to defend yourself. Hang on a minute."

He left the room, and Raymond heard him opening and closing a couple of drawers in the desk in his den, and when he returned he had a black object about 6 inches long in his hand. "Here, take a look at this."

"What the heck is it?" It resembled an ink pen, but was made of metal and weighed more than a regular pen.

"It's a Gerber tactical pen," Wayne told him. "You see this?" He pointed to a metal tip just above the opening at the end of the pen. "That's tempered steel. You can use it to punch out the glass on a car, or to put a real hurt on somebody who's attacking you. A lot of cops carry them. Besides being excellent pens that can even write in the rain, they're a last-ditch defense weapon. Not nearly as good as gun, but better than nothing if you're in trouble."

Raymond turned the pen around in his fingers. It was well tooled, and obviously a quality item. "Where did you get this?"

"I bought a couple dozen of them a while back," Wayne told him. "In my business it's always a good idea to give the office managers and nurses, and even the doctors, a little something now and then. They're handy because they can put them in a pocket like any other pen, but walking out to their car at night or whatever, it provides them with a little bit of extra security."

"That's pretty cool," Raymond said, handing it back to him.

Wayne was taking another drink from his beer and shook his head. When he swallowed, he said, "Keep it. Just stick it in your pocket whenever you go out. You never know when one of those assholes is going to come back again."

"Thanks," Raymond said, slipping it into his pocket.

"Now, what's this stuff about your old man and some kind of score? Either your mother has gone all the way over the edge or she's implying he's some kind of serial killer. Or, from what you've told me about her and the way she feels about him, maybe both."

"I don't know," Raymond said. "None of that makes any sense. But when I asked him about it, Royce definitely got hot under the collar."

He handed Wayne the papers that Norma had printed out for him. "Here, check these out."

"What are they?"

"I guess you could say my family tree. I didn't know anything about my father or his side of the family at all, and Norma was able to find this stuff pretty quickly on Ancestry.com."

"Interesting," Wayne said, reading through the papers. "Was she able to come up with anything else?"

"No, it was getting late so we called it a night." Wayne was probably the best friend he had ever had, but Raymond wasn't comfortable talking about what had happened between him and his former assistant manager. "I was amazed at how quickly she was able to find things. She said she'd do some more research and get back to me."

"Oh, there's a lot out there on the Internet to be found," Wayne said. "And there you were, wasting your time with fishing reports."

"I'm thinking I want to get online and see what else I can find out."

"Do you really think this can help your case, Raymond?"

"What do you mean?"

"I mean, it's interesting to know where your family came from and all that I guess, but what does this have to do with what's going on with you right now?"

"I don't know, Wayne. I'd still like to know what my mother was talking about, and why it got Royce so mad."

Wayne shook his head, then shrugged. "Who knows? I don't think there's anything to that. I mean, from what you told me, your old man was running around screwing anything that moved. But as far as some kind of score, and dead people? That doesn't make any sense. Like I said before, it makes him sound like a serial killer or something like that, which is nonsense. If he had killed somebody, wouldn't he be sitting in jail?"

"I guess you're right," Raymond agreed. "But still..."

"Look, I don't want to tell you how to live your life, but right now I think you've got a lot more to worry about than whatever this is. Once this is all behind you, then you can trace your roots all the way back to Robin Hood or whoever. But for right now, my advice to you would be to focus on the problem at hand. And besides, you could be opening a can of worms. Have you thought about that?"

"What are you talking about?"

"Just for argument's sake, let's say your father *had* killed somebody, as ludicrous as that sounds. But what if he did? If that came out, do you really think it would help your case? I can just see those TV reporters talking about the bad seed. Do you really need that extra grief, Raymond?"

He couldn't deny that Wayne was right, even though he really wanted to know what his mother had been talking about. Then again, what would it accomplish?

"Anyway," Wayne said, getting up from his chair, "I'm pretty beat. It's been a long three days on the road. I think I'm going to take a shower and hit the sack."

"Sounds like a good idea," Raymond said. "What's your schedule like the rest of this week?"

"I've got a lot of paperwork to catch up on from this trip," Wayne told him. "And a couple of conference calls tomorrow. So I'll be around here. I'll have to check my calendar, but I think I've got some appointments down in Melbourne and Vero Beach on Friday."

"Sounds like a plan. I'll see you in the morning."

Raymond sat there for a while longer, reading through the printouts Norma had given him, and his mind went back to what had happened at her place. It had been completely unexpected, and while he couldn't deny that it been pleasurable, he still felt a certain sense of guilt. Yes, he and Sheila were living apart now and their divorce was making its way through the legal process that would put an end to it. But he still *was* married. Shouldn't that count for something, even if the marriage had been no more than in name only, almost from the start? He wondered if Royce had managed to justify his own cheating in much the same way.

Chapter 35

Raymond was awakened by the sound of the doorbell ringing persistently, and then loud talking from the living room. He pulled on jeans and a T-shirt and walked down the hall, hearing Sheila's voice shouting, "Where is he, Wayne? I want to talk to him right now!"

"Calm down, Sheila. Whatever this is, I'm sure..."

Raymond had turned the corner into the living room, and seeing him, Sheila pushed past Wayne and charged, slapping Raymond on the side of his face. When he pulled backwards, she dug her fingernails into his cheek. "You no good, rotten bastard, how could you? I'll kill you!"

Raymond tried to cover up with his arms and stumbled back as Wayne grabbed the enraged woman around the waist from behind and pulled her away.

"Let go of me, Wayne! I'm going to kill him," Sheila screamed.

But Wayne held tight and said, "Stop it! Stop it right now, Sheila. Whatever this is, you're out of control and you're only makeing it worse."

"How could you, Raymond? Doesn't anything matter to you except what you want? It's bad enough that you were a terrible husband and father, that you were screwing that whore, but this? How could you do this to your own children?"

"I don't know what you're talking about," Raymond said. "Christ, Sheila, have you lost your mind?"

"What I'm talking about is our children's college fund. It's gone! How could you do that to them?"

"What?"

"Oh, don't you try to make excuses, or act like you don't know what I'm talking about. My attorney was doing an audit and found that you transferred the money from the account. What did you do with it, Raymond, spend it on that whore of yours?"

"What?"

"You heard me Raymond. Don't act so innocent. I've already called those detectives. Oh, you're going to pay, mister! You're going to pay for this!"

"Sheila, I never touched the kids' college funds."

"Right, Raymond. Just like you never cheated on me with that whore. Just like you never killed her. Just like you..."

"Okay, that's enough," Wayne said, his arms still locked around her waist. "Come on Sheila. It's time to go."

He got her out the front door with some resistance, and while Raymond couldn't hear the conversation between them, it obviously wasn't pleasant and went on for several minutes before Sheila turned and went back across the street, her back rigid.

Wayne came back inside and shook his head. "Are you okay, man?"

"Yeah," Raymond said, pulling a tissue from a box on an end table and dabbing at his cheeks. "Sorry about that, Wayne."

"That is one pissed off, crazy bitch."

"Thanks for pulling her off me. I think she would've killed me if she had her way."

"Do you have any idea what she's talking about?"

"We had an account set up for the kids to help with college," Raymond said. "Apparently the money is gone, and she thinks I took it and gave it to Holly."

"How much was it?"

"I'm not sure, to be honest with you, Wayne. Somewhere around $11,000 or $12,000."

"Was this a joint account?"

"Yeah, but it wasn't one we ever used. When my mother's parents died, they left each of the kids a couple thousand dollars and we put that into it, and then added to it over time. To be honest, I never really thought about it. In fact, when Mr. DeLeon asked me about our assets I didn't even tell him because I never thought of it as our money. It was for the kids."

"Well, that much money has to have a paper trail," Wayne told him. "It shouldn't be hard to find out where it went."

***

"$13, 673. That's a lot of money that you never told me about," DeLeon said, reproachfully.

"I didn't even remember of it," Raymond told him. "It was an account that we set up for the kids a long time ago. I didn't even know how much was in it."

"According to this," DeLeon said, looking at the bank statement on his desk, "you took it out almost three months ago."

"I never touched it. Please believe me on this, Mr. DeLeon, I wasn't trying to hold out on you or something. I just forgot about it."

"You forgot? Not to be rude, but you're not a rich man, Raymond. If you were a millionaire I could see where you might forget a few thousand laying around here and there. But you're not."

"It wasn't *my* money. It was something put away for the kids. And I have to say, I really don't appreciate your attitude right now."

"You don't appreciate *my* attitude? What's the one thing I said to you right up front, Raymond? In case you forgot, it was that I needed total honesty from you. Total honesty. Not 75% honesty or 80% honesty. Total."

Raymond felt his face growing hot, and said, "I have been honest with you. And yes, I forgot about that money. Because it wasn't my money. It wasn't Sheila's money. It wasn't *our* money. It belonged to the kids. If you don't believe me, maybe it's time I found myself a new attorney."

"That's certainly your right, sir."

"So that's it? Your dropping me as a client, just like that?"

"I'm not dropping you. It sounds like you're firing me."

"If you don't believe me, how can you defend me when this gets to court?"

"That's my point, exactly," DeLeon said. "How can I?"

They stared at each other across the attorneys desk, both men angry and both waiting for the other man to decide if their relationship was going to continue or end right there. Finally, DeLeon said, "Alright, I'm going to give you the benefit of the doubt on this one, Raymond. But I'm telling you right now, no more surprises. Got it?"

Raymond was tempted to get up and walk out of the office but he knew he needed DeLeon more than the attorney needed him, so he nodded and said tightly, "Got it."

"Okay, then."

"Now what happens?"

"I would expect we are going to be hearing from the detectives very soon now if your wife contacted them like she said she would. In the meanwhile, do you want to file an assault charge against her for what happened this morning?"

"No," Raymond said, shaking his head. "All that will do is add fuel to the fire."

"You're probably right, but you've got to draw a line somewhere, Raymond. A restraining order goes both ways and she violated it when she came to Mr. Lamb's house this morning."

"I don't want to push it. I can understand where she was coming from, and if I had been in her shoes, I might have done the same thing."

"That doesn't make it right. And as this divorce progresses, the incident today could be valuable ammunition for you."

"No," Raymond said firmly "This is bad enough as it is. I'm not going down that route."

"It's your choice," the attorney said, raising his hands in surrender.

"Yes it is, and that's my choice. I've done enough to hurt my family already, I'm not going to lock my kids' mother up, too."

"You're a nice guy in a bad situation," DeLeon said, "and while that may be noble, keep in mind what they say about nice guys and where they finish."

Seeing that Raymond was not going to change his mind on the subject, DeLeon said, "Well then, for now, just go about your business and keep yourself available. I'm sure we'll be hearing from our good friends at the police department before too long."

***

It was early afternoon and Raymond and Wayne had finished lunch when the call came. Wayne was in his home office when Raymond knocked and poked his head in the door. "That was DeLeon. I have to meet him at the police station."

"Do you want me to come along?"

"No, there's nothing you can do anyhow. I guess I'll see you when I see you."

Wayne pushed his chair back from the desk and got up. "It's going to be okay, Raymond. No matter what else, if both of your names were on that account, yours and Sheila's, then no matter if the money was earmarked for the kids or not, it's not illegal for you to take it out. I mean, I know you didn't take it, but even if you did, it's not a crime."

"Thanks, Wayne. I'd better get a move on."

Driving to the police station, Raymond's mind tried to work through

Black Friday

the maze that had become his life recently. Where had the money gone? The kids didn't have access to it, only he or Sheila could have taken it. And if it wasn't him, it had to be Sheila. But the rage she had displayed that morning at Wayne's was real. Then again, all of Sheila's rages had been real. All of his musing got him nowhere, and before he knew it, he was pulling into the parking lot of the police station. He felt the same tightness in his chest and queasiness in his stomach that he had on his visit four days earlier.

He was comforted to see DeLeon standing on the sidewalk waiting for him, and as they walked inside, the attorney said, "Just like last time Raymond. Answer their questions but don't volunteer anything. And listen to my instructions if I tell you to shut up, got it?"

"Did I ever tell you how much I'm beginning to hate the term *got it*?" Raymond asked.

"Yeah, yeah, you're beginning to sound just like my wife. Come on, let's go."

They kept them waiting for over 45 minutes, and Raymond grew restless and began to fidget in his chair in the lobby. "What's taking so long?"

"Nothing," DeLeon said. "It's all part of the game, Raymond. Hurry up and wait. They hope you'll get rattled, and then they can manipulate that to their advantage."

"Well it's working."

"Don't let them get to you," DeLeon warned. "This is just a fishing expedition to see what they can come up with."

"How can you sit there so relaxed?" Raymond asked. "Doesn't this bother you, too?"

DeLeon shook his head and chuckled, "Not at all. I've been through this many times before. Besides, it's billable hours, and you're paying for it. That ought to give you something else to think about for a while."

Before Raymond could think about that too much, a door opened and Detective Acosta said, "Mr. DeLeon, Mr. Winters? Come on back."

Chapter 36

He led them down the same hallway to the same room, making Raymond wonder how many times he'd have to take this same trip before all this was behind him. Detective Harrison and Assistant District Attorney Morrison were waiting for them. They greeted his attorney, but ignored Raymond until they had been seated.

Detective Harrison opened the meeting by looking at Raymond's face. The bruises had faded quite a bit by then, but there were three angry red welts on his cheek from Sheila's attack that morning. "It looks like you managed to get yourself into some more trouble, Mr. Winters."

Raymond didn't say anything, just stared back at the man.

"Mr. Winters, I understand that you came in on Monday to file a police report about an incident that happened on Friday," Morrison said. "I apologize for the way that was handled. And when we're done here, I'll be happy to personally see that a report is taken, if you wish."

"Don't bother," Raymond told her. "It's over and done with."

"Sir, you do have the same rights as any other citizen in this county. And that includes the right to equal protection under the law."

"It's over," Raymond repeated.

"As you wish."

With that behind them, Harrison opened a folder and said, "We received a phone call from your wife today, Mr. Winters."

"That's what I hear."

"According to her, and according to bank records, you removed several thousand dollars from an account that was set aside for your children's education. Is that correct?"

Before Raymond could say anything, DeLeon spoke, "Mr. Winters has told me that he did not touch those funds, and that he does not know what happened to them."

"Mr. Winters says a lot of things," Harrison replied. "I'm just curious, Mr. Winters. Could this be another one of those cases where you forgot that you took the money? Kind of like you forgot that you knew Holly Coulter? Or when you told us you didn't leave your house at all after you were with her in that motel room, because you forgot you spent some time visiting with your neighbor across the street?"

"Detective, stop it. My client says he didn't have anything to do with that money going missing. But even if he did, technically it was community property in that both he and his wife were signers on the account. That would make it a civil matter between them that can be hashed out during their divorce. So what's the point of all this?"

"The point," Morrison said, "is that we've been looking at some more of the e-mails and text messages exchanged between Mr. Winters and Ms. Coulter. And guess what we found?"

"I'm not going to play guessing games with you, Ms. Morrison," DeLeon said. "If you've got something to tell us, stop beating around the bush and get to it."

"Very well then," she said placing two pages of transcripts in front of them. "Mr. Winters, what do you have to say about this?"

We have to talk – Ray
Im kinda busy right now - Holly
It's important – Ray
Okay, whats up – Holly
It's about that money – Ray
What about it? – Holly
You said it was a loan. I need to get it back into the account before S finds out – Ray
I know, I'm workin on it. Just need a little more time – Holly
How much more time? – Ray
Geez you act like I'm stealing from you or something – Holly
No I just need to get this taken care of – Ray
It's not like you ain't rich or something. – Holly
I'm not rich or anywhere close to it – Ray
Compared to me you are. We get together and do our thing and you go back to your fancy house and I'm still right here – Holly
Don't go there. We've had this conversation before – Ray
And that's all we ever do is talk about it – Holly
These things take time – Ray
How much time? – Holly

Where are you? – Ray
Are you coming? – Ray

Holly? – Ray
Sorry got hung up – Holly
Are you still coming? – Ray
Sorry can't make it. Maybe tomorrow – Holly
You promised – Ray
I'll make it up to you – Holly
Do you have any of the money for me? – Ray
No not yet. I'm workin on it - Holly
Damn it, you promised!!! – Ray
It's not like you didn't get somethin in return - Holly
Not fair! – Ray
Not fair is you go home to your wife and I'm all alone – Holly
I need to see you. We need to talk about this – Ray
That's all we do is talk about it – Holly
Okay, okay what time tomorrow? – Ray
Holly? – Ray
Holly? – Ray

"Mr. Winters?"

"I don't know what to tell you. I never texted that woman before and I never sent these texts"

"How long are we going to play this game?" Harrison asked. "Doesn't any of this bother you at all, Mr. Winters? I mean really, how do you sleep at night?"

"That's enough," DeLeon warned.

"No, seriously. How do you do it? You cheat on your wife, you steal from your kids, you kill this woman. Are you that cold? Doesn't it get to you at all, Mr. Winters?"

"Enough!" DeLeon said. "My client has already told you he never exchanged e-mails with the victim in your case, and that he didn't kill her, so where are we going with this? Or is this just more harassment on your part, Detective?"

"Do you really expect us to believe anything he says at this point?"

Before DeLeon could reply, Morrison said, "Listen, this isn't getting us anywhere. What if we see if we can't work something out and put all of this behind us?"

"What are you talking about?" DeLeon asked.

"Your client makes a full confession, leaving nothing out, and I'll accept a plea to second-degree homicide. He was under a lot of pressure, he had given the victim a lot of money that she never repaid him, the affair was coming to an end, and he cracked under the pressure. It happens. That takes Murder One off the table and spares him the death penalty. Who knows? 20, 25 years and he might be out, with good behavior."

DeLeon laughed but there was no humor in it. "You must be joking. My client is innocent. He has stated that over and over, and you don't have any evidence to the contrary."

"Evidence? Evidence like proof that he was in the room with Ms. Coulter when she was killed? Evidence that they had sex in that room? We have his DNA, we have the records of him checking into the room."

"And you have nothing that shows he killed her. All your proof does is show that they had a one-time thing, which he has already acknowledged. Extramarital sex does not make one a murderer, Ms. Morrison."

"That would be great, if it was a one-time thing, as you say. But these texts? The statement from the victim's sister when they were on Mr. Winter's street that her boyfriend lived there? Not exactly a one-time thing, Counselor. It sounds more like an affair to me. An affair that turned bad and left Ms. Coulter dead."

"And where did this affair take place? Because there's not another hotel or motel within 50 miles that shows his or her name on a registration card," DeLeon said. "And her neighbors say they never saw a man at her apartment."

"Maybe he used a fake name wherever they were getting together."

"So you're saying he used a fake name all the while they were meeting for this alleged affair, but the day he supposedly killed her he used his real name? Who uses their real name when checking into a motel with a woman and then kills her? Does my client look that stupid to you?"

"Oh, I'm not questioning your client's intelligence, Mr. DeLeon," she said. "I know he's an intelligent man. But I don't think he's as smart as he gives himself credit for. Mister Winters, we do this for living, and you're way out of your league. You are in over your head, sir. And you just keep sinking deeper and deeper. Think about my offer, because it's not going to be on the table very long."

"Are we done here, or do you plan on trying to intimidate my client some more?"

"No, we're done here, Mr. DeLeon. Mr. Winters, you have my card. Think long and hard about your future, sir."

Black Friday

Detective Acosta, who had not said anything during the entire meeting, led them back down the hall to the lobby. "You gentlemen have a nice day," he said, and turned and went back the way they had come.

Raymond took a deep breath as soon as they were back out in the parking lot.

"Now what?"

"Now you buy me a cup of coffee."

***

"We have to figure out where these e-mails came from," DeLeon said, after they were seated in a coffee shop near the police station. "Whoever is behind this is working very hard to give them a solid case against you. I keep coming back to your wife, Raymond. It just makes sense. She's in the house where your computer is, she had access to the bank account. It's real obvious there was no love lost between the two of you. Who else could it be?"

"I don't know," Raymond replied. "I just can't see Sheila doing all of this. Why would she? I mean, I could see her killing me in a fit of rage. At least then she'd get some life insurance out of it. But this? What's in it for her?"

"Who else hates you that much?"

"Nobody that I know of. I'm not the kind of guy that makes enough of an impact on people's lives that they would hate him."

"What about that woman?" DeLeon asked.

"What woman? Holly?"

"No, what was her name, the one from the store who claimed you had sexually harassed her? Nancy somebody?"

"Nancy Chambers."

"Is this something she could pull off?"

"I don't see how," Raymond said. "How could she have access to my computer?"

"Did you take your laptop to work with you?"

"Once in a while, but not often. And the times they show me sending these texts and e-mails I was at home. So how could she do that? Besides, I don't think she's smart enough to come up with something like this. Then again, to be honest, I don't think Sheila is either."

"What about your kids?"

"How can that be possible? And why would they?"

"Hell, Raymond, these days kids in grade school know more about computers than you and I ever will. And as for a motive, you said you don't get along that well with either one of them. In fact, it sounds like you and your daughter have butted heads more than once. Could one of them have figured out some way to get the money out of that account and then set you up to cover it up?"

"Come on, one of my kids didn't kill that woman."

DeLeon sipped his coffee and nodded. "I guess you're right, and I guess that there's no way your wife could have followed you and then figured out some way to get in that room and kill the victim either. But even that doesn't make sense. No, somebody spent a lot of time setting this whole thing up. And the thing is, we don't know if you were the target or if Holly Coulter was."

"What do you mean?"

"Well, you said her husband told you she slept around a lot, and it seems like she wasn't above taking advantage of a guy whenever she could. She lived a high risk lifestyle. Could this whole thing be a jilted lover getting even with her?"

"That doesn't make sense either," Raymond said. "Let's say that's what happened. How did this lover of hers arrange to be right there when she and I went to that motel? Was he stalking her, just waiting for the right time? And what about the rest of it? What about her pointing my house out to her sister? What about her telling her ex-husband about this big deal she was working on? I keep going over it in my head and none of it makes sense."

"Well, there is *some* good news," DeLeon told him.

"Well whatever it is, don't hold out on me because I need all the good news I can get right now," Raymond said.

"Janet Morrison offering a deal tells us that their case isn't as strong as she would like us to believe. Because if it was open and shut, she'd be going for Murder One. The fact that she's willing to bargain tells me that she isn't convinced she has a guilty conviction locked up."

"But she still wants to put me away for a long time," Raymond said.

"That's true, but I meant what I said in there, Raymond. All they can prove is that you were in that room and that you had sex with Holly Coulter. There is no proof that you killed her. Absolutely none. And a jury has to find you guilty beyond a reasonable shadow of doubt. That's why she's willing to cut a deal."

Black Friday

Raymond took some comfort from the attorney's words, but even more so when DeLeon continued. "And I owe you an apology, Raymond. That money coming up missing and you saying you forgot about it, that was a curveball that I wasn't expecting. But you're my client and I do believe in you. And like I told you when we first started down this road, I'm with you all the way, got it?"

"Yeah, I got it," Raymond said. "But I still hate those two words."

"No problem. You hang in there, because there are two words you are going to hear eventually that you're really going to love."

"And what are they?"

"Not guilty."

Chapter 37

Raymond stopped at a Staples office supply store on the way home and purchased a Toshiba Satellite laptop computer. Back at Wayne's house, his friend looked at the box and asked, "Did you buy yourself a new toy?"

"Yeah, I thought I'd try to learn a little bit more about my old man."

Wayne frowned. "I'm all for technology, but like I said last night, you should probably be focusing on your case right now. I know your attorney has that investigator of his poking around, but I keep wondering if there's something we can't be doing, too."

"Like what, Wayne? What could we find out that a professional investigator hasn't?"

"I don't know. But after all, you were the one who found out about this Holly woman telling her ex she had some big deal working. Granted, it cost you an ass whipping, but still."

Raymond couldn't help but laugh.

"Look, buddy, I'm just saying it's *your* life on the line, and nobody, no lawyer, no private eye, and damn sure no cop, has as much to gain as you do by figuring out what that woman was up to and how it went wrong and she got herself killed."

"I know, I just..."

"Hey, whatever works for you. If nothing else, you can keep up with where the tarpon are biting. Anyway, you're still walking around free so I guess the cops didn't have anything all that important to talk about today."

"Oh, they had lots to talk about," Raymond said, then told him about the interview, and about DeLeon's opinion that the offer of a plea bargain showed that the district attorney's case against him was shaky.

"Interesting, I guess. And I guess there are some guys who'd take the deal."

"Why would I do that?" Raymond asked. "I'm innocent."

"I know that, I'm just saying that facing the death penalty, some people would take any kind of deal they could get. I guess they'd figure 25 years in prison is better than getting a needle stuck in your arm."

"If it came to that, I would just want them to stick it in my arm and get it over with quick," Raymond said. "I can tell you right now, Wayne, I couldn't handle being locked up. I won't do that. If it comes to that, I'll hang myself in my cell or something."

"Hey, enough of that kind of talk," Wayne said. "We're not even going to think along those lines. How about I throw some burgers on the grill and we have a beer while they cook?"

"That sounds good," Raymond told him. But as Wayne went through the kitchen and out the back door to the patio, Raymond realized that what he had told his friend were not empty words. He could not live in prison, and if it came to that, he would find some way to end his life. Maybe he should rethink Wayne's suggestion about getting a gun.

They stood on Wayne's back patio sipping beer and listening to the burgers hissing as they cooked. Wayne used a spatula to flip them over, sending up a brief flame as the grease hit the fire below. He set the spatula on the platform on the side of the grill, then looked at his friend with concern in his eyes.

"Tell me you're not seriously thinking about doing something stupid."

"What do you mean?"

"You know what I mean, Raymond. I know things suck right now, but tell me you're not going to do anything to hurt yourself."

Raymond couldn't meet his eyes when he responded, "Okay, I'm not thinking about anything like that."

"Hey, I'm serious," Wayne said. "Dammit, Raymond, don't be thinking that way!"

"I'm not."

"Then look me in the eyes and promise me that."

"Yeah, okay."

"Don't bullshit me," Wayne said forcefully.

"I'm not!"

"Then why are you avoiding looking at me?"

"Give me a break, Wayne, I just..."

"You just feel like life is so screwed up that ii's not worth living right now. I understand that, buddy, I do. But no matter how bad it gets, doing something to hurt yourself is not the answer."

"I know, but until you've been where I am, it's hard to understand how helpless..."

And then Raymond was crying. He hated himself for it, hated giving in to his weakness and hated his friend seeing it in him, but he couldn't stop himself. Deep sobs shook his body and he began to tremble, which only made it worse. Wayne set his beer down and wrapped his arms around Raymond and held him while he cried.

"I'm sorry, I..."

"It's okay," Wayne told him. "It's okay man, let it go. Just let it go."

Raymond had spent his entire life holding his emotions in check. It was something he had learned early on when some childhood tragedy from the past which he could not even remember had happened and he had run crying to his mother for comfort. "Oh, stop being such a baby," she had scolded him as she pushed the boy away. "The world isn't always all sweetness and light, and the quicker you learn that, the better!" It had not taken him more than two or three experiences like that to learn that sympathy was no more than a word in his family. It had been the same with any accomplishments he had made growing up; he remembered coming home excited with the news that he had made the seventh grade honor roll, and his mother's reaction to it; "Big deal, you went to school and learned your lessons. Isn't that the reason you're there, Raymond?"

And, of course, it had been the same with Sheila. News of every promotion he had received at work, every award for productivity, had been met with the same sneer from his wife, who only wanted to know if it came with a pay raise, or how much time it was going to take away from his chores at home.

As a result, he had learned to celebrate his victories and suffer his defeats in silence. Anything else was only going to bring ridicule. But now he could not help himself as he let the pain pour out of him and shared it with his friend. At any other time he would have been embarrassed, even horrified, at this display of weakness. But he had reached a breaking point and now it didn't matter.

For his part, Wayne just held him close, patted his back, and absorbed all that Raymond was letting go of. Finally, and it could have been a minute, or five, or thirty for all he knew, Raymond ran out of tears and his body stopped shaking. He took several deep, ragged breaths and was finally able to compose himself. Feeling the difference in his body, Wayne released him and Raymond stepped back.

"I'm sorry. These days every time I turn around I'm crying like a little baby."

"Nothing to be sorry for," Wayne assured him. "It's okay."

Raymond suddenly felt very weak and sank into a chair on the deck. Wayne turned the fire off under the burgers, which had begun to burn on one side, and sat across from him.

"I don't know what came over me," Raymond said, trying to explain his breakdown.

"Hey, it's been building for a while, and the dam just burst," Wayne said. "Perfectly understandable, and it's okay. I'm your friend Raymond, and that's what friends are for."

"I owe you so much, Wayne. You've been here for me through all of this, giving me a place to stay, bailing me out of jail. There's no way I can ever repay you."

"That's the thing about real friends," Wayne told him. "They don't keep score, because they don't care. All they care about is being there for you when you need them."

"I hope you know I'd do the same for you," Raymond said. "Seriously, anything you ever need, anything I can ever do..."

"What you can do," Wayne said, interrupting him, "is to do what I asked you a little while ago. Look me in the eyes and tell me honestly that you're not going to do anything to hurt yourself."

This time Raymond was able to meet his eyes when he said, "I promise you, I'm not going to do anything stupid and I will not do anything to hurt myself."

Wayne smiled and asked, "No matter how bad it gets?"

"No matter how bad it gets."

"Okay then, let's eat," Wayne said standing up. "I don't know about you, but it's been so long since I've eaten that my stomach thinks my throat's been cut."

Raymond felt so drained that it was hard to stand up, but he smiled back at his friend and did, then followed him inside to eat.

***

After they finished their meal, Wayne said, "Let's fire up this new computer of yours and see what it's made of."

Raymond took the Toshiba out of its box, plugged in the power cord, and Wayne talked him through the simple set up procedure.

"Let's see," Wayne said, "twelve gig of RAM, one terabyte hard

Black Friday 221

drive, Intel processor. Looks pretty good, buddy. You want me to install the anti-spyware and malware programs I did on your other computers?"

"I'd appreciate it, if you have the time," Raymond said. "I know you're busy with reports and all."

"No problem," Wayne said, "I'm pretty much caught up. Give me an hour or so with this thing and I'll have you up to speed."

Raymond busied himself washing the dishes from dinner and in less time than predicted, Wayne called out, "All done."

"I installed AVG antivirus software, Malwarebytes, and Super AntiSpyware. That should keep you from getting a lot of cookies and other stuff that slows down your computer and also protect you when you go to those nasty porn sites. And I deleted some of the junk that all computer manufacturers stick on their new machines that you're not going to use anyway. It just takes up space, though you've got plenty of room on this hard drive, anyhow. Here, take it for a test drive."

"How do I get online?"

"That's easy," Wayne said, "click on the blue icon there in the bottom bar and it will take you right to the Internet. Oh, I've got you set up on my Wi-Fi network here, but write down your password in case it kicks you off for some reason and you need to get on sometime and I'm not here."

Raymond picked up a pen and notepad sitting on the table next to the computer and said, "Okay, what is it?"

"All caps," Wayne said, "the letters I and D and then the number 10 and then T and then a space and your name, all in caps."

Raymond wrote it down, and it took him a minute to realize what he was looking at, ID10T RAYMOND.

When he looked up, Wayne was smirking at him.

"Thanks a lot, buddy!"

"That's computer geek humor for you," Wayne said. "Have fun with your new toy, I've got a couple of phone calls to make before it gets too late."

Raymond first checked his e-mail. Aside from two messages about updates to one of the fishing websites he followed, and a dozen or so assorted spam messages telling him about male enhancement products, hot college coeds who are looking for a man just like him, offers to consolidate his credit cards, and one from a nice man who had been the bookkeeper for a deposed Nigerian dictator who wanted to deposit $26 million into Raymond's bank account, the only other message was from Doug Kuykendall, who had been his roommate his senior year at college.

Doug's family operated a small chain of grocery stores in North and South Carolina, and he had tried to hire Raymond away from Palmetto pantry several times over the years. The pay and benefits package had been attractive, but he enjoyed his job and knew that Sheila would never leave her mother and sister, no matter how good a move might've been for his career. He opened the e-mail and read it.

Raymond, I know you've got a lot on your plate right now, but I know it's all a big mistake and that you didn't do anything wrong. When this blows over, give me a call. I've got a place for you in our organization. We need three managers, so you can take your pick of stores. I need you here, buddy. Keep the faith!

Doug

In the past, Raymond would have sent back a quick reply thanking Doug for the offer but repeating that he was happy where he was and didn't foresee any changes. But now there was no reason not to think beyond Palmetto Pantry, beyond Titusville, and even beyond Florida. Though he had lived there most of his life, he couldn't see himself remaining, once this was all over. He had meant what he had told Wayne that he would always be *that* guy.

Then again, would this really be over someday? And when it was, would he have the freedom to make any choices for himself, or would his future be life in a prison cell until they strapped him to a gurney sometime in the distant future and wheeled him into the execution chamber. No, that was one choice he still reserved for himself. Because he knew that he had lied to Wayne. If he were found guilty of Holly's murder, he would find a way to end things on his own terms.

He logged onto the Ancestry.com website, used his credit card to open an account, and spent the rest of the evening learning how to navigate his way around. He was surprised to find how easy it was to do basic research. He was able to find both his maternal and paternal grandfathers' World War II draft cards, all four of his grandparents listed under the Social Security Death Index, and even a link to the Find A Grave website where he found the Ohio cemetery where his father's parents were buried, including pictures of their headstones.

He didn't realize several hours had slipped past, but when he took a break to use the bathroom, he noticed Wayne's bedroom door was closed, and it was after midnight. He was fascinated with the information he was finding, though he did wonder if Wayne hadn't been correct, and that while it was an interesting diversion, he should be spending his time finding some way out of his legal predicament, though he wasn't sure how he could go about that. He reluctantly shut off the computer and went to bed.

Chapter 38

The sound of Wayne knocking on his bedroom door woke Raymond the next morning.

"You awake?"

"I am now," Raymond said, sitting up.

"Get some clothes on, there's something you need to see."

Raymond dressed quickly and went into the living room, where Wayne stood with a grim expression on his face.

"What's up?"

"Come out here," Wayne said, leading the way out the front door.

Raymond felt his stomach lurch when he saw his pickup truck. All four tires had been slashed and someone had spray painted KILLER in red letters on both sides of the truck.

"Damn it," Raymond said, looking at the damage that had been done to the truck.

"That's not all they did," Wayne told him. "Look at the house."

If Raymond had felt anger at what had been done to his truck, it was nothing compared to the emotions that went through him when he turned and looked at the front of the house. The same graffiti artist had also written KILLER and MURDERER in red paint across the front. The paint had dripped like blood down the white surface of the building.

"Oh man. Oh shit, Wayne, I am so sorry!"

His friend's jaw was set in a hard line and he didn't reply.

"This is getting out of hand," Raymond said. "It's time for me to check into a hotel or something. You don't need this crap, Wayne."

"Stop it, Raymond. This isn't your fault. I'm just pissed."

"No, it is my fault," Raymond said. "They wouldn't have done this to your house if I wasn't staying here."

Wayne brushed off his comment with a wave of his hand. Raymond turned to look around the deserted street and noticed that the door to his former home was open and his daughter was standing there looking at him. Except for a quick glance as they came and went, Raymond had not seen either of his children since Sheila had thrown him out of the house. Their eyes met for a brief moment and then Kimberly extended her middle finger at him and closed the door.

***

"Probably kids," said the uniformed officer who took the police report on the vandalism. He was a young man with a face full of freckles, red hair, and a name tag that identified him as patrolman O'Rourke.

"Yeah, I didn't really think it was a CIA operation," Wayne said.

His sarcasm was lost on the policeman, who said, "There's not really much we can do, I'm afraid. I'll ask the neighbors if they saw or heard anything, and drive around the neighborhood, but to be honest with you..."

"I get it," Wayne said.

"You might want to consider putting up a couple of security cameras and some motion detector lights," O'Rourke suggested. "That way, if they come back, it might scare them off. Or at least you might get video of them in the act."

When the policeman left, Raymond didn't know what to say. He felt guilty for the fact that his situation had spilled over onto his friend, but Wayne seemed to take it in stride, brushing his comment off when Raymond again suggested that it might be best if he found someplace else to stay.

"Forget it, this is America, and I'm not letting some punk kids tell me who can stay in my house and who can't. I'll call Bobby Guerra and have him slap some paint on the front of the place, and we'll call a tow truck to come and take your pickup to the tire shop."

"That takes care of today," Raymond said, "but what about tomorrow? What happens if they come back and do it all over again?"

"Let them try," Wayne said with a hard edge to his voice. He walked down the hall to his office and returned a moment later with a zippered canvas pouch. He opened it and held up a large black handgun.

"Whoa, where did you get that thing?"

"I've had it a long time. I carry a lot of drug samples when I'm on the road and there's more than one druggie who would love to get their hands on them, and wouldn't mind hurting me in the process."

He held it out to Raymond, who shook his head. "No thanks, like I said before, with my luck I'd shoot myself in the foot. Or worse!"

"Suit yourself," Wayne said, "but it doesn't hurt to know how to use one, just in case."

"What is that thing, anyway?"

"It's a 9mm Browning Hi Power."

"Where did you get it?"

"It's an old family heirloom," Wayne told him. "Belonged to my dad before he died. This design has been around forever, and there have been a lot of knockoffs made. But this is one of the original ones made in Belgium back in the late '60s or so, I think. It holds thirteen rounds in the magazine and one in the chamber. It was the standard military and police sidearm in a lot of countries around the world for many years."

"I guess I never saw you as a gun toting kind of a guy," Raymond said.

Wayne laughed and said, "There's a lot about me you don't know, old buddy. It's no big deal, I have a concealed carry permit. I've never had to use it, thank God, but if I had to, I would."

"I just don't think I could ever shoot anybody."

"You might be surprised what you're capable of, when it gets right down to the wire," Wayne told him.

"Well let's hope it never gets that far," Raymond replied. "But seriously, Wayne, you can't just shoot some kid for showing up with a can of spray paint. Much as he might deserve it."

"I know that," Wayne said, "but how do we know this really was kids? I mean, you had those two guys jump you at the boat dock, and then that girl's father accosted you right here in the yard. Maybe it was somebody like that."

"I hope not. I just keep wondering how long this is going to go, on and how much worse it can get."

Raymond had no way of knowing that it *was* going to get worse. A lot worse. And it wouldn't take long for it to happen.

***

Bobby Guerra was a short, wiry Cuban with a reputation in the community for hard work and honesty that had made him the handyman to call whenever anything needed repaired. Be it a leaking roof, broken water line, or balky air conditioner, if Bobby couldn't fix it, he would figure out how to, or else bring in one of his many cousins, whose combined knowledge seemed to cover anything and everything that a homeowner could ever need.

He surveyed the damage done to the front of the house, shook his head, and said, "Don't you worry, Mr. Wayne, I call my two sons over here. You give us an hour, maybe two, we have that covered up."

"I appreciate that," Wayne told him.

Bobby was on his cell phone telling his sons what equipment to bring with them when the sound of speeding cars drew all three men's attention to the street. Two police cruisers screeched to a stop at the curb and four officers jumped out, guns drawn. All three men in the yard instinctively raise their arms over their heads.

"Raymond Winters, down your knees right now, and keep your hands where we can see them!"

In some form of terrifying déjà vu, Raymond found himself face down as his hands were handcuffed behind him and he was pulled roughly to his feet, patted down, and pushed into the back of a police car. He wanted to ask what was happening, but he had enough experience with the police in the last few weeks to know better than to say anything until DeLeon was there. The last thing he saw as the police car made a U-turn in the middle of the street and left the neighborhood was his daughter Kimberly, again standing in the doorway of her house.

***

They kept him in a small holding cell by himself for over two hours before a uniformed guard came for him. The scene in the interview room was the same as it had been the last time, and the time before that, with the two detectives and the assistant district attorney on one side of the table and DeLeon on the other. At a nod from Harrison, the guard removed Raymond's handcuffs and he sat down next to his attorney.

"Mr. Winters, before we do anything else, I want to read you your rights," Harrison said, and then recited the same Miranda warning that Raymond had heard before. When he had finished and Raymond acknowledged that he understood his rights, the detective said, "You've been busy, haven't you, Mr. Winters?"

Raymond wondered how they had learned of his trip to The Villages and could only guess that his father had called to complain about the visit. But he remembered DeLeon's previous instructions and didn't say anything.

When he didn't respond, Harrison said, "Do you really think you could do it again and get away with it?"

"I have no idea what you're talking about," Raymond told him.

"I'm talking about Norma Swirensky."

"Norma? What about her?" Raymond felt a sense of dread even before the detective spoke again.

"She's dead, that's what about her."

Black Friday

Chapter 39

Raymond's throat constricted, he felt hot pinpricks of red behind his eyes, and had a sensation of falling that caused him to press both hands hard against the tabletop. His stomach churned and he had to swallow hard to keep from vomiting. The detectives and Morrison watched him with no expression on their faces. When he could finally get his breath, he shakily asked, "What happened to her?"

"Why don't you tell us?," Harrison said.

"I don't know. When? How?"

"When she didn't show up for work yesterday morning, the store manager called her house and nobody answered. He tried again an hour or so later and still didn't get an answer. Apparently Ms. Swirensky was quite punctual, so he became concerned. He gave it another hour and when she still hadn't come in or answered the telephone, he drove to her house. Her car was in the driveway but she didn't answer the door, so he called the police to do a welfare check. When an officer got there, the door was unlocked and he went in and found her in her bed. She had been beaten and strangled. Does any of this sound familiar to you, Mr. Winters?"

"It's unfortunate that this woman is dead," DeLeon interrupted, "but what does that have to do with my client?"

"The victim worked with Mr. Winters here. In fact, she was his assistant manager at Palmetto Pantry. Isn't that right, Mr. Winters?"

"You already know that."

"And did you have a personal relationship with Ms. Swirensky?"

"Not while we were working together."

"What does that mean, sir?"

"After I got fired we met for lunch a couple of times and…"

"And what, sir?"

"And the other night I was at her house."

"What day would that have been, Mr. Winters?"

"Thursday."

"Thursday. The same night she was murdered. Would you care to tell us what happened while you were there?"

Raymond glanced at DeLeon, who nodded his head.

"We had a couple of drinks and she showed me how to look up some stuff on the computer."

"What kind of stuff?"

"Genealogy. Family tree stuff."

"And that's all that happened?"

"No.... we had sex."

"My, you do get around, don't you, sir?"

When Raymond didn't answer, the detective said, "Tell me about the sex."

"It was just sex."

"Just sex? Nothing kinky? Maybe rough sex?"

Raymond felt dead inside as he shook his head. "No, just sex."

"And what happened after you had sex?"

"We both decided that it probably wasn't a good idea, given my situation."

"Was this the first time you and Ms. Swirensky had sex?"

"Yes."

"And then what?"

"I got dressed and went home."

"When you say home, do you mean Mr. Lamb's house, where you are staying?"

"That's right."

"And she was alive when you left?"

"Yes."

"So let me get this straight, Mr. Winters. You and the victim worked together for what, five, ten years and there was no hanky-panky between the two of you. But then, after you're charged with murdering one woman, and after you're fired from your job, you two suddenly start having an affair? Is that what you're telling me?"

"It wasn't an affair," Raymond said. "It was just something that happened."

"It just happened? How does this just keep happening to you?" Detective Acosta asked. "It seems like every time you turn around, you find yourself in bed with some other woman. And then she winds up dead. How do you explain that?"

"Detective, stop baiting my client," DeLeon said.

"I'm not baiting him," Acosta replied, "I just don't understand how this keeps happening to him. You're telling me that you and the victim never had anything going on between you, and then all of a sudden you find this mutual attraction that you can't resist, and now she's dead. I'm sorry, but that just defies logic to me. Are you sure nothing had been going on between you two for a while, Mr. Winters?"

"No," Raymond said, "It wasn't like this mutual attraction thing you're talking about. I didn't go there expecting to end up in bed with Norma. In fact, she's the one that came on to me."

The minute the words had been spoken Raymond regretted them. Both detectives laughed derisively, and when DeLeon shot them a stern look, Harrison said, "I'm sorry, but this guy lives in some kind of fantasy world, Mr. DeLeon. Who else do you know who keeps having women come on to him out of the blue, and then they end up dead?"

"Enough," DeLeon said. "Janet, if you can't make these detectives act like professionals instead of schoolboys, this conversation is over right now."

The look she sent him made it obvious that Morrison did not appreciate the attorney using her first name during an interview, but she did say, "Let's get back on track, gentleman."

Harrison didn't seem the least bit repentant, but he did sit back in his chair for a moment, staring at Raymond.

"What time did you get to Ms. Swirensky's house Thursday afternoon?"

"A little after four."

"How much is a little? 4:10, 4:15?"

"I didn't look at the clock," Raymond said. Maybe 4:15, give or take a couple of minutes."

"And how long were you there?"

"I left a little before nine."

"Why did you leave?"

"What do you mean?"

"You said that you and Ms. Swirensky did something on the computer, then you had sex. I'm curious, Mr. Winters, why didn't you spend the night?"

"I don't know. I guess it just didn't seem appropriate."

"What do you mean by that, sir?"

"We just... I don't think either one of us wanted that."

"Why would that be? Was there a problem, maybe something that happened while you were in bed that spoiled the mood?"

"No, I think we both realized that it was a one-time thing."

"A one-time thing? Isn't that what Holly Coulter told you, too? Right before she was killed?"

"Enough, Detective," DeLeon warned. "Are we here to talk about the Coulter case or what happened to Ms. Swirensky?"

"You have to admit, the coincidences are pretty strong," Morrison said.

"We're right back where we were with the first case," DeLeon said. "My client admits he was with the victim, he admits they had sex, but that doesn't mean he killed her."

"So this is all just some crazy coincidence? Is that what you're saying, Mr. Winters?"

"I don't know what to tell you," Raymond said. "I didn't kill Holly Coulter, and I didn't kill Norma Swirensky."

"So lightning struck twice in the same place, and missed you both times? That's amazing," Harrison said.

"Ms. Morrison, do you intend to charge my client with something today? Because if you don't, we're out of here."

"Don't you find it rather unbelievable that this could happen twice and he's *not* involved?"

"There's no question that he is involved," DeLeon told the assistant district attorney. "But being involved doesn't make him guilty of anything."

"So what, this is some big conspiracy directed at your client? Are you telling me that somebody is running around killing women who suddenly find themselves attracted to Mr. Winters here and go to bed with him?"

"I'm telling you that if you don't intend to charge my client, we're done here. So what's it going to be, Ms. Morrison? Put up or shut up."

Morrison glowered at the attorney, and then looked at the two detectives for a moment. When she turned back to Raymond and DeLeon, her jaw was set. "Oh, I do plan to charge Mr. Winters with the murder of Norma Swirensky. Maybe not today, but rest assured, I'm going to charge him. And that deal that I offered you the other day? Forget it. It's no longer under consideration. I intend to prosecute Mr. Winters for two counts of first degree homicide, I intend to get a guilty conviction, and I intend to be sitting in the front row when theyexecute him. No matter how long it takes."

Black Friday

***

The drive back to Wayne's house was quiet. It wasn't until they pulled into the driveway that DeLeon said, "I don't know what's going on, Raymond. When this all started out, I really thought it was about Holly Coulter somehow or another. But this... this just doesn't make sense."

"I wish I had an answer for you," Raymond said. "I know it sounds crazy. Why would someone be doing all this to get at me? I just don't know what to think anymore. I keep going over it and over it, and none of it makes sense."

"Well, those women didn't kill themselves. Somebody did it, and we need to figure out who, and why, pretty quick. Because there is no question in my mind that Janet Morrison is going to charge you with this one, too. And I'm not sure the judge will leave you out on the street much longer. She's got her own professional reputation to take into consideration."

"So what do I do?"

"Just keep doing what you're doing," DeLeon told him. "Obey the terms of your release, keep your mouth shut, and for God's sake, Raymond, don't go to bed with anybody else until this is over."

***

His truck was gone from the driveway, but Wayne's car was there. He looked at his friend with concern when Raymond came in the door.

"Are you okay? A cop showed up here asking me what time you got home last night, and if you went anywhere after that, but he wouldn't tell me what was going on. I called DeLeon's office but his receptionist didn't know anything except that he was at the police station, and the police wouldn't tell me anything. What happened, Raymond?"

"It's Norma. She's dead, Wayne. Somebody killed her."

"Oh no! Shit, man. Here, sit down. Do you need something to drink? Water? Beer?"

Raymond sank into a chair, put his head back, and closed his eyes. "No. No, I'm okay."

"The hell you are. How could you be?"

"I'm just numb. What the hell is happening, Wayne? And why Norma? How did she get dragged into all of this?"

"I don't know, buddy. I wish I did."

"I keep asking myself, over and over again, what I ever did to anybody that would make them want to do all of this, and I just can't come up with anyone. I go to bed every night thinking it was all just a bad dream, and every morning when I wake up, the nightmare seems to get worse."

"There has to be something," Wayne said. "Was there ever a lawsuit you were involved in that somebody felt they got screwed over or something? Maybe a real estate deal?"

"No, never. I've never been in any kind of lawsuit in my life."

"Think real hard, Raymond. Somebody you fired?"

"No. Actually, manager's can't fire anybody at Palmetto Pantry. That comes from corporate, and Stan Kirtridge handles it."

"But could somebody have gotten fired and blamed you?"

Raymond shrugged. "I guess, but it's been so long since anybody left, fired or just quit, that I can't remember."

"Okay, I'm just throwing ideas out here to see if anything jogs your memory. If it wasn't an employee or a former employee, could it be somebody's husband?"

"What do you mean, Wayne? I never messed around with my employees. Not once."

"No, that's not what I mean. I know that. But could some employee's husband think there was something going on between you? Or maybe somebody that worked for you got divorced and her husband blames you for some reason?"

"I don't know," Raymond said dully. "Not that I know of."

"What about this Nancy Chambers, the one who went on TV and all that? Could it be her husband or boyfriend or whatever? I know nothing ever happened, but could she have been telling him something was going on?"

There was a throbbing behind Raymond's eyes that made it hard for him to concentrate, and all he could do was shake his head and say, "I just don't know."

Realizing that his friend was emotionally and physically exhausted, Wayne let it drop and said, "Why don't you get some rest? We'll talk later, okay?"

Somehow, though he didn't know where he got the strength, Raymond nodded and managed to make it to his feet, and down the hall to his bedroom. The last thing he remembered hearing as he closed his eyes was the sound of a telephone ringing, back in the living room.

Black Friday

Chapter 40

The afternoon shadows were long when Raymond awoke from a troubled sleep, in which grotesque visions of both Holly and Norma's battered and abused bodies haunted him. He washed his face, brushed his teeth, and found Wayne watching the evening news on television.

"What's going on?"

"You don't want to know."

Raymond's eyes were drawn to the screen, where the front of Norma's cottage was displayed under a graphic that said Second Woman Murdered. The voice of the woman reporter was overlaid, saying, "In a dramatic revelation, police have identified the name of the woman who was killed inside this home sometime between Thursday night and Friday morning as Norma Swirensky. The victim worked as an assistant manager at the Palmetto Pantry on Cheney Highway. This is the same supermarket where Raymond Winters, accused of the murder of Holly Coulter on Black Friday, was the manager before he was arrested in that murder investigation. While police would not reveal what kind of relationship, if any, this victim and Mr. Winters may have had, one store employee told us, off the record, that they had worked closely together for several years."

The scene switched to the studio, where the anchorman asked, "Laura, have police said if Mr. Winters is a suspect in this latest homicide?"

"They wouldn't go that far," she replied, "but they did admit that he was questioned at police headquarters after the body was found, and later released."

"Released? How could that be possible?"

"It's a mystery to me. But it's just one of many unanswered questions in this case that just seems to get more complicated by the hour."

The news moved on to a story about Christmas decorations being vandalized in one neighborhood, while in another, people were complaining about one home's excessive display of lights, which some neighbors said was disruptive and drawing too much traffic to their street. Wayne hit the button on the remote control to turn the television off and said, "There have been about a dozen calls from reporters, and one was parked out in front with a news van for a couple of hours, but they left a little while ago."

"Will this madness ever end?"

"Sooner or later it has to, one way or another."

Raymond didn't want to consider which way that might be, so instead he asked where his pickup was.

"I had it towed to Reed's Tire Shop after the cops came for you. In fact, they called an hour ago and said it was done. They're open until six. Want to go and pick it up?"

Raymond didn't want to leave the house. He wasn't sure if he ever wanted to step out the door again, but he knew that wasn't realistic, so he just nodded.

***

Someone had covered the graffiti with black paint, and though it wasn't pretty, it still looked better than it had that morning.

"I had Bobby's sons cover it up," Wayne said, reading his thoughts. "I figured you'll want to get it repainted once this is all done, but it will do in the meantime."

They went inside, and when the store's owner saw Raymond the smile left his face. "Mr. Winters, I didn't realize that was your truck when Mr. Lamb here had it towed in, or I'd have told him to take it somewhere else. I'd appreciate it if you found another shop to do business with in the future."

"I've been a customer for over ten years, Ted."

"Yes sir, but you're not welcome here anymore."

"That's bullshit," Wayne said. "This man's money is as good as anybody else's."

"Not here, it's not. Now I'll thank you to pay your bill and both of you get off my property before I call the police."

Raymond's hands were shaking as he handed the man his credit card, and his normally neat handwriting was illegible as he scribbled his signature on the receipt. Back outside, Wayne shook his head. "Forget . Raymond, he's just an asshole. There are lots of places that will be

Black Friday

happy to take your money."

"I don't know," Raymond said, climbing behind the wheel of the pickup. "Maybe not in this town, ever again."

"Forget this guy. You can't change how people are going to think, Raymond. But when this is all said and done and the truth comes out, people like him are going to regret jumping to conclusions."

Raymond didn't say anything. He didn't know what he could say. And he really didn't believe that if he ever was vindicated, people would change their minds about the way they thought of him anyway. He was always going to be *that* guy. The man who was involved in the murders of two women in one small town.

"Have you eaten anything today?"

Raymond realized that he had not, but he wasn't the least bit hungry. He shook his head and said, "I can't even think about food right now."

"You need to eat something," Wayne said. "Let's stop and get a burger on the way home."

"I'm really not hungry. And the last thing I want to do is see anybody else."

"Okay, I understand. How about when we get home I order a pizza. You don't even have to go to the door when the delivery guy comes. I will."

Raymond nodded, though he still did not have any appetite.

A few blocks from the tire store, Raymond stopped for traffic light and while he was waiting for it to change he glanced into the next lane to find a beat up yellow pickup beside him. It took him a moment to realize that the two men in the cab of the pickup were Donald and Kyle Erickson.

***

The brothers apparently recognized Raymond a fraction of a second sooner, because Donald quickly stepped on the gas pedal and made a hard right turn, blocking Raymond's truck from escaping when the light changed. Both men jumped out of the Chevy, and before Raymond could lock his door, Kyle wrenched it open.

"Come on out of there, you murdering bastard," he said, reaching toward Raymond who tried to slide across the seat to get away. In doing so his foot slid off the brake pedal and his pickup rolled forward a foot or two and hit the side of the Blazer. Neither brother seem to notice as they grabbed his legs and tried to pull him out onto the pavement. Raymond kicked as hard as he could, feeling his foot connect with one of them and hearing a grunt of pain, but it didn't slow the brothers down. He felt himself sliding back across the seat toward the open doorway, and the next thing he knew he fell out, landing hard on the pavement. Pain shot from his tailbone up his spine, and he struggled to get to his feet. But before he could, the night was shattered by a gunshot.

"Get your hands off of him and back off right now," Wayne ordered, pointing his pistol at the brothers. "Do it, or the next one won't be in the air!"

"How about you mind your own damn business, mister," Donald said.

"I'm not going to tell you again," Wayne warned them. "Back away right now or you're both dead." He was holding the Browning in a two-handed stance, feet apart, and his finger on the trigger. There was no doubt that he meant business.

"Put your hands on top your heads and back up to the curb there," Wayne ordered. The light had changed and traffic and began to build up behind the scene. A couple of horns honked, but those nearest the altercation sat still, afraid to move and be caught up in the middle of the drama.

Once Donald and Kyle were on the curb at the edge of the street, Wayne said, "Raymond get in your truck and get out of here."

"What are you going to do?"

"I'm gonna make sure these guys don't try to follow you. Now go!"

Far away, there was the sound of sirens headed in their direction. Raymond didn't want any more interaction with the police department at that point, so he followed Wayne's orders and climbed back in his truck and backed up and around the Chevy. A moment later, Wayne was in his car and following him.

When they got back to Wayne's house, Raymond's hands were shaking so hard that it took three tries to turn off the ignition in his truck. He climbed out, weak kneed, but his friend seemed to have enjoyed the altercation.

"I don't think those two rednecks are going to be bothering you again anytime soon," he said with a grin. "I think I put the fear of God in them."

"I don't know about them, but you damn sure put the fear of God Jesus, Wayne, you were like Marshall Dillon or somebody out there."

The other man laughed and said, "Now if I could just find my own Miss Kitty. Let's get inside and order that pizza, I'm starved."

***

"You really do know how to use that thing, don't you?" Raymond said, as Wayne pulled the gun and its clip-on, inside the pants holster from his belt and set them on a bookshelf in the living room.

"Damn straight. That's the first time I've ever had to point it at anybody, but I've spent enough time on the range to know what I'm doing with it."

"Do you think somebody took your license number and the police are going to show up here?"

"Who knows? I guess it could happen, but I'll worry about that when it comes to it. *If* it comes to it. Under the law I was stopping an assault, which is justifiable."

"You've done your homework."

"Raymond, if you have a gun, it comes with a huge responsibility. I've taken firearms safety classes, and even a couple of tactical shooting classes. So yeah, I've done my homework. Guys like you, who aren't comfortable with guns, really shouldn't have one. Too many people think they can just buy a gun and that makes them qualified to handle any situation that comes along. It's not like that. But I have to say, if I hadn't been following you from the tire store tonight, things could have gotten a whole lot worse. I still think you need to give it some serious consideration."

"I hear what you're saying, but I still don't think I could shoot anybody. But I'm damn glad you were there tonight!"

"The thing is, I'm not always going to be there," Wayne told him. "Think about that."

Chapter 41

Ever since Detective Harrison had told him that Norma had been murdered, Raymond's brain had been mired in some sort of haze. He had gone through the motions of the police interview, and picking up his truck at the tire shop, and even managed to eat two slices of pizza after the confrontation with Holly's brothers. But through it all, it felt like he was outside of his body, looking down on the events of the day.

It didn't really hit him until he went to bed that night. That's when Norma's face seemed to float before him, and the impact was like the kick of a mule. If Raymond had felt a sense of loss at the death of Holly, a woman he had only spent a few hours with, what he felt about Norma was a deep, penetrating grief that tore at his very soul. In all the years they had worked together, he had been somewhat irritated with her sometimes bossy ways more than once, but overall it had been a very good professional relationship. He knew that Norma was always there to make sure the job got done, and he credited her with much of his success as the manager of the Palmetto Pantry.

Still, he had never really considered the two of them friends. Coworkers, yes. A good fit as a management team, certainly. But until their lunch at the Dixie Crossroads, he had never thought about Norma as anything more. Even after that, while he was comforted knowing that there was a friendship there, and that she cared about him and his future, he had never felt a strong attachment, let alone an attraction toward the woman.

Thinking back to their intimate encounter, he had certainly enjoyed it. While Norma may not have been as creative in bed as Holly had been, she was a woman who knew what she enjoyed and didn't hesitate to let him know that. And between the two, Raymond realized that he had enjoyed his encounter with Norma much more so than with Holly. Thinking about it, he knew it must be because of their long history together and the fact that they had meshed so well for so many years. Had he been in love with her? He didn't think so, but then he wasn't sure if he even really knew what love was. Certainly he had never been exposed to it as a child growing up, and it had never been a part of his marriage to Sheila. But now, he lay in bed and cried. Cried for the loss of a friend, cried for the loss of a good woman gone too soon. And yes, maybe, he cried for the loss of what might have been.

Finally he cried himself out, but still sleep would not come. He tossed and turned, and stared into the darkness at the ceiling for what seemed like hours. He got up and took a long, hot shower, hoping that would relax him enough that he could fall asleep, but it didn't help. Eventually he dropped off, but jerked awake a short time later. He finally gave up and got out of bed. Pulling on his jeans and slipping a T-shirt over his head, he went out into the darkened hallway and into the living room.

The digital clock on the microwave said it was 5:35 AM when he passed the kitchen entry. He didn't want to turn the television on for fear of waking Wayne, so he sat at the dining room table and turned on his laptop. The mail icon indicated he had three messages, so he logged onto his mail account.

Two were spam that he ignored, but the third was from the Palmetto Pantry corporate offices, informing him that the internal audit at his store had been completed and that no discrepancies had been found, therefore $19,637.25 would be payable to him to close out his profit sharing account, and asking him to contact the accounting department to tell them where to send the check.

After reading the e-mail, Raymond clicked on the two spam messages and sent them to his spam folder. When the icon showed three messages there, he clicked the touchpad to find an e-mail from Norma that had been misdirected.

Seeing her name in the sender's line took him aback, like discovering a message from the grave. But the timestamp showed it been sent at 11:55 PM Thursday night, almost three hours after Raymond had left her.

Raymond, I don't want you to think I'm stalking you, but I couldn't sleep so I did some more research. It took me a while, but I found this link on Google, and wanted you to see it. Wow! Now we know what your mother was talking about. Call me, day or night.

Norma

He clicked the blue link Norma had attached to the e-mail and waited

Black Friday

until the website opened. It was a newspaper story from Pensacola, dated May 15, 1982. He started to read it, then sat back in shock and stared at the screen, his heart pounding.

Three Shot In Pensacola Motel

Pensacola police responded to a report of shots fired at the Dancing Seahorse Motel on West Strong Street Friday night, and found two people dead and a third clinging to life. Detective Herbert Niedermeier identified the deceased as Melvin Hall 52, and his wife Patricia, 35. The third person, who was shot twice, has been identified as Royce Winters, 39. He was transported by ambulance to Pensacola General Hospital, where police said he was in serious condition. No other details were available at this time.

Raymond read the story a second time, then clicked on the search bar at the top of the newspaper's page, typed in his father's name, and two more links from the paper's archives appeared on the screen. The first was another newspaper story, dated two days later.

More Details On Motel Shooting

Pensacola police have released new details on the double homicide at the Dancing Seahorse Motel on West Strong Street Friday night. In a news conference this morning, Police Chief Darrell Clinton said that the motel manager reported a disturbance in Room 14 just after 9 PM.. While he was on the phone with police, he reported hearing gunshots. When officers arrived on the scene, they found Melvin Hall, 52, and his wife Patricia, 35, dead, and Royce Winters, 39, with two gunshot wounds to his back. Chief Clinton said the shootings were witnessed by Melvin Hall Junior, the 11-year-old son of the deceased couple. According to the boy, his father had driven them to the motel and his father left him in the car while he went into the room, where Mrs. Hall and Mr. Winters were in a compromising position. The boy got out of the car and followed his father to the room's door in time to see him shoot his mother and Mr. Winters, and then turn the gun on himself. Police said that Melvin Hall owned Hall's Ford-Mercury-Lincoln dealership in Pensacola, and that Mr. Winters was employed as a salesman at the company. The boy, the couple's only child, is being cared for by relatives.

Raymond felt sick to his stomach. His mother's comments about him trying to match his father's score now made sense to him, and he understood the animosity she had held for her ex-husband for so long. Curious to know more, he opened the second link to another newspaper story, this one dated two weeks after the shooting.

Affair Led To Murder Suicide

Police have learned the apparent reason for the shooting at a Pensacola Motel two weeks ago that left a couple dead and a third man seriously wounded. Police Chief Darrell Clinton said that a private detective hired by Melvin Hall, who killed his wife and shot Royce Winters, who was in the room with her before killing himself, has told police that less than two hours before the shooting, he gave Mr. Hall photographs he had taken of his wife, Patricia, and Mr. Winters going into a room at the Dancing Seahorse Motel on West Strong Street. The private detective, whom chief Clinton identified as Theodore Ambrose of Pensacola, said that he told his client it was not the first time he had seen the couple meeting at the same motel. The couple's son, Melvin Junior, age 11, said that he was not in the room when his father and Mr. Ambrose met, but that after the private detective left, his father told him they needed to go out somewhere. That somewhere turned out to be the motel where the shooting took place. The boy, who witnessed the shooting but was not injured, has been living with his father's sister Elizabeth and her husband Daniel Lamb since the tragedy occurred. Melvin Hall was a well-known Pensacola businessman and a self-made millionaire who was active in the automotive and real estate investment business. Friends and business associates say he had been withdrawn in the last few months and seemed to be troubled about something, but would not tell anyone what was on his mind.

Raymond felt the same red pinpricks going off in his head as he read the story. He had to read it a second time, not wanting to believe what he saw on the computer's screen. He wanted to believe that this was yet another bad dream, but he knew it wasn't. Never, even in his worst nightmares, had he ever felt the horror that those words seared into his heart like a red hot branding iron.

"So now you know."

He had been so absorbed in what he was reading that he had not heard Wayne come into the room or realized that he was standing behind him. The only light in the room was the glow of the computer's screen, but it was enough to see the pistol in Wayne's hand.

Black Friday

Chapter 42

"Why, Wayne?"

"Why? You just read why. It's payback, buddy."

"But I was just a kid, like you. My father was the one who was having the affair with your mother."

"You were never a kid like me," Wayne snarled. "You didn't hear your mother begging for her life before she died screaming. You never saw your father's brains sprayed across a motel room wall. You got to come here and live your life like any other kid. So don't you dare say you were ever anything like me!"

"Wayne, I..."

"Shut up! Shut up or I'll kill you right now," Wayne shouted.

Raymond held his hands up, palms forward.

"You go on and on about what a bitch your mother is," Wayne said. "Do you want to know what my life was like? Do you know how many shrinks I saw over the years? Do you know how many nights I woke up screaming, reliving that night over and over again? Do you want to hear about how I pissed the bed until I was in my twenties?"

Raymond started to say something, but Wayne thrust the Browning forward and he closed his mouth.

"Do you have any idea what it's like to go from being a kid who had it all, a nice house, and a beautiful mother and a successful father, to being the kid whose dad killed his mother and then himself when he found out she was a whore sleeping around behind his back? Do you know how many schoolyard bullies kicked my ass growing up?"

By now Wayne was screaming, and his finger was white on the trigger of the big pistol. At any second Raymond expected an explosion of fire to erupt from the barrel and to feel a bullet tear through his flesh. His mind raced, trying to think of something to say or do, but he was too terrified to make a move. All he could do was watch the gaping muzzle of the pistol like a cobra watching a snake charmer.

"But it didn't stop there. Oh no! My aunt and uncle didn't give a damn about me. All they cared about was getting their hands on the money. So they shipped me off to boarding school and had a good old time spending everything my father had worked all his life to build up. And none of it would have happened if your father would have just kept his pecker in his pants! But not Royce Winters. Oh no, he had to screw every woman he laid eyes on, whether she was married or not. It didn't matter that my father gave him a good job and treated him like a brother. No, nothing ever mattered to him except getting his dick wet. And my family were the ones who paid the price."

Finally Raymond managed to work up the courage to speak. "I'm sorry, Wayne, I really am. But why me? Why not Royce?"

"He's an old man," Wayne said. "He'll die soon enough on his own. But so what? No, somebody needed to lose everything just like I did. So I tracked you down. It was easy, really. You can find anything on the internet. And there you were, just coasting through life with your nice little job and your nice little house and your nice little family. Well, not exactly nice. Your kids are a couple of spoiled losers and that bitch you're married to is the most miserable woman who ever lived. But I will give her this, she's good in the sack. Especially when she's pissed off at you and needs to work off some steam."

Wayne laughed cruelly at the look on Raymond's face. "What, you don't believe me? Just because you're not man enough to do anything for her doesn't mean she doesn't like to get her rocks off. It took me a month to start screwing her after I moved in. Yeah, old buddy, while you were out fishing on that silly assed boat of yours, my pole was getting a workout, too."

"I don't believe you."

"You don't? Then how do I know about that crescent shaped birthmark on the inside of her right thigh just above the panty line? Or the little mole next to her left nipple? Yeah, I've seen them a lot over the past couple of years. But don't take my word for it, I've got video, too, if you want to see. It's amazing how much detail a small camera can pick up if you put it the right place in a bedroom. I've got them everywhere. Even in that pretty little daughter of yours' bedroom. In fact, I'm thinking that after this is all over with, she's going to need some nurturing from her Uncle Wayne, don't you? We all know a girl needs a strong father figure in her life, and you haven't quite measured up to that, have you?"

When Raymond didn't respond, Wayne reached to the light switch on the wall and turned it on. "You still don't believe me, do you? See that little box up there in the corner up there by the window? Yeah, buddy I'm going to get to relive this moment over and over again. All of the moments. But hey, why should I have all the fun? That's not fair, is it, Raymond? What about you? Would you like to see your old lady getting off with a real man? Maybe that would get you going, buddy. You might find out that you're a closet voyeur."

Raymond had never been a violent man, but he wanted to take the gun away from Wayne and pound his head into mush with it. Maybe his body tensed, signaling some intention that he didn't realize he might act upon. But as if he was reading his mind, Wayne warned, "Don't even think about it, you pussy. We both know I'm a better man, in bed or out, than you'll ever be. You'll be dead before your ass ever clears the chair."

Wayne laughed again. "You know, Raymond, it cost me a lot of money to set this all up, but believe me, it was worth every penny to watch you squirm as your whole world dissolved around you. *Oh woe is me, life isn't so wonderful anymore.*" Poor, poor Raymond. And I was right here for you, every step of the way, wasn't I? Patting you on the back and listening to you cry like a little girl. And all the while I was laughing inside "

"My life was never perfect. Far from it."

"Shut up," Wayne shouted again. "Do you know why it was so miserable, Raymond? Because you're a spineless wimp without the balls to stand up to anybody. Not your mother, or your sister, or your wife. Hell, not even your kids. But if you thought it was bad before, or that what's been happening has been rough, wait until you get to prison. They're going to stick you in a cellblock full of hard corps cons, and your soft little ass is going to get a good workout. Yeah, the whole cellblock is going to love their new bitch."

"You killed two women to get even with me for something my father did over thirty years ago?"

"Actually, I only planned to kill Holly. She was easy. Such a typical slut. I convinced her that I was in love with her and that I needed her to help me with a big scheme I was working on. I told her your family was rich and that we'd be able to blackmail you for big bucks and she was more than glad to go along with it. Of course, she didn't know that she was disposable. She thought that as soon as you left that motel room and I came in, we'd be ready to put our big scheme in motion and we'd be on easy street. She was a good piece of ass, but you know that, right?

But it's no big loss, the world is full of women like her. She won't be missed."

"So you were there all the while we were in that room together?"

"Sitting right across the street in a parking lot watching the door of that room. Except for when I went to Holly's van and took those tablet computers out to help convince the cops you're a pathological liar. But don't worry, they won't go to waste. I mean, after all, since I was the one who convinced Sheila your kids really needed them, I'll be sure they make their way under the tree for them from good old Uncle Wayne."

"Why did you have to kill Norma? How did that fit into your plan?"

Wayne gave him a mock frown. "That one hurt, didn't it? I think you were sweet on that one, buddy, weren't you? Actually, she didn't fit into any of this. But when you came home telling me all about how she was into genealogy and all that stuff and how much she had found for you online, I figured it was just a matter of time until she stumbled onto something. So as soon as you fell asleep the other night, I slipped out and paid her a little call. If it's any consolation to you, she woke up when I came into her bedroom and called your name. I bet not many women have done that. Am I right?"

"You'll never get away with this, Wayne."

"Of course I will. Do you think the cops are going to believe anything you say? Hell, man, you're a psychotic murderer. And even if you weren't, who would believe a wild story like this? But what the hell, it will give you something to talk about in the cellblock. When you're not busy making the rest of the guys happy, that is."

"You're crazy."

"Not according to all of those high priced shrinks I used to have to see. No, I'm traumatized by what I went through, but rest assured, I'm not crazy."

"I'm not going to prison, Wayne."

"Sure you are. That's going to be the best part of all of this. I mean, seeing your life implode has been great, but all good things must come to an end. But don't worry about old Wayne, I'll be just fine. You see, Uncle Dan and Aunt Elizabeth had an unfortunate accident when I was sixteen. Something about a propane heater and a faulty carbon monoxide detector at their cabin up in the Smoky Mountains. Man, I'm sure glad I left to go back to school the day before that happened! The good news is that they had adopted me and given me a brand new name, and I got to inherit enough money left over from my father's estate to keep me

Black Friday 255

afloat for a long time. And to pay for this fun little adventure we shared. And as much as I like it here, and enjoy your wife's favors, I think after you go to prison I'll just be too broken up to stay here much longer. But don't worry, I promise I'll write you every week. And you write back too, okay? I want to know everything that's going on with your life in the joint."

"I'm not going to prison, Wayne. You can kill me right now and save them the trouble, but I'm not going to prison."

Wayne pouted. "I really don't want to do that, Raymond. I need to know that you're alive and suffering every day for the rest of your miserable life. Besides, you promised me you wouldn't off yourself."

"Kill me now, Wayne, because if you don't, I'm going to take that gun away from you and stick it up your ass."

"I don't think so," Wayne said. "You're too much of a coward for that. You know it and I know it. But go ahead, make your move. I won't kill you, but I'll gut shoot you, and make sure you stay alive until the ambulance gets here to take you to the hospital. I did mention that I'm an excellent shot, didn't I?"

"And how do you plan to explain that, Wayne?"

"Explain it? Shit man, by the time I'm done telling them about how I caught you sneaking out of here, ready to go on the lam, and tried to stop you, and how you came at me and I had to shoot you to protect myself, they'll probably give me a medal. Oh sure, some people will say I should have realized how evil you were to start with, but hey, I'm a good friend who just wanted to believe in you. I'll be an emotional wreck for a while. Yeah, that's probably why I'll have to go away someplace."

Raymond knew that as outlandish as Wayne's plan was, it could well succeed. Who was going to believe anything he said to try to expose it, or even listen to him, for that matter?

"You know what? On second thought, I think I *am* going to shoot you," Wayne said. "It wasn't part of the original plan, but I'm all for improvising. Yeah, I think I'll shoot you in a kneecap before I call the cops, just for kicks. But I'll tell you what, since we're such great pals and all, I'll let you pick which one, just for old time's sake."

"You really are crazy."

"No Raymond, I'm *traumatized*. Haven't you listened to a word I've been saying? Now which is it going to be, right or left?"

Raymond stared at him, trying to muster the courage to attack.

"You can't decide? That's one of your many faults, Raymond. You're always so indecisive. Okay, let's do it this way. Eeny, meeny, miny, moe, pick a..."

The doorbell rang and then somebody pounded heavily on the door. "Titusville police. Search warrant. Open the door!"

Wayne turned toward the sound, and before he knew what he was doing Raymond found himself rushing him, closing the few feet between them and slamming into the other man's body. The pistol roared and a hot pain lanced through his left arm, but he ignored it as they hit the floor together. Wayne punched him in the throat and Raymond gagged. Wayne was bigger than him and stronger, and he effortlessly rolled on top of Raymond and locked his fingers around his throat. Raymond heard pounding coming from far away and wasn't sure whether it was coming from the police at the door or from inside his head. Above him, Wayne had a wolfish snarl on his face as he choked harder.

Raymond couldn't make his left arm work and was powerless to release the other man's grip. He felt himself beginning to black out as his oxygen starved brain began to shut down. His right arm fell away from Wayne's hands and flopped onto the floor. His right hand hit something hard and round and his fingers closed around the Gerber tactical pen in his jeans pocket. With the last of his strength, he pulled the pen out, brought it up in a wide arc, and slammed it into Wayne's temple with everything he had in him. The other man's eyes bulged and Raymond felt the grip loosen on his throat as Wayne collapsed on top of him. He managed to roll out from under Wayne just as the front door crashed open and Detective Acosta and two uniformed police officers rushed into the room, guns leveled at him.

"Don't move," Acosta shouted. "I'm warning you, Winters, if you so much as twitch, you're a dead man!"

The only thing that moved were Raymond's eyelids as they closed and he fell into a deep pool of darkness.

Chapter 43

The sound of something beeping woke him up. Raymond opened his eyes to see a large black woman in a hospital style scrub top leaning over him, a digital thermometer in her hand. He felt her press it against his forehead and closed his eyes again. When he opened them a second time, he was alone and his bladder felt like it was going to burst. He tried to sit up but it hurt to move and he felt something hard around his right wrist. He looked down to see a handcuff attached to his wrist, the other end locked around the bed rail.

He tried to ignore the pressure but couldn't. "Hello?"

"What do you need?"

He turned his head to the left and saw a uniformed police officer sitting in a chair.

"Where am I?"

"Parrish Medical Center. For now, at least. As soon as the doctors cut you loose you'll be going to the jail."

It hurt to talk, but he managed to say, "I need to go to the bathroom."

"Not my problem."

"Please, I really have to go!" His voice sounded raspy.

"You'll just have to hold it."

"I can't. I'm about to wet myself."

"Jesus Christ. They should have shot you when they had the chance."

The policeman walked to the side of the bed and pushed a button on a plastic cord. A moment later there was a knock on the door and a nurse poked her head inside.

"Yes?"

"He's awake and says he needs to take a leak."

She came into the room and took Raymond's pulse. He couldn't help squirming in discomfort and she said, "Stay still, please."

"I really have to go to the bathroom," Raymond said.

"Okay, hold on." She went into the bathroom and came back with a plastic urinal. "Can you manage this on your own?"

Raymond tried to move his left arm but it felt too heavy and when he looked he saw that it was incased in a cast. "I don't know how," he said.

"Do you want to help me out here?" the nurse asked.

"Sorry, that's not in my job description," the policeman said.

The nurse sighed and shook her head. "Fine." She pulled the blanket away from Raymond, raised his gown, and held the urinal over his penis. At any other time he would have been humiliated, but his need was too great and he let the flow go, feeling release as the pressure went away. If the nurse, who was a trim young woman with brown hair and eyes, felt any discomfort in the process, she did not let it show. When he was done, she took the urinal back into the bathroom, noted how much he had passed on a chart, and then emptied it and flushed the toilet. She washed her hands and returned to the room and asked, "How is your pain level, on a scale from 1 to 10?"

"I don't know, maybe a three or four, at the most," Raymond answered.

"Okay, if you need anything else just, let the officer know."

"Hey, I'm not his errand boy. He doesn't need anything except a quick trip to Raiford, and that's where he's going."

The nurse ignored him and left the room. Raymond was asleep again before the door completely closed.

It was dark outside the window the next time he woke up, and he could smell food. He looked to his left and saw a cafeteria tray sitting on a stand next to the bed.

"Looks like he's awake."

He looked past the tray to see a different policeman sitting in the same chair. Then Detectives Harrison and Acosta moved into his view.

"How are you doing, Winters?"

It still hurt to talk, but he said, "I'm okay."

"You were lucky, the bullet broke the ulna in your left arm and went right on through. You were even luckier that you passed out when you did, because if you had made another move, we'd have killed you," Acosta said.

Raymond didn't feel lucky. He wanted to ask them why he was handcuffed and under guard, but he didn't have the energy. All he wanted to do was close his eyes again and sleep forever. But the next words from the detectives brought him out of his stupor.

"Raymond Winters, you're under arrest for the murders of Norma Swirensky and Wayne Lamb."

"Wayne's dead?"

"What did you expect?" Harrison asked. "You drove that damned metal pen right through the side of his skull."

"He did it," Raymond said. "He..."

"Yeah, right, he stuck it in his own head. Makes sense to me. People do that every day," Harrison sneered.

"No, he..."

"I don't want to hear it," the detective said. "You can tell it all to the judge. Who, by the way, is really pissed that she gave you a break and you went out and killed two more people. She knows her career is shot because of this, but the last thing she'll want to do before she leaves the bench is to make sure you get the death penalty."

"They'll discharge you in the morning," Acosta told him, "And then you'll be transported to the county jail. In the meantime, don't even think about trying to pull anything funny, because in addition to the officer here in the room, there's a second one right outside the door. And they won't hesitate for a second to blow you away if you give them half the chance."

"You should eat your dinner," the guard in his room advised after the detectives left. "Hospital food's not great, but it's the best thing you're ever going to get again."

Raymond had no appetite, so he didn't bother to ask how he was supposed to eat with one arm shackled and the other in a cast. Instead he just stared at the ceiling, listened to the noises of the machine next to his bed, and contemplated what life would be like in prison until the day he was executed. He wondered if he had the courage to try to escape from the hospital bed to force the guard to shoot him. He was trying to figure out how to do it when he fell asleep.

**

Early the next morning the two detectives and two uniformed police officers stood guard while a doctor examined Raymond and pronounced him well enough to be transported to the county jail. They attached leg shackles to his ankles, and his right arm was handcuffed to a chain that was connected to a separate one around his waist. Bowing to hospital policy, they allowed him to ride down the elevator and to the entrance in a wheelchair pushed by one of the policemen. But once they were outside, he was put into the back of a van and locked to a thick eyebolt that was attached to a metal bench along one wall. One of the uniformed officers drove the van and the other sat up front with him, while the detectives sat on a bench across from Raymond.

Nobody said a word during the drive to the jail. When they arrived he was booked and placed in a small cell by himself at the end of the corridor.

"This is for your own protection," said the guard, as he locked the door behind him. "There are some guys in here who'd like to make a name for themselves by taking out the Titusville Terror."

Seeing the look on Raymond's face, he said, "That's what they're calling you on the news. You don't look all that terrifying to me. But my job isn't to judge anybody in here. You keep your mouth shut, do as you're told, and we'll get along just fine."

Raymond couldn't remember the last time he had eaten, but he had missed breakfast and had to wait until lunch, when the same guard brought him a tray with a sandwich, an apple, and a nutrition bar that had the consistency of sawdust, but at least it helped fill his stomach. He washed it down with tepid tea that tasted like it had sat in the pot for days.

There was nobody to talk to, not that he wanted any company, and no radio or television within earshot. He spent his time doing what he had been doing ever since the two detectives first came to the Palmetto Pantry and took him to the police station to be interviewed. Thinking about the case, re-examining every detail, and wondering how he had been such a fool as to not see how Wayne had been manipulating not just him, but everybody, since he had first moved in across the street.

The news of Sheila's infidelity had hurt him, not because he was innocent by any means, but because all the while she had denied him she was sleeping with the man who he had thought of as his best friend. His only real friend. He could not help but wonder how things would have been between him and his wife if Wayne had not been in the picture. But then he realized that Sheila's venomous anger toward him had been there long before Wayne arrived on the scene.

There had to be some way to get people to listen to him, to expose Wayne's elaborate plan to destroy his life for something that had happened when they were both children. But who would listen to him?

Black Friday

***

His opportunity came late that afternoon when two guards appeared at his cell and told him he had a visitor. As they had done on the trip from the hospital, his ankles were shackled and he was handcuffed to a chain around his waist as he was led down the corridor. Other inmates either hooted at his presence, or suggested the guards put him in with them so they could see just how tough he really was.

He was taken to a small interview room where DeLeon waited. But any hope that the attorney would listen to his revelation of what had been taking place was short lived. Before he could say anything except that he could prove he was innocent, DeLeon held up his hand.

"Stop it, Raymond. Just stop it, okay? I don't want to hear it."

"But, I'm trying to tell you..."

"No, you need to listen to what I'm telling you. You're a sick man, Raymond. At first I believed there was some other explanation. I even began to buy into your theory that somebody was setting you up. But the truth us, you're insane. Nobody in their right mind would do all of this."

"I'm not crazy," Raymond interrupted. "It was Wayne. He did all of this!"

"No, Raymond, Wayne is dead. You killed him. Just like you killed Holly Coulter and Norma Swirensky. Now, you may believe there was some kind of big conspiracy. You wouldn't be the first person who committed crimes because of some paranoid delusion. Now all we can do is damage control. I think that with an insanity plea, we may be able to avoid the death penalty and get you life in the Florida State Hospital in Chattahoochee.

Raymond started to protest, but DeLeon raised his hand to silence him. "That's it, Raymond, take it or leave it. But if you persist in claiming you're innocent, my only recourse is to ask the judge to let me be excused and you can have a court appointed attorney represent you. If you go that route, I guarantee you'll be on Death Row before you know it."

He stood up and said, "Your arraignment on the Swirensky and Lamb murders is at 10 tomorrow morning. I want you to think long and hard about what I told you. I'll arrange for us to have a few minutes together before we go into the courtroom. I'll need your answer then."

Black Friday

***

Raymond spent a sleepless night tossing and turning on the thin mattress that covered the steel bunk bolted to the wall of his cell. If he knew that he could not handle being in prison until his execution date, how could he spend the rest of his life in a facility for the criminally insane?

He had read of prisoners of war who had maintained their sanity by escaping with their minds. In one case, a POW in Vietnam who had been an avid golfer had spent his days replaying every course he had ever been on. Could reliving his days spent fishing on his boat, the only truly peaceful moments of his life, get him through for the next thirty or forty years? And then what? Was it better to claim he was insane and die an old man in a cell? Or to let the legal process do its thing and end it strapped to a gurney?

And *was* Deleon right? Was he really insane? Had he killed three people in some mindless delusion. More than once he had heard that crazy people did not know they were insane and truly believed the reality they had created inside their heads. Was he the monster that everyone said he was? Was the Titusville Terror real?

Somewhere in that long night, Raymond came to a conclusion. He did not know if he was insane or not, but he did know that it didn't matter anymore. Either way, his fate was sealed. He was going to die. It didn't matter if it was through execution in a year or two or three, or at the end of decades, sitting in a secured room in a mental hospital. But the end result was going the be the same. Nothing he could say or do was going to change that fact. And once he accepted that, it was just a matter of choosing how to do it under his own terms.

Chapter 44

His last meal was reconstituted scrambled eggs, two pieces of thin bacon, half of an English muffin, and coffee. He expected them to come for him right after breakfast, but nobody did. Raymond had first planned to attack the guards as they put his shackles on, but then he realized that would not work. They were unarmed, but could quickly summon enough help to overpower him. They did not need lethal force to accomplish that.

But he knew from his first arraignment that the guards in the courtroom were armed. He went over his plan again and again, looking for any flaws. He knew he would have to act fast, and he knew he would only get one chance. Grab Deleon, wrap his arms around the attorney's neck, and start dragging him toward the door. He didn't want to seriously hurt the other man, but he knew he had to do enough to make one of the guards shoot him to stop his escape attempt. He just hoped DeLeon would not be injured in the process, but reminded himself that desperate times called for desperate measures.

There was no clock in the cell, so all he could do was estimate the time. Eventually he called out to a guard and asked when he was going to be taken for arraignment.

"What's your hurry. It's not like you're going to get out on bail," was the only response he received.

Lunch was served, some sort of vegetable soup, crackers, another nutrition bar, and more of the bitter iced tea, which was just as bad as the day before. Raymond asked the guard who brought his tray why he had not been taken to his arraignment.

"Who knows? Monday mornings are always busy. Probably lots of drunks and weekend warriors ahead of you.

When they finally did come, it was the same routine. He was handcuffed and shackled, but this time he was led to an elevator and down to a sally port in the basement. When he stepped out, he was greeted by four armed guards and led to a van just like the one he had been brought to the jail in. Raymond looked for a momentary slip on their part that would allow him to attack them and end it all right there, but they were experienced in prisoner handling and did not give him an opportunity.

"Where are we going?"

"Shut up."

"I'm supposed to be arraigned."

"And I'm supposed to be rich and banging some twenty year old redhead," the potbellied guard said. "Life's a bitch and then you die."

For a moment Raymond wondered if they were taking him someplace away from prying eyes to assassinate him in an "escape attempt" to save the state the cost of a trial, and he welcomed the fantasy. Instead, the van stopped at the police department.

He was led down the same hallway to the same interview room, but this time there was a difference. Besides Assistant District Attorney Morrison, the two detectives, and DeLeon, there were two other men in the room. One was the freckle faced patrolman named O'Rourke who had taken the report of the vandalism to his truck and Wayne's house, and the other was an older man with carefully trimmed gray hair and manicured nails, wearing a three piece suit.

Raymond was surprised when his shackles and handcuffs were removed, and Morrison said, "Please sit down, Mister Winters." He sat next to his attorney, which put him directly across from the young policeman. Raymond wondered how quickly he could jump across the table and grab his weapon from its holster, and hoped that no one else would be shot when the two detectives drew their weapons to stop him. Maybe he could make it out into the hallway to avoid anyone else being injured in the small room. When should he act? Better late than never, he decided, tensing to make his move.

But before he could, the older man said, "Mr. Winters, I'm Police Chief Holcomb, and I believe you've met Officer O'Rourke before."

Raymond nodded at the policeman, not knowing what the expected protocol was when an accused murderer was in such a setting, but not wanting to telegraph his intentions. He wondered if he stuck his hand out, if O'Rourke would respond in kind out of reflex, making his attack easier. He started to extend his hand when the police chief said, "You owe Officer O'Rourke here a big thank you. He saved your life. And we all owe you a big apology."

Raymond wasn't sure what was happening, but the police chief's words and the chagrined look on everybody's faces told him it was something big.

"What do you mean?"

"It seems that Officer O'Rourke is a bit of a techno nerd, and while he was securing the scene at Mr. Lamb's house after you were arrested on the warrant for Ms. Swirensky's death, he noticed your laptop computer on the table. The screen saver was on, but when he swiped his finger across the touchpad he found the story on the screen about the death of Mr. Lamb's parents. I'm afraid our two detectives here would not listen to him when he tried to tell them that there was more to the story than what they were seeing. I'm afraid sometimes policemen make the mistake of looking at the obvious and going from there instead of digging a little deeper to see what else they might uncover."

Raymond felt a roaring in his ears and tried to concentrate on what he was hearing.

"When he couldn't get anywhere with Detectives Harrison and Acosta, Officer O'Rourke called me at home late yesterday. That, by the way, is what's called going way out on a limb by a young police officer. And his instincts were right. He recognized the small cameras that Mr. Lamb had hidden all over the house, and once we were able to review the video from them we saw exactly what happened yesterday. Including Mr. Lamb's statements about the deaths of Ms Coulter and Ms. Swirensky."

Raymond began to sway in his seat and DeLeon put a hand on his shoulder to steady him.

"So I'm not crazy?"

"No sir," Chief Holcomb said. "You're not crazy, you are a victim. And very soon you're going to be a free man."

Raymond thought that he had cried himself out after Norma's death, and did not believe his tear ducts were capable of anything else. But suddenly the tears were flowing again and he could not stop them. He didn't even try.

Eventually he got control of himself, and the police chief told him that while the investigation was ongoing and that the computer forensic technicians were still examining all of the data on Wayne's computers and the tiny wireless cameras secreted not only in Wayne's house, but also in the home Raymond had shared with his wife and children.

"There are some things in the video files that we have recovered so far that are rather delicate," Holcomb told him.

"My wife with Wayne?"

"Yes sir. I'm sorry."

Raymond was too numb to feel anything and just nodded in response.

"How did he do it? I mean, all of the e-mails and text messages that were supposed to be from me?"

"That was easy, from a technical standpoint," O'Rourke told him. "You trusted him to keep your computers up to date, and he installed a program that ran in the background that allowed him to control them remotely, and even to send e-mails and texts that looked like they came from you."

"So now what happens?"

"Well, Judge Stewart is waiting for us, and we just have to go through the formality of her dismissing all of the charges against you. And then you're free to go."

"Where?" Raymond asked. "Where do I go?"

The police chief seemed to be taken aback by the question. "Ahh... anywhere you want to go, I guess. It's a free country and you're a free man."

Chapter 45

Raymond spent the next three weeks like a man walking through a dream. He had walked out of the interview room for the last time, without shackles or handcuffs, and had been taken before the judge, who had dismissed all of the charges against him and told him that he was free to go. He remembered the police chief, detectives, and Janet Morrison shaking his hand and apologizing, and then it was DeLeon's turn. "I'm sorry Raymond. I should have believed you."

All he could say in reply was, " At the end, I don't know if I even believed me."

Wayne's house was a crime scene, but they allowed him to go inside, accompanied by Officer O'Rourke to retrieve his clothing, computer, and the rest of his possessions. Then, with nowhere else to go, Raymond had taken a motel room on a weekly basis.

Calls came in from television and newspaper reporters, including from two nationwide weekly news shows, but he didn't want to talk to any of them. There were calls from Doug Kuykendall, asking him to come to North Carolina to talk about his future with his company and assuring him he could have his choice of stores, or even a district manager's position, with a compensation package that would dwarf what he had been earning with Palmetto Pantry. There were also calls from DeLeon and the District Attorney's office, keeping him updated on the progress of the investigation into Wayne Lamb's background and activities. An investigation had been reopened into the deaths of his aunt and uncle, though so much time had passed that little was to come of it. DeLeon informed him that investigators had discovered proof that it had been Wayne who had diverted the money from his children's college funds, and that while it would take time, the money would be returned from Wayne's sizable estate. He added that he was sure a lawsuit against the estate for damages would be successful. Raymond declined to pursue it, though he heard through the grapevine that Sheila was retaining an attorney to do so.

And then there was Sheila. A week after the charges were dismissed against him, she called. Seeing her name on his caller ID, Raymond did not answer. The message she left was contrite.

"Uh, it's me, Raymond. I really don't know what to say. Look, we both made some mistakes but... well, I miss you. And the kids miss you. Call me, okay?"

Raymond deleted the message.

The next day he went to the cemetery and spent a few minutes alone at Norma's grave. More tears were shed and some solemn words were said. Then he drove back to the motel, hitched his boat to his pickup, and drove out of the parking lot.

As he had so many times in the past, he paused when he came to Interstate 95. A right turn would take him north to a good job with good pay and a secure future. It was the sensible thing to do, and all of his life Raymond had always done the sensible thing. A left turn would take him to the Keys that Hemingway had loved and Jimmy Buffett had made famous with songs of margaritas and living on island time. He knew that was a myth. These days there were more tourists than palm trees, and condos had replaced the shacks the first Conchs had lived in. But the water was blue, the weather was warm, and the fish were always biting.

He turned left.

Thank you for reading Black Friday. If you enjoyed it, here's a sneak peak at one of Nick Russell's most popular books, Dog's Run.

Two boys playing hooky from school to go squirrel hunting found the young woman's body lying face down in the muddy creek at the bottom of Dog's Run. At first, Wayne DeCross thought it was a dummy and started to approach it, but his buddy Chance Carver grabbed his arm and pulled him back.

"No, Wayne, that ain't no dummy, that's a real woman and I think she's dead!"

"Naaa," Wayne told him disdainfully, shaking the other boy's hand off his arm. "You got too much imagination, Chance. Besides, even if it was a real woman, I ain't scared of no dead body. Are you?"

"I'm not scared," Chance said with a shake of his head, even though he was. "I just don't want to be messin' with no dead body."

"Well what do ya think those squirrels hangin' off your belt are? Ain't they dead bodies?"

Chance couldn't deny the reasoning but he still didn't want to get anywhere near the thing laying in the creek. "That's different. These are animals and pretty soon they'll be food. That there's a dead person."

"Ain't people animals, too?" argued Wayne. "And if we don't get her out of that water pretty soon she'll be food too, for the crawdaddies."

"I ain't touching her!" Chance said. "We need to go tell the Sheriff."

"I swear, you are such a sissypants. Dead is dead, ain't it? Don't matter if it's a squirrel or a chicken or a person."

"Well I ain't never been haunted by no squirrel or a chicken before!"

"And when was you ever haunted by a dead person?" Wayne asked.

"I wasn't. But you ask Pete Ledbetter about gettin' haunted. He'll tell ya! He was haunted by his mother-in-law after she died 'cause they never got on."

"Pete Ledbetter?" Wayne scoffed. "Hell, you know well's I do that old Pete's drunk most of the time, and he's got a worse imagination than you. If he heard a tree branch scrapin' the side of his shack, he'd swear it was old Bessie Green scratchin' on the door tryin' to get in!"

"I don't care. I ain't touching no dead body!"

"Fine, then hold my gun and I'll do it. I ain't scared of nothing!" Wayne said, handing his old Savage single-shot .22 to his friend and walking up to the body.

And there was no doubt that it was indeed a body he determined when he got closer. A hank of long, curly yellow hair waved off to the side in the muddy water and the back of the woman's white dress had ridden up, exposing her upper thighs and the cheeks of her butt. Being a normal thirteen year old boy, Wayne couldn't help pausing to admire the curve of her rear end for a quick moment before he put his hand on her shoulder and tried to pull her over. She was surprisingly heavy for such a relatively small woman. He called out to Chance, "Stop bein' such a baby and come here and help me."

Chance hesitated for another moment, then screwed up his courage. He wasn't a Catholic, in fact he wasn't much for Sunday School of any kind, but he crossed himself like he had seen that priest in the Saturday matinee at the Rigley Theater do last week, then laid the three squirrels they had shot, Wayne's rifle, and his beat up old Savage 20 gauge on the creek bank and joined his friend. The water covering his ankles was cool, but that wasn't what made him shiver.

"Who is it?"

"Don't know," Wayne said. "Guess we'll find out when we roll her over. Here, give me a hand."

They grabbed the woman's right arm and pulled her onto her back and were greeted with the sight of a fat crawdad hanging from the corner of her left nostril by one pincher.

All thought of false bravado disappeared as both boys screamed and ran splashing out of the creek, leaving their guns, the dead squirrels, and the body behind them as they fled Dog's Run.

Black Friday
Chapter 1

Police Chief Lester Smeal took a bite of his meatloaf sandwich and smiled at Mary Jo, nodding as he chewed. "That's just delicious, darlin'," he said as he swallowed.

Mary Jo beamed and said, "I'm glad you like it Les. Anything else I can get you?"

"Well I can think of several things I'd like," the chief said. "But most of them are immoral, and I'm pretty sure a couple are flat-out illegal."

Mary Jo blushed and cackled, slapping his arm playfully. "What am I going to do with you, Lester J. Smeal? You're incorrigible!"

"Yes ma'am, I am," the chief said with a wide grin, before taking another bite. That's just one of the reasons you love me."

"Oh, I love you, do I? I think you're assuming a lot there, big fella."

"Well, if it ain't love, it must be lust," the chief said, drawing another loud laugh from the waitress.

Their daily flirtation was interrupted when the door to the Sunshine Café burst open and two muddy, excited young boys rushed inside leaving a trail of footprints across Mary Jo's linoleum floor.

"What in the world are you boys doing stomping in here like that?" Mary Jo demanded. "You take yourselves right back outside and wipe your feet and then come in and close the door like gentlemen!"

Normally Wayne and Chance were well behaved boys, but this day they were too excited to even hear her, much less obey.

"Chief, we found a dead body! Come quick!"

"What? What dead body? Where?"

"Down in Dog's Run. She's lying in the water and a crawdad was eatin' her face," Wayne said.

Chief Smeal knew the boys by sight, though he didn't know their names. They were like most of the youngsters from Dog's Run; often unwashed, dressed in hand-me-down clothes, and allowed to run free most of the time with little parental guidance. Dog's Run was a shabby collection of shanties and thrown together houses on the east side of Elmhurst. The town attracted refugees from West Virginia, Kentucky, and Tennessee, who came to Ohio looking for work in the factories around Toledo and a better lifestyle than the coal mines and hardscrabble farms they had left behind could offer. Most were decent, hardworking folk, but there was also a hard element among them that included moonshiners, petty thieves, and ne'er-do-wells.

"Slow down boys. Now just where did you find this body, and who is it?"

"She's down in the creek at the bottom of the Run," Chance told him. "Just upstream from the bridge. I don't know who it is, we just looked and ran when we saw the crawdad eating her."

Mary Jo's face had gone pale at the boys' revelation and she said, "Oh my Lord!"

The chief looked at the boys sternly, and asked, "You sure about this? You boys ain't just pulling my leg? Because if you are and you come here interrupting my lunch like this, we're going to have a problem."

Both boys shook their heads vigorously.

"No sir, it's a dead lady and she's layin' there in Dog's Run!"

***

Dog's Run is a steep-sided ravine that begins somewhere just across the line in Michigan and continues southward to the west side of town before petering out at Swan Creek. Chief Smeal parked his Buick Roadmaster under a hickory tree near the bridge and followed the boys down a worn footpath to the water's edge.

"Where is she?"

"Right up there around the bend," Wayne said. "I ain't going no further. I don't want to see her again."

"No, you're both going to show me exactly where she's at," Lester said. "I still don't know what you found, but until I get to the bottom of this, I'm not letting either one of you out of my sight!"

Reluctantly the boys led him upstream and around the short bend, where the chief stopped abruptly. "Holy shit! You boys stay right here and don't you go nowhere, you hear me?"

Both boys nodded emphatically, relieved not to have to get too close to the body again.

Chief Smeal walked a few yards farther and surveyed the scene. The woman lay twisted onto her left side, her upper torso in the water. Nearby, on the creek bank, he saw a rifle and shotgun and the dead squirrels the boys had left behind. Walking out into the water, he felt it rise to just above his ankles as he squatted next to the body. The crawdad that the boys had seen was no longer in evidence, but small marks on the woman's face told him that it'd been there.

The woman had been pretty in life, but in death there was little left to show of what she had been at one time. Studying the body, the chief noted the dark bruise on the side of her face, that her left ankle was twisted at an odd angle, and that the scrapes and abrasions on her arms and legs had come from something more than crawdads.

"Oh Wanda Jean, what's become of you now?" Lester asked the woman.

Made in the USA
Coppell, TX
25 April 2021